FOUND IN TIME

J.K. KELLY

ISBN: 978-0-9994099-0-9 (paperback)
ISBN: 978-0-9994099-1-6 (ebook)

Contact:
J.K. Kelly
P.O. Box B
Media, PA USA 19063
jkkellybooks@gmail.com
jkkelly.com

Dedication

Found In Time is dedicated to the brave men and women who put themselves in harms way to protect their fellow man.

Recognition

A very special thank you to my Lisa. Your unlimited patience and encouragement meant the world throughout this adventure

Christie: Enjoy the ride! [illegible]

1

Berlin, Germany 1945

THE CHERRY BLOSSOMS may have come and gone in D.C., but the late spring warmth was a stark comparison to what they found on arrival early that morning overseas. As U.S. Marine Major James Jackson looked around, all he could see was rubble. The buildings that surrounded him and his T-1 team of six looked just as they did in the photos he'd studied before they arrived, taken just after the war ended. The smell of smoke hung heavy in the air. The only sound they heard came from a hungry dog barking way off in the distance.

The vibrant city had crumpled under the assault of Allied bombers. What had once been a warm and sophisticated city of science, culture, and art was now little more than a shell, a ghost town. But the team had seen it all before, in Iraq and Afghanistan, bombed and burned out buildings.

"Night goggles would be nice," Captain Wilson muttered.

JJ peeked around the corner at the rear of the Reich Chancellery, and the emergency exit of Adolph Hitler's Bunker. Just twenty yards away. His heart raced at the realization they'd actually made it this far. The intel taken from the tons of photos, maps and interviews they'd studied was dead on. And not a soul in sight. Other than the remaining loyal Nazis guarding their Fuhrer and his guests.

"Is my eyesight screwed or do you see only five guards?"

"Roger that," Wilson responded. "My bet is, with everyone knowing the war's over, most of the Krauts have run off. Only the extreme shit-heads will stay behind to protect the bastard."

JJ nodded. The briefing had also stated that, by now, most of the German military had run out of ammo and headed for the hills.

The five German soldiers huddled around a fire drum to keep warm. The flames' orange light picked out black SS officer's hats and uniforms, red armbands high on their sleeves, holstered Lugers, assault rifles riding shoulder straps. Four black Mercedes Benz sedans, untouched by the destruction around them, were parked nearby. JJ waved up three other T-1's, leaving Corporal Richard to watch their backs.

On the whispered count of three, five German-made rifles, operated by the most elite 21st-century combat fighters on the planet, and modified with state-of-the-art silencers, took out the guards with simultaneous headshots. They rushed the bunker door.

Taking the lead, JJ was within five feet of the door when it suddenly swung open. A lone guard, returning with steaming hot coffees in both hands, stared at JJ with more curiosity than shock. Wilson opened fire. The guard took one lunging step then went down hard. JJ winced as the ceramic cups hit the cement and shattered.

"Go!" he whispered. And they slid quietly into the bowels of the infamous Nazi lair.

2

The Pentagon – 2015

MARINE GENERAL DICK Stewart, Chairman of the Joint Chiefs, sat in the crowded room at the long conference table. For nearly seventy-five years, men and women in this room had made decisions that cost hundreds of thousands of lives—and saved just as many. It had already been a long day, with far too much time debating the same issues that never seemed to get resolved. But it was this last presentation that made his heart lurch and brought him up straight in his seat.

"You've got to be kidding, Colonel," he said, unable to stop from interrupting the leader of the United States Special Operations Command.

"No, General," Colonel Petty responded, looking him directly in the eyes. "I'm dead serious. I've participated in the experiments personally. We have developed a technology that allows us to send troops into the past, and return them safely to current time."

A murmur of shock and disbelief rose up around the immense oak table. Stewart took in the stunned expressions.

For a moment, the room fell silent. Then questions and shouts flew, and all was mayhem.

"Stop!" Stewart commanded. He waved them all to silence. *What the hell!* He knew that Petty wasn't a jokester. And yet…this was almost too outrageous to give credence to. "All support staffers and liaisons, out of the room," he ordered. "Only the Chiefs stay."

Within seconds staff had gathered notebooks, laptops and briefcases, and quickly shuffled out of the room, tossing each other puzzled looks. The seven Chiefs remained, sitting anxiously, waiting for Colonel Petty's next words.

Stewart was aware of the colonel's impeccable reputation within the armed forces leadership. He wasn't a man to waste anyone's time, or take his position lightly. The logical part of Stewart's mind told him that what he'd just heard couldn't possibly be true. Another part—the Marine who longed for the perfect weapon that would keep his men from harm and win every battle, changing the game of war forever—told him to listen to the man.

He fixed a steely gaze on Petty and said, "Go on."

Before Petty could speak, Army General Brooks barked out, "So you're telling us you've got some sort of time machine?"

Air Force General Shields laughed. "Can you also send them into the future, Colonel? I'd like to retire and could use some help with the Powerball numbers."

Contemptuous laughter filled the room but stopped abruptly when Petty's expression remained serious. Stewart stood up, took a bottle of water from a beverage tray and threw a few to the men who sat forward and raised an arm. Clearly at this late hour they would prefer beer or something stronger, but there was more work to be done. And the seriousness of Petty's announcement meant alcohol was definitely not on the agenda.

Stewart took a sip of water, looked out the window at the rush hour traffic jamming I-395. Beyond the highway was Arlington National Cemetery, where many of the nation's heroes lay at rest. How many graves wouldn't be there today if the U.S. had a weapon that the enemy couldn't fight?

He turned back to the powerful men seated at the table. "I guess it goes without saying, that at various times in history, the atomic bomb, heart transplants, and walking on the moon were thought to be science fiction. It wasn't until brilliant men and women of imagination, invention and problem solving delivered these breakthroughs that we could take them for granted. Let's give the Colonel a chance to fill us in. I, for one, don't want to miss the opportunity to be at the forefront of the next great discovery." He let his words sink in as he looked around the table at each of his colleagues. "Just look at what we get to fight with these days—smart bombs, stealth fighter jets, drones." He shook his head and hoped to hell that Petty hadn't lost his mind. That he had something of substance to tell them.

For the powerful figures seated at the table, protecting the country they had spent their lives defending might have just become an even more complicated endeavor. At the same time, racing through his mind, was the fear that, if these experiments were as Petty promised, there would be unscrupulous types desperate to use this new technology to advance their own personal and political aspirations.

Stewart gave a nod to Petty. "Colonel, if you'll continue with your briefing?"

"Thank you, General." Petty took a deep breath as

though to order his thoughts. "As I was saying, using innovative technology only recently developed, we've sent a small team, a team of six with their equipment, back in time." He glanced at Shields. "Sorry, General, we've not been able to go forward. As proof that our experiment has worked, we sent the team back to West Point and then to Annapolis, in November 1976. Their mission was to infiltrate the living quarters of two of the Joint Chiefs who are here today."

"And?" Stewart prompted when Petty seemed to hesitate.

"With all due respect, I can inform you that, contrary to Army and Navy academy regulations regarding contraband, the team found that one cadet clearly had a fondness for twelve-year-old scotch and the other for Playboy magazines. The team found these items under their bunks while the cadets were away for Thanksgiving holiday."

The room erupted in laughter.

"That sounds like the private stash in every upper-level office here at the Pentagon and at the Capitol," Stewart shouted over them. "Now let's get down to the details, Colonel."

Petty pursed his lips, folded his hands on the table in front of him. "I suspected that might be your reaction. So, with your permission, General—I'd like to bring one more person into the room. She heads the team that has been working on this project. She's waiting just outside the room now. Her name is Doctor Andrea Moretti. She's a brilliant and fascinating woman. She's got a pretty extraordinary story to share with us today."

Stewart gestured impatiently toward the door. Petty immediately stood and left the room, returning in less than a minute with a short, gray-haired woman who looked to be in her nineties. Those around the table exchanged skeptical looks, but Stewart hoped they'd hear the woman out. He trusted that Petty knew what he was doing.

Dr. Moretti chose to stay standing as she spoke. Although her body appeared rather frail, her gaze was sharp and her voice strong.

"I was born in Italy," she began. "My mother died when I was only a year old. My father didn't know how to raise a child and wanted a better life for his daughter. So, he put me on a ship with my older sister and sent us to live with our cousins in New York. I will not waste your time with details or false humility, but only tell you that I excelled in school; they called me a prodigy. I breezed through college, earned my Masters, my PhD, and then was recruited to work for the government at the start of World War II."

"Madam, we're a bit too busy to listen to your life story," Brooks grumbled. He turned to Petty. "This wasn't on today's agenda. Why don't you just tell us about this so-called technology, so we can get on with our God-damned day!"

Stewart gave an inward sigh. Brooks, the most senior officer in the United States Army, had got where he was by playing politics rather than earning his position through performance. The other Generals and Admiral got along with him, for the most part, but his brash behavior sometimes put the others on offense. Stewart, for one, wasn't in the mood for his antics today.

"My apologies, Dr. Moretti. General Brooks must have a hot date in Georgetown tonight. Please go on."

Brooks didn't look happy with the rebuff, but remained silent.

Andrea Moretti picked up where she'd left off as if

nothing unsettling had happened. "Back then, during the war, I was the only woman chosen for my department. But I can say, in all humility, that I was smarter than many of the male scientists I was selected to work with. My peers were tough on me, shunned me—and that made me work even harder. I was determined to prove myself. And I did."

"When a few of the other scientists tried to take credit for my work, I isolated myself as best I could and continued the research the military had directed me to do—in a private laboratory. After many years, I not only earned the respect of my peers, I was given the opportunity to work on whatever I wanted." She looked up and around the table with an innocent smile. "I also outlived every one of those men."

Petty spoke up now. "Andrea and I have been friends for a long time. I hope she doesn't find this offensive but, I honestly thought her better days were behind her. When she came to me with what she'd found, I realized how wrong I'd been." He shook his head, as if still trying to wrap his mind around her discovery. "It was a meteor, we are sure of that much. Where it came from, or exactly what it is made from, no one has been able to ascertain. It's being stored in Area 51."

Moretti held up a hand to bring their attention back to her. "I'll spare you the technical jargon and the long version of our years of research. What I came up with was just enough material to develop twelve activators. We call them pulse devices. Six of these devices form a ring and are the power behind time travel."

For a moment, no one said anything.

It was Stewart who broke the silence. "I know a Marine Major who would be perfect for this assignment."

Brooks cleared his throat to speak. "That's funny, Stew. I was just thinking of an Army Officer on my staff who would be a great choice."

Navy Admiral Horton sat forward. "Hey, you two can fantasize all you want about who leads the charge, but don't forget we've got the Seals and damn fine high fliers who know how to kick ass, too."

The other officers laughed at the ongoing rivalry between the service branches. For now, though, they would learn as much as they could about this new technology, and wait to see what cards the others might deal.

Stewart said, "Let's give the colonel a chance to finish what he came here to tell us."

"Absolutely." General Burns, commander of the National Guard Bureau, leaned into the discussion. "I find this intriguing. What, for instance, would happen if you tried to slide a seventh person into the middle of a trip? It would seem they'd just be cargo."

Petty shook his head grimly. "There are plenty of dead guinea pigs buried out in the Nevada desert, General. It's six at a time, one pulse device for each beating heart. No more, no less."

Petty went on to recommend the formation of a top-secret, black ops time machine program, using the acronym BOTM. The technology worked, he assured those present in the room, but now they needed real-world testing. In his judgment, highly qualified operatives needed to be rigorously tested, to see how they performed under stress and in reaction to the people and situations they encountered.

"I leave it up to you gentlemen to decide what to do with it. I think it's imperative that we put this newest technology in the U.S. arsenal. Special Ops teams could be sent back in time on covert missions to do whatever is needed."

"Thank you, Colonel, for bringing this to us," Stewart said. "I'd like to excuse you for the time being so the rest of us can discuss this amongst ourselves a bit further."

"Good work, Colonel," General Shields added. "And Dr. Moretti, this is amazing news. Thank you." The others offered similar congratulations and thanks as the colonel accompanied the scientist out of the room.

Stewart stood at the end of the table, facing his fellow officers. "The job just got a bit more interesting, wouldn't you say, men?" Affirmations circled the table. "This is an unprecedented historical accomplishment for American ingenuity and for the U.S. Military." He looked at his colleagues. "The question, however, is whether it is appropriate to use such a powerful weapon. Do we have the moral right to change the course of history? What would we change? What would we choose to let happen? We have no idea of what the long-term, downstream effects might be."

From a practical standpoint, they could easily hide the program's existence and expense within their clandestine planning and operational Department of Defense budgets. At the onset, it seemed to Stewart, the cost would be minimal. But that was irrelevant. Politics within the Armed Forces, and between them and the legislative, judicial, intelligence, and executive branches of government, were complicated enough—furthering the need for secrecy.

Therefore, they might need to keep this new technology to themselves, at least for now. Black Ops—operations that can't be traced back to those who ordered them—have always been in existence; however, since 9/11 their number had increased exponentially. BOTM, if given the green light, would be the blackest op to date.

The officers continued to discuss possibilities. They could send teams back in time with the sole goal of protecting the United States. The time travelers could use any and every tool available to them as spies, saboteurs, kidnappers, and terminators. The air in the room felt electric with possibilities.

"I wonder what the global population would be today if World War II had been averted," Admiral Horton said.

"I was just now considering that myself," Shields sighed. "I did the math and we'd have roughly five- to ten-million more people on the planet today if we used this technology to eliminate the threats that evolved in Germany and Japan. People think jobs, food, and water are getting tight now. But can you imagine needing to provide for another ten million?"

"I used to tell my brother he should practice instead of procreate. Hell, he's got seven children for Christ's sake," Brooks remarked.

Stewart steered the debate back to issues more important than the Brooks family's vigor. What about germs? Might a 21st-century team expose people in the past to diseases they'd not yet developed immunities and treatments to fight them? Conversely, could the BOTM operatives accidentally carry something back with them with the potential to infect and wreak havoc on today's population?

"The spin off from that topic is biological warfare," Army General Brooks said matter-of-factly. "We could send a deadly strain back to wherever and whenever we want. Eradicate an enemy before they are even born."

Admiral Horton straightened up, elbows on the

conference table. "That contradicts the very basis of what we are talking about here. We've spent hours discussing the unknown ramifications of changing the past, and now you are suggesting we wipe out a continent. Are you talking China, Japan? Maybe stopping Hitler and his entire military before they went ape shit? Where do you start and where would you stop?"

Marine General Turza, spoke up for the first time. "We're getting ahead of ourselves, gentlemen, way ahead of ourselves." He gave Stewart a look.

"The Vice Chairman is right," Stewart said. "Let's make sure the damn thing works before we start blowing shit up."

Shields gave an impatient groan. "This is a ground-breaking discovery and those always come with risks. Let's not talk this thing to death." He looked across the table at Brooks and then at Stewart. "Can we agree to have no more suggestions of taking out entire countries or societies? Let's establish the rest of the ground rules and green light a test program. One that will start out soft. Once the real missions begin, the teams will need to carry out surgical strikes, with little notice or collateral damage left in their wake."

"I agree," Brooks said. "We'll assemble teams, test them and the equipment for at least a few months. That will give us more time to plan what we're actually going to do with this thing once we are sure of its capabilities. In addition to going back and looking at preventing some of our past conflicts, I suggest that we send a team back a week in time and plant listening devices in the Kremlin or Nanjing Palace. Then go and retrieve them. I think Petty said something about the near-past being an issue but I'll still put those on my list for early tests."

"Fine," Stewart said. "I need to ask if everyone is on board with this project. We can't afford leaks or infighting, gentlemen."

Unanimously, they agreed to the top-secret program and its charter. They would keep BOTM to themselves and not divulge its existence to any non-essentials. That meant excluding the CIA, the Secretary of Defense, Vice President, and even the President.

Finally, General Stewart brought discussion to an end. "I suggest we all take the weekend to review everything that has been said in this room today. Then consider specific missions you would like to propose, the pros and cons of the program itself, and the bigger question of changing time's path. Whatever we choose to do will involve crawling before we walk and then run."

"And then what?" Shields asked.

"We'll meet again and again in the Joint Chief's conference room until we've talked through every possible element of the program. First on the agenda will be mapping out a more detailed charter, establishing ground rules, a chain of command, accountability, contingencies and staffing. Outside of these meetings, worrying about the possibilities and pitfalls of this newfound capability will cause some of us to lose sleep, while others will embrace the technology and think of the ways in which our lives may be changed for the better by it."

Stewart had already placed himself firmly in the latter category. He couldn't remember another time he'd been this excited.

3

THEIR CHARTER WAS clear and simple. Initially, the technology would only be used for Research & Development. All members of the Joint Chiefs agreed with General Stewart that the program's participants would not perform intelligence operations involving the executive, legislative, or judicial branches of the United States. After a trial period, the Chiefs would meet to evaluate the program and begin to execute operations designed to weaken or eliminate threats to the country.

BOTM was to focus solely on American interests and not include or involve allies. Stewart believed that this new technology needed to be developed slowly, cautiously—unless an urgent need or imminent threat to national security arose. Basic standards and principles must be followed.

All U.S. service organizations already operated under the credo that nobody was ever left behind. The BOTM project took this a step further—operatives would be under orders to never leave anyone or *anything* behind. While on a mission they weren't allowed to take videos or photographs, or remove objects, people, or souvenirs of any kind from the target time-period.

To enable the travelers to better blend with the locals they were likely to encounter, they could wear or bring from the 21st century only material or objects that also would have existed in the period they were traveling to. Stewart knew someone who could help them with the proper dress and any weapons deemed necessary for the assignment.

Since secrecy was of the utmost importance, team members were forbidden from speaking of their experiences outside of a briefing with their BOTM commanding officers. The travelers were to act *only* as observers of history. Although the precise consequences of breaking the rules weren't discussed, it was understood that anyone guilty of gross violation might be tried for treason—a capital offense when operating under the orders of the highest military authority and as black ops. Punishment would be quickly and quietly carried out.

At this high level, accidents did happen and people disappeared in an instant.

To further insulate the Chiefs should the existence of the program ever be discovered, they agreed that one man would bear responsibility for BOTM. The vote for Stewart was unanimous. If things went sour, he would be the fall guy. Then again, in all his years of service he'd always landed on his feet.

"What will you do if the program is exposed," Shields asked once they'd made their decision.

"I'll say that BOTM is still in development. In my judgment, it wasn't ready to be presented to the DOD Secretary or the President." Stewart took in the solemn faces around the table. "At this point the only thing that scares me is Mrs. Stewart!"

The men laughed along with Stewart, but the room fell almost immediately silent as it occurred to the others that the General was serious. Elizabeth Stewart was a strong woman, a well-established attorney specializing in international law. She was also a Gold Star mother.

After the Stewarts lost their son Mathew, killed in action in Afghanistan, their world changed drastically. Dick Stewart remained strong on the outside, although crushed inside. He and Mathew were buddies from the day he was born. Despite serving on opposite sides of the world at times, they managed to remain as close as possible. Elizabeth was a tough woman who agreed with the General's feelings on weak leaders, destroying evil, and protecting their country—but she could no longer bear to see her husband in uniform every morning as he prepared for work at the Pentagon—and so, she left DC. Her only defense against her heartbreak was to move as far away as possible from everything that reminded her of the military.

Stewart spoke with her three or four times each week, ending each call by asking when she was coming home. She always responded: "The day that uniform comes off for good."

Each branch of the armed forces has a special, elite group known to the public as Navy Seals, Army Rangers, or Green Berets. But within the Marines there is MARSOC, which stands for Marine Special Operations Command. It is a newly formed group and in typical Marine fashion they were expected to be the best of the best while relying on minimal budget and resources. It was from that group, at the direction of BOTM Chairman Stewart, that a team of elite Marine Raiders—Time Team One, or T1, was to be assembled.

From the first day when they began discussing the new

technology, Stewart knew who should be involved. He handpicked the team commander, whose job it would be to properly staff T1 and establish their T2 back-up team.

Stewart's choice was Major Jim Jackson. "JJ" to his friends. Jackson's father had served in the Air Force and coordinated missions with Stewart around the world. They were also best friends. When Jackson's mother was taken by cancer the father and son were devastated. Jackson's dad continued to serve his country and looked after his son until he himself was diagnosed with lung cancer and died a very short time afterward.

JJ was destroyed. Days later, tears running down the teenager's face, he stood at attention as his father was buried at Arlington National Cemetery. His parents would, once again, be together. It was a week before Memorial Day, and the Stewarts opened their doors and their hearts to the young man. They returned to Arlington, at his insistence, and attended the solemn event at the Tomb of the Unknown. Jackson was surprised but very proud when the President of the United States took a moment after delivering his address to extend his sympathies to JJ and the Stewarts. Then they spent the rest of the weekend barbequing and doing everything they could to keep their new guest occupied.

Two weeks later, the Stewarts attended his high school graduation and watched as he went off to celebrate senior week at the outer banks in North Carolina. For the most part, his friends kept him busy and out of trouble. He returned with only a bad sunburn and a worse case of too much partying. But they were disappointed to learn he had broken up with the girl he had dated throughout high school. His only explanation to the Stewarts was that he didn't want to be involved with anyone for a while.

His emotions were worn thin; he was tired of losing, scared of losing people he cared for. They understood the words he often said: "If I'm not in love with anyone, then I can't get hurt." They hoped that time would heal his wounds. They supported him and gave him the wide berth he needed.

Throughout his youth, JJ had every expectation of following in his father's footsteps. But after the funeral his focus changed and he expressed an interest in going into research and finding a cure for cancer. He had been raised to fight. Trying to stop this evil disease before it stole more lives seemed a noble cause.

He took chemistry and microbiology summer school classes at the community college to learn exactly what life as a researcher might involve. By Labor Day, he knew that science wasn't for him. He hated it. The classes were boring and didn't make much sense to him. He was frustrated and felt, even worse, that he might be letting his new mission and his parents down.

On the morning of 9/11/01, sixty years to the day from when construction on the Pentagon began, the building was attacked. JJ and Elizabeth watched the TV screen in horror as security footage showed the explosion and fire—knowing that Stewart was working there that day. Luckily, their mentor and husband survived without a scratch and quickly called home to tell them he was all right. He was on his way to a command center to prepare for what many thought would be a day of relentless attacks across the country.

JJ knew what he had to do. Without hesitation, he joined the Marines the following morning. His passion and focus changed overnight. He was now going after another type of evil. He wanted to find and destroy the terrorists who had attacked his country and the man who had stepped up when he lost his parents. He had grown up around military men who taught him well. He was born for this.

After boot camp at Parris Island, South Carolina, he qualified for special training in California and was sent to Officer Candidate School in Quantico. Continuing to build a resume, he also served on Embassy Duty in Tel Aviv and Berlin as part of the Marine Quick Response Team. He saw action in Iraq and Afghanistan and, when the opportunity came to try out for MARSOC and become a Raider, the elite of the elite, he signed up and made the grade.

After Mathew was killed, Stewart feared he'd lose JJ, too. He transferred JJ to Quantico to teach strategy at the War College. JJ resented and resisted the transfer. He didn't want to appear to be receiving preferential treatment or being pulled out of harm's way. Stewart denied those were his motives. But, in truth, he wanted JJ close and knew Elizabeth would be lost forever if anything happened to the other young man in their life.

Eventually, JJ accepted his enforced departure from the Raiders. He sensed that he was exceptional and on a fast career track, so he trusted Stewart's assurance that something special would come along, and when it did he'd get the call.

Now a Major, Jackson looked and acted the part of the handsome, ass-kicking, beer-drinking, dog-loving, freedom fighter that Hollywood cast as its action heroes in war movies. He was the type of guy you wanted to party with, and to have at your back in a fight.

With the birth of BOTM, and JJ's taking command of

General Stewart's new program, any tension between the two men disappeared. The more JJ learned about the mission, the more excited he felt. This was going to change the world; and he would be a part of it.

Six weeks after JJ got the BOTM assignment it was go-time. At Andrews Air Force Base, he hand-picked his team and arranged their transfer from posts all around the world. Andrews would be ideal for a base. Security was super tight. Government Suburbans came and went 24/7. The team could easily blend in there. While undergoing extensive physical and psychological testing they would have little time for anything other than maintaining their weapons, meals, and grabbing some much-needed sleep.

To set the tone, Major Jackson assembled the team for the first time at 17:00 and immediately took them to a favorite bar for introductions. Dark-paneled walls were decorated with photos and posters that reflected the fighting history of the Marines, Army, Navy, and Air Force. It was rare for a local to drink there. They knew better.

"Okay, welcome to our T1 meet-and-greet." Captain Tommy Wilson, second in command of the BOTM program, waved everyone to a table for six. He ordered five tall beers, a double scotch for himself, and two rounds of tequila shots. This was the first of the casual meetings JJ hoped would build camaraderie within the group. Sharing war stories, drinking stories, jokes about the other military branches, and dates gone bad was all part of fitting in. Without a close bond, his team would find the challenges ahead of them harder to face.

"I like this guy already," Marine Sergeant Christy White, the only woman on the team, joked when the drinks arrived.

"Here, here!" Navy Corpsman Abrams seconded, raising his mug.

"Thanks for getting right down to it, Captain Wilson," JJ said. He and Wilson already had a special bond; Tommy was his brother-in-law.

JJ told the team that, while there was a clear chain of command in their program, they would need to become accustomed to exhibiting less formal behavior around one another. That meant less saluting and "yes sir, no sir" in their everyday life and, particularly, when they were carrying out their missions. Everyone knows you don't salute an officer on the battlefield; it puts a huge target on their back. Now they'd have to learn to detune even further.

Since the first day at Boot Camp, the Marine way of walking and talking had been pounded into them, until it became programmed behavior. The news that, from now on, things would be different meant reversing what had become second nature to them. But it was essential that they blend into the native population. Presenting themselves in a less rigid, less disciplined way was essential.

"No Gunny's going to stick his foot up your ass. Well, Wilson might, but you're safe with me." JJ smiled, sensing that he already had their attention. Good. He paused to take a long draw on his beer. The rest followed his lead and lightened their mugs. Despite his intention to loosen things up, and the initial light banter around the table, he was aware that his team was laser focused and anxious for him to continue.

"I've got a ton of training and experience," he continued. "And everyone at this table is qualified to do what we need or else we wouldn't have chosen you. For anyone who doesn't know it already, I've got a decent resume with the Corps and will share that in greater detail tomorrow morning." Jackson looked around the table at their intent faces. "I know what it took to work the gigs you've worked and then some. That's why we hand-picked you to be a part of this new program. So, as I said the good news is—for reasons that will become clearer at our first formal briefing tomorrow, *and I can't stress this enough,* we will be a bit looser than you've been trained to be."

Several of the team exchanged glances. He knew they must be consumed with curiosity by now.

"But one thing won't change," he said. "We are Marines and we will perform flawlessly. We complete the missions assigned, and we bring everyone home. That will never change." Gesturing to their surroundings, JJ said, "Normally we'd be doing this in a briefing room, but I know this place." He took another swig and studied the crowded bar then the room crammed with busy tables. "Ninety-nine percent of these people have top-secret clearances. There are people in here who work on the big blue 747s. There are special ops and contractors and Langley types mixed in. They'll stick to their shit and leave us to ours." He locked eyes with Wilson, who nodded in agreement. "So, let's move on with the warm and fuzzy stuff and leave the business for the base. If anyone in here ever asks what you're working on, let me know because that bastard will find himself in a world of shit."

"Okay, boss." Sharif gave a cautious laugh.

Captain Wilson ordered up a quick refresher, then JJ asked everyone to take a turn and introduce themselves. He nodded at Abrams to take the lead.

Benny Abrams, lowest in rank began: "First off, I'm not a Marine. I'm a Navy Corpsman. I grew up in Brooklyn. I'm Jewish, but don't do synagogue much. Hell, I don't do it all. I watched the Twin Towers fall and knew I'd sign up as soon as I could. Becoming a Corpsman, keeping our guys patched up and kicking ass works for me. I'm single now, but I want a wife and kids someday." He grinned shyly.

JJ went on to tell everyone how he met Benny on Embassy Duty in Israel. "I was stationed there with the Rapid Response Team. There was an alert; a woman who appeared to be pregnant was in the Embassy lobby, wailing that the baby was coming any second. We arrived to find her on the floor, screaming. One of the guards thought she might be faking it and was up to something."

"Like she might be concealing a bomb under her clothes?" White said.

"Right. She hadn't gone through the x-ray machine yet. Hell, they couldn't x-ray a pregnant woman and were preparing to pat her down when she hit the floor. Anyway, the scene was pretty chaotic. We're all trying to check her out, and here comes Abrams. He's in port with the Navy. He gets down on his knees, lifts her dress and, voilà , yells, 'I see the head!' Problem solved.

"From that moment we hit it off. A bunch of us who were in the lobby when the kid popped out went out drinking that night." Abrams smirked at JJ.

JJ laughed. "It was quite an experience. The thing is—this guy knows how to patch people up, but he can knock them down pretty damn well when he's pissed off. Some shithead at the bar found out we were Americans and decided to describe Abrams mother in an unflattering light."

"The prick ate a few of his own teeth that night," the corpsman said.

"Benny comes very highly recommended for continued field service supporting Seals and our Raiders. You can count on him to do whatever's needed to protect us Marines or anyone who needs help."

Benny Abrams nodded. "I get conflicted sometimes when the job means I have to patch up some piece of shit we just captured who was injured during an op. But I keep telling myself that saving a bad guy who can give up intel is worth it. Hell, I can stop the bleeding and establish an airway on anybody. But…funny thing is, my memory isn't always so good. Sometimes I forget to give those assholes anything more than saline for the pain."

Groans mixed with laughter. Sharif slapped Abrams on the back. "Good man!"

JJ was pleased that the alcohol was flowing and the team seemed to be relaxing nicely. "By the way, I know most of us are accustomed to calling the medics 'Doc,' but we already have a Doc on board. You'll meet her soon, so Benny here is Abrams—plain and simple."

Wilson reached across the table and gave Benny a high five. "Okay, ladies, these shots aren't going to down themselves!"

"Speaking of *ladies*—White, you're next on deck," JJ said. "Fair warning, guys. Marine Sergeant Christy White is the deadliest woman—whether her chosen weapon is martial arts, hell she is a weapon, or a sniper rifle—any Special Ops team has ever seen. Go, Sergeant."

Christy shrugged. "Nothing much to tell, Major. I grew up in Oakland. Learned to protect myself on the streets before I escaped to the Marines. Already knew how to curse and kick ass as good as I could shoot," she said matter-of-factly.

"You learned to shoot in Oakland?" Abrams asked.

JJ watched the cocoa-brown skin of her face darken slightly. "There were a few run-ins with the local police. Past that now. Got a new life, thanks to the Corps. My only other loyalty is to the black and silver of the Oakland Raiders. Long as none of you have an issue with that, we'll get along just fine." She let out a big laugh at the heads nodding around the table. "Guess I should also say I'm not married. Don't want to be and never even thought about having a kid. Oh, and yes, I do have ink. I usually show it off after beating some bitch, I mean a man, at arm wrestling, but you boys will get to see it for free." She rolled up her sleeve to reveal a skull wearing a football helmet with the words "Raider Forever" high on her right arm.

JJ guessed that once she became a Marine Raider, the first female Raider ever, it gave her ink even more significance. He knew from studying her record that she always pursued the extraordinary. When he offered her a chance to transfer to his new unit, she immediately did so—but, with the reservation that she could opt out and return to the elite special op group at any time. JJ had promised her she'd never be bored.

"Sweet ink," Sharif said. "I want one!"

Wilson was the one who recommended they enlist Sharif, and JJ agreed after hearing his credentials. He and Wilson had served together in Iraq. His special skills made Omar Sharif more than qualified to do the job.

"Guess it's my turn," Sharif volunteered. "Don't let my

size fool you," he said with all seriousness. "I'm the stealthiest Marine at this table. Because I'm short I can access tight spaces to plant or locate hidden explosive or monitoring devices. Plus, I'm double jointed as hell and that makes the guys I hang out with laugh their asses off. I also have a better understanding of the cultural differences between the various religious and ethnic factions that make up the world. I was raised in Michigan. I'm a Muslim. My father is Egyptian and my mother is from Dubai. I grew up speaking Arabic in our home and English in school."

White laughed. "Yeah, English might come in handy. You girls going to do the next round or am I drinking alone?"

They took a break to raise their second round of shots, and down they went. "Another round please, and this time make it Jaeger!" Christy White called out to the waitress.

"Well shit, there goes another month of memory," JJ laughed. "Go on Sharif, what else ya got?"

Not as accustomed to tequila as the rest of the team, Omar winced as the alcohol burned its way down his throat. "Anyway, I'm used to everyone busting on me because of my name. Just like the actor in that movie Genghis Kahn. He was a bad ass Mongol who conquered Asia, the Middle East, and part of Europe. I'm Omar Sharif, badass Marine! Single but do want to settle down someday."

Jackson leaned back in his chair and listened as his team chattered on. He'd always felt that he could learn a lot about someone by getting them drunk. Were they a happy drunk? Did they become belligerent, quiet, talkative?

If you've been sworn to secrecy, but discuss, or worse yet, brag about your business after a few shots in a bar—as far as Jackson and Wilson were concerned, you were gone. No gray area there. So far everyone had done just fine. JJ felt confident that he and Tommy have made the right choices. But they would retest their team from time to time. Meanwhile, the warmth of their camaraderie was exactly what he had hoped for. Their chemistry seemed excellent.

He set aside his analysis of personalities and tuned back into the conversation.

"So, what's with Havasu? You still awake over there JR?" Wilson asked.

Marine Corporal JR Richard was born and raised on the outskirts of Lake Havasu in Arizona. He hauled himself up straight on his chair, showing signs the shots were having their predictable effect.

"Sir, yes sir, I mean yes, um, Tommy." Richard grinned, a bit wobbly. "Oh, you guys want to hear about me now? Okay. I been told I've demonstrated great skill in desert warfare. Saw a lot of action in the Middle East since entering the service five years ago. My specialty is sniper. I can also drink most of you under the table. Heck, I know I can drink any Army or Navy squid under any table any time!"

Abrams cleared his throat and looked at JR as if considering offering a challenge.

Wilson laughed at his buddy. They'd served together.

JJ said, "I heard there was a special story about you and Tommy on R&R in Germany last year?"

Richard smiled and responded, "That's classified, sir. I mean, JJ."

Wilson was still laughing. "Of all the Marines I know, this one has it made—I mean really *made*. He loves beer and bikinis, so he spends his leaves at his grandfather's beach house in Southern California." Richard may have been selected because of his abilities and his history with Wilson, but JJ knew there was much more to his being chosen. The grandfather Wilson mentioned was someone who had intimate relationships within the Pentagon and Washington.

Richard smiled and added one last point, "By the way, I am bi-lingual. Like most people who grew up in the Southwest, I speak a bit of Spanish but *pendejo* is my go-to word. It's the only one I know that everyone seems to understand. Single and lovin' life!"

The steady flow of beer continued as everyone got to know their teammates. But the Jaeger shots brought an early end to Sharif's night. "That stuff tastes like Robitussin and Red Bull," he muttered as he stood up unsteadily to head for the taxis waiting outside.

"An acquired taste," White admitted with a smile. "So, JJ, when are you going to tell us why you got us all transferred here?"

He stared at her for a moment, glanced at Wilson, then leaned forward, elbows on table. "I think we'll call it a night. We'll assemble in the briefing room at 0800 sharp. We'll get into it then, *Sergeant*."

White looked away, as if she thought she might have messed up. She'd been drinking and started to talk business.

Wilson settled the bill. They caught up to Sharif, piled into two taxis. Minutes later they were back on base.

JJ felt as satisfied with the night as he could have wished. He hoped Team One of the BOTM Program got a good night's sleep. Tomorrow morning he'd deliver the news that would change their lives forever.

4

CURRENT DAY, BOTM Briefing Room 0800

"Yep, that's what I said." Major Jim Jackson looked around the table at his team—eyes wide, jaws hanging open. Many in the military had the same reaction almost fifty-five years ago when it was announced Marine John Glenn was going to be strapped into a capsule with a little window and rocket-launched into an orbit around the Earth. "The United States now has the capability to take another dramatic step. We can, and will, go back in time."

Colonel Petty entered the room with Doctor Moretti. He could tell from their expressions that they might perceive a presentation by someone who looked a lot like Mother Theresa as a joke. But he related the same bio he'd told the Joint Chiefs, and the atmosphere in the room slowly changed.

"She's a bad ass!" White remarked.

It took a lot to impress this audience, but after hearing her story T1 seemed to forget her age and they refocused on the colonel. Petty presented an outline of the charter, reminding everyone in the room of the top-secret nature of the program. He then turned presentation of the basics of how the program would work to Moretti.

The Marines and Navy corpsman had seen a lot in their lives, but what they are hearing left them skeptical to say the least. "Listen up," JJ raised his voice to get their attention. "I had a million questions when I first learned of this technology and I had another million a week later. You will, too. But, luckily, we've come up with just about all the answers. We're going to sit down and go through all of it, together. But to get right to it, we felt it made the most sense to take you on a ride and show you firsthand that the science works. If anyone needs to hit the head, you have five minutes. Then meet us in the assembly room next door."

Nobody moved. "Forget that! Can we go now?" White asked, seconded by the team.

Moretti laughed and, with a smile, handed Petty a ten-dollar bill. "You win. They *are* chomping at the bit."

Everyone on the team had ridden roller coasters, jumped out of airplanes, gotten shot at, and put an end to the lives of some murderous bastards. It took a lot to get them excited. But JJ had no doubt their adrenaline was pumping.

Moretti gave each team member a small pulse device, mounted on a neck chain. JJ imagined that, in the future, these devices would replace their military identification tags. Moretti demonstrated that they had to be worn against the skin, as close to the beating heart as possible. She moved the team, one at a time, onto a small round piece of material. It looked like a throw rug. Standing in a very tight circle, shoulder-to-shoulder, face-to-face, all they could do was what comrades in arms always did—bust on each other.

"Sharif," Wilson said, "I don't know what kind of

donkey butt you ate for breakfast, but tear gas would smell better at this point. If our first trip takes us anywhere near wildlife, they're going to be on you like flies on shit."

The laughter caused them to step away, adding in more jokes and comments, until JJ got serious. "To this day, I still don't understand how airplanes stay up, so I'll leave the rocket science to the lab coats and leave the extraordinary to the Marines. Come on, let's do this."

General Stewart had explained to him what Moretti had expressed in the team briefing, that it had taken years for this brilliant, dedicated woman to develop these six devices. For whatever reason, the six had to be within two feet of each other to form a solid connection—a chain. Anything in contact with the team members' bodies would stay with them. Clothes, watches, shoes, pocket change and, at times, weapons and ammunition, would travel with them. Unfortunately, communication equipment didn't work between the past and present day, due to the electro-radioactive nature of the pulse devices. There would be no contact between those who journeyed into the past and the support team back at Andrews. Among traveling team members, radio communication only worked when they were at least fifty-five feet away from their pulse devices. Stepping away from your ticket home, your lifeline, was risky.

One of the strangest things Dr. Moretti had to figure out was the connection of the boots or shoes to the floor surface. She discovered this the hard way when first experimenting with mice and then monkeys before moving on to human trials. You can't travel if connected to a stationary object like a floor. Even if you were allowed to, you can't bring back a car if you are riding in it, due to the six-foot range constraints of the ring.

It took time and many experiments, but something as simple as using a sheet of aluminum foil as a launch pad seemed to do the trick initially. That is until a malfunction during a test. The test dummy's boots heated up, due to the prolonged electrical/radiation interaction, and caught on fire. Fireproof boots the solution? But what if the boots were lost during the trip? Or they interfered with the team's ability to blend in?

The simplest, but most impractical thing to do was to have everyone jump in the air to break contact with the ground surface. The test team in the desert had pushed back enough over time that Moretti finally developed a six-foot round mat made of a special material that addressed the issues. All they needed to do now was roll it out, step on, and get tight. On arrival, they'd roll it up and stow it away until they were ready to depart. Not very high tech, but functional. The one problem—if they ever lost it, back in time, they might never be able to return.

Most of the actual development and testing was done between two warehouses in the desert at Area 51 and at Edwards Air Force Base in Nevada. They tried all sorts of ways to test the process. Sending a team back in time to the base newsstand to read newspaper headlines was easy. They'd then return with the information and date. Moretti had been on base for so long it was easy for her to orchestrate the simple missions. With everyone operating under TOP SECRET clearances the operatives comings and goings were never questioned. She grew very frustrated with their inability to go back to recent times but the overall capability was now functional and reliable. She had proven her discovery. Her technology worked and it was ready for action.

"Okay, the shits and giggles are over ladies." Jackson looked at Wilson. The two men stepped back onto the mat. The rest of the team followed. Their pulse devices rested against their chests, close to their hearts. Abrams was chewing gum. Wilson gave him a look; the chewing stopped.

"Okay, JJ, you are ready for the count?" Moretti said.

JJ nodded. Moretti and Petty stepped back against the wall and waited for the team leader to engage.

"See you on the flip side Team One," JJ said. "3-2-1!"

And they were gone.

JJ looked around. He and his team were standing on the mat in a hotel room, curtains drawn. They stepped away from each other, eyes blinking, amazement on their faces, trying to process what had just happened and where they might be. JJ walked to the nearest window and pulled the curtain back. Sharif stepped up behind him.

"Holy shit!" Sharif shouted. A million lights blazed across a cityscape of towering buildings. "It's Times Square. We're in New York City." The streets below were jammed with people.

The rest of the team joined them at the window. They could hear the crowd shouting, whistles blowing, air horns bellowing.

"What the fuck," White said. "It's 2000!" She pointed to her right at the illuminated ball, reaching the apex of its climb. Immense numbers announced the start of the new millennium.

Faces pressed up against the glass to take in all they could of this incredible moment. They were making history!

"Happy New Year, JJ," Wilson proclaimed, hugging his

friend in celebration of their successful first journey. "My God, we made it! Do you believe this?"

"Wait a minute." Abrams stepped away from the window and stared around the room. "Whose room is this? And how did they know it would be empty? How'd you know to come to this spot, at this time, on this date?"

Everyone was listening now. "Easy. Colonel Petty rented this room with his wife all those years ago. At this hour, at the stroke of midnight on January 1, 2000, he and Mrs. Petty were dancing and drinking way down below us in the ballroom of the Marriott Marquis Hotel."

The reality of the moment was starting to sink in. While most went back to watching events unfold in the streets outside, Wilson and Abrams looked at each other with one thought in mind.

Wilson stepped forward. "Hey, JJ, let's go downstairs and celebrate with the mob!"

JJ shook his head and smiled. "You guys know better. We aren't dressed for the occasion. Besides, this is enough for now. Time to head home."

Wilson might have been joking, but Abrams shook his head. "No, wait a sec. My parents were out in that craziness that night—*tonight*! They left me home to watch it on TV with my sister while they came down here to celebrate."

JJ stepped up and patted him on the shoulder. "That's cool. But we can't. This is one of the reasons we're going to test the crap out of this technology. Listen up, everyone, that reason alone—coincidence—is why we have to consider everything that might happen on a mission, and be prepared to handle it or avoid it. This is a whole new ball game. Now, let's circle up and get back to Andrews."

Wilson had been checking out the room and discovered the minibar. He reached down and picked out a tiny bottle of Johnny Walker Red. "Happy New Year, all!" He raised the unopened bottle in a toast then returned the bottle to the fridge. The team seconded his wishes. Back to business, he walked to the door and threw the security chain. JJ pulled the curtain shut again.

"Wait a minute, how's Petty and his wife going to get back in here?" Sharif asked Wilson as they stood shoulder to shoulder.

"Not my problem! Hit it JJ."

In the blink of an eye, the six were back at Andrews, standing in a circle, as if they'd never left.

"Ten minutes flat, not bad for a first flight!" Colonel Petty called out.

The next two hours were filled with congratulations and questions as Team One was debriefed. Petty and Moretti threw out an avalanche of scenarios and circumstances for discussion. JJ was pleased with the results. That first day brought the group of eight together. As days went by, relationships developed, and plans for their futures in the past were born.

Major Jim Jackson also had the responsibility of assembling a second team of Marines and a corpsman, but relations between T1 and T2 weren't as positive. T2 resented being a back-up team; they wanted to see some action of their own.

For the most part, all they were given the opportunity to do was conduct tests to identify "near-past" time constraints. For reasons, as yet unexplained, traveling to recent pasts had proven inconsistent and unreliable. Some in T2 wondered whether they were being given busy work. Surely those in the know must be already aware of the technology's capabilities. They also resented being led by an Army officer, Captain Josh Scott.

The Marines talked and complained amongst themselves. Would they get to see any real action as long as they were under this Army implant?

The fact was, in order to get the BOTM charter green lighted, with himself at the lead, General Stewart was forced to make a deal with Army General Brooks—who insisted that an Army officer had to lead T2. It was non-negotiable. Stewart accepted on the condition that Brooks' choice was ranked below Jackson, and whoever it was would follow Major Jackson's orders. The deal was made and things took shape.

As the Corps and the program charter mandate, for the most part T2 members followed orders without question, keep their bitching to a minimum, and watching from the sidelines. They might as well have been firemen sitting around the station waiting for the bell to ring. They were to maintain a state of readiness so they could respond when needed.

Whenever T1 was away on a mission, there would be two members of T2 standing guard with Dr. Moretti. One Marine and their Navy corpsman. The remaining four Marines would keep the facility sealed and secure. Only Colonel Petty and General Stewart were allowed absolute access. The system seemed foolproof to JJ, and he did trust his teams, but he was wary of one member, the outsider. Scott might be an officer stationed at the Pentagon, but some wondered if "mole" shouldn't be added to his resume. There had been rumors. He decided that Scott needed to be watched.

Meanwhile, he'd make sure T2 got their chance for a

ride into the future. He just wanted to take baby steps, see for himself what the other six were was really made of.

In an attempt to get to know each other better, JJ and Wilson invited Scott and his SIC Jones to join them at a local pub for drinks. After only ten minutes Scott began to dig himself into a hole.

"Hey JJ, who were those two hotties you were just talking to?" Scott asked as he watched two women head for the ladies' room. "I haven't seen tail like that since I hired two hookers in Cabo. Wilson, which set did you like the best?"

Wilson looks at JJ, then Jones, and finally at Scott. "Well, the one in the v-neck sweater had the nicer set. She's JJ's wife, Michelle. She's also my sister. The other one has a better ass, her name's Anne and she's their neighbor. They work with special needs kids in Bethesda. You want to change the subject now or should we continue down this road?"

Scott's face reddened with embarrassment but he seemed to take the put down in stride. JJ figured he'd tasted his foot before and grown accustomed to it. "My compliments, men, and my apologies. Now let's get off boobs and talk baseball."

JJ's attempts to get to know his T2 counterpart didn't go anywhere that night. It was clear to him that the man would continue along whatever path he'd set for himself. And the Marines beneath him would continue to have issues with the Army officer.

JJ did notice another relationship that seemed to be evolving much better.

Team Member Abrams, the medic, always kept an eye on Dr. Moretti, recognizing that the nonagenarian appeared frailer as time passed. "With everything you know Doc, you sure you didn't invent a way to extend life?" he often asked.

Moretti just shrugged her shoulders and raised her hands as if to say, "Who knows?"

Smiling, Abrams suggests, "Maybe someday we'll take you with us. Colonel Petty said you like movies and sports. Would you like to watch them film Roman Holiday with Gregory Peck back in the 50's? I remember watching some of his movies. He was in Moby Dick, too. Or you could see the Olympics in Rome, 1960? What do you think, Doc?"

Moretti's response was the same every time. "Someday I'd like to go back to Italy. Someday, just not today."

One afternoon, Colonel Petty stopped by the hanger at Andrews to visit the teams and to check in on Dr. Moretti. "It's her birthday today, JJ," Petty whispered. "Want to take her out tonight? She lives alone, and she really likes you and the team."

"On it, Colonel. I'll get everyone together. Our guys never pass up a chance for beer and cake. It's their favorite combo. Go figure. Be sure to reserve a private room. I know our guys won't talk business, but who knows what the Doc is like with a few *chiantis* in her."

Hours later, after many rounds of celebratory drinks and toasts, and entirely too much Italian food, Dr. Moretti waved off the birthday cake and candles. "I'd rather just talk to the team, if that is okay with them."

The waiter closed the door behind him and they were left to continue their party in private. "So, we all know why we are here—not to sing to this old bag of bones—but to celebrate something nobody ever has done before."

White interrupted jokingly, "If there's no cake, Mama

Mia, I'm outta here! There's some Army stiffs at the bar I can arm wrestle for some fast cash!"

Moretti smiled at her and then at each of the others. "Thank you for this tonight. It is a special night for me, but also one for you all. You are like the astronauts getting ready to launch into space for the first time. So far all that you did was drop into an empty room and pop back out. Who knows how your next mission will go. There will be more risk. We've done all we can to make sure you are as safe and prepared as possible."

Everyone raised their glass and toasted their guest of honor with "Cent' Anni!" "May you live one hundred years."

"Grazie," Moretti replied. "I will be one hundred before you know it. But, like I was saying…what the hell was I saying?"

They all laughed. The more time they spent with the doctor the more they enjoyed and appreciated her company.

"Yes, I wanted to ask each of you one thing. Let us fantasize for a moment. If you had the ability to go back in time, anywhere not military related, where would you want to go?"

JJ was sure they'd all given this some thought. Before long they were taking turns revealing their wishes.

JJ began. "Doc, if I could go anywhere back in time, I'd go check out the Samurais in Japan. I loved that movie *The Last Samurai.*"

"You just liked that guy's hot wife," Wilson needled him. "You always had a thing for Asian women. Me, I'd like to go back and check out the dinosaurs. They must have been impressive to watch in action. Growing up in Montana I got to see a lot of dino fossils. I know we weren't supposed to be around back in their day but to see them even if just for a few minutes would be amazing Plus, I'd take a bazooka just in case!"

Richard laughed, "I can just see you now, knocking your cave girl over the head and dragging her in to make supper!"

Wilson stared at Richard and the room went quiet until Wilson burst out laughing, "You guys know me pretty well, don't ya!"

Moretti was laughing, too. "That's interesting. What about the rest of you?"

Sharif spoke up next. "I'd like to see how they built the pyramids. I know from an engineering standpoint how they did it, but it would still be cool to see it for myself."

JJ shouted, "Aliens built them, Sharif. Don't you watch TV?"

Abrams had been quiet but finally offered his wish. "Okay, if I could, I'd be standing at Logan Airport in Boston on 9/11 with a special present for those fucking hijackers!"

Moretti protested immediately. "Whoa now, my boy, you can't change history and we said no military ideas."

JJ nodded his head in agreement. "I saw those towers fall. It freaked me out, freaked a lot of people out. Nobody knew what was going to happen next. But just seeing all those people's lives shattered—" He sighed deeply. That was a day he'd never forget.

The room stayed quiet for another minute until JJ spoke again. "As a teenager, I sat helplessly watching cancer take my mother and, later, my Dad. I couldn't do a damn thing about that evil. Stewart, General Richard Stewart to you, was in the Pentagon when the plane hit there. It's bad enough what those bastards did with those airplanes, but when they tried to kill Dick Stewart, the man who stepped up to take me in when I had no one else, that was it for me. There's a lot of evil in the world that we can't do anything about. But this was something I *could* do. I joined the Marines the next morning with the intention of hunting down and killing everyone involved in those attacks. The Navy Seals did an excellent job getting Bin Laden, but there's still a lot of assholes out there. Hopefully with the good doctor's help we can do even more to take care of business."

Wilson was watching everyone's faces as their leader spoke. "Sounds like a recruiting video, doesn't he?"

That broke the tension in the room. Everyone laughed.

"But I'll tell you this," JJ's second in command continued. "JJ here is the finest Marine I know. He's also one of the quietest. Some think that's ego or arrogance. It's neither. I've learned that he prefers to listen and figure things out. So, hell, there must be something in the water here because this is the most he's said in one sitting since I've known him." A few heads nodded in agreement. "JJ's got a lot of heart and cares about each and every one of you. I really don't know why but he does." Grins, all around. "He's selected each of you because he knows you have what it takes to do this unique job. Hell, I've never seen a better group of highly trained killing machines, who can also adapt to their surroundings and situations better than con men…or even politicians. Just do your job and he'll never let you down!"

JJ appreciated his friend's words. "They say a Captain's job is the loneliest one. Tommy Wilson here might be tough on you, but you can count on him. No matter what." By now, the table had grown quiet.

Colonel Petty must have decided the party had taken a too-serious turn. "Hey, enough of the warm and fuzzy crap! I wish I'd been a witness to what I think is the most important event of all time. I'd go back to the Ed Sullivan Theater and watch the Beatles make their first appearance on American television. No, seriously." He held up two hands at the burst of laughter in the room. "I grew up listening to their music, and my parents said the whole country went crazy when that show came on. That's what we need more of. Things to bring us together."

JJ said, "Now that's an idea. How about you, White? We haven't heard your must-see."

She thought for a minute and then said with a smile, "Okay, but if I tell you I might have to kill you!"

Wilson chuckled. "Fair enough. Let's have it."

White's face saddened. She took a deep breath before speaking. "I'd like to have been at my parents' wedding in Oakland. My grandmother told me that's the only day my father didn't give my mother any shit."

The room stilled.

"Buzz kill, White," Wilson murmured. "You're going to have to buy a round of shots at the bar to make up for it. You with us, Doc?"

"No, no, not me. There was a time when I could have gone wild with any of you. But not now. Well, then, I must thank each and every one of you for this evening. It is very special. Now Colonel, remember you're going to transfer Abrams here to some special duty. Maybe the South Pole?"

Laughter again filled the room and reminded everyone why they were there that night. "No, I think Major Jackson here will square him away if the look he gave him didn't already." With that, and another frown directed to his friend Abrams, JJ wished the Doctor a happy birthday. He gave her a hug and, to his surprise, she held him tightly for a moment. Once again, he wished her the best and he headed for the door.

"Wait a minute, JJ. We need to get a group picture," Wilson called out.

"Doc, give me your cell so we can mark this moment," Abrams said.

Pulling it from her pocket, she held it up. "This old thing? It doesn't take pictures anymore."

"Dude, we need to get you an upgrade. I think that's an original iPhone!"

With a smile she responded, "It's vintage, like me. You know, in all my years I've never been called dude before. Now someone get me back to my bed. Andiamo! I need my beauty sleep."

5

Team One

IN ADDITION TO the months of physical testing, JJ was most concerned with the operational and philosophical issues that had to be addressed. No matter where and when they chose to time travel, T1 needed to determine the exact, safest spot to "land." Their initial experimental trips were to be to famous historical sites and events—because these moments in time offered a degree of control. They could be researched and the team would arrive knowing, more or less, what to expect.

Whether they went to Dallas 1963, Pearl Harbor 1941, Appomattox 1865, or Egypt 500 B.C.—they couldn't be seen arriving or leaving. They needed currency. They needed clothing and accessories designed to look the part, enabling them to blend in. They might have to naturally alter their physical appearance, not by using makeup or special effects. If long hair was in order, they'd grow it and that took time.

"This is bullshit," White protested. "I can't possibly walk around Andrews with hairy pits and legs while all you guys have to do is shave your heads."

Grow it, cut it, lose weight, gain weight, get sun, or stay out of the sun, whatever it took. Tattoos were taboo, because it is too hard to ensure they wouldn't be discovered. White's Oakland Raider tattoo that transitioned to a Marine Raider version had to go or she'd be off the team. The scar left behind by the laser would be easily explained as an injury from a fire, fight, or abuse.

"Remember, White," JJ cautioned her, "you're an out-spoken, intelligent, beautiful black woman. You might not be able to act the way women do in our time. Can you act?"

JJ, Wilson, Jones, Sharif, and Abrams all looked at Christy White, waiting for her answer.

"Well, I hate you dipshits, but you can't tell now, can you?" she answered with a sugary smile. "I can act. Just ask the last guy I dated."

Wilson gave her a high five. "Semper Fi, sister."

"Oorah," she quickly responded.

They studied the ways in which people spoke, starting with accents then learning phrases, colloquialisms and slang, and jokes from each time target. They must fit in as naturally as possible. The Tarantino film *Inglorious Bastards* was one of their favorites, but the three-fingered type giveaway in the bar scene was something none of them could ever allow to happen. Germans used their thumb and two fingers in ordering three drinks. Brits and Americans ignored the thumb and raise the next three. They were to avoid interacting with the locals at their time travel destinations, but it made perfect sense to be prepared.

When it came to acquiring the right period pieces, they lucked out. Corporal Richard's grandfather, Bill Griffiths was a well-connected film producer in Hollywood. Higher ups in all branches of the U.S. Government in Washington, including Stewart, had come to rely on Griffiths for everything from Halloween party costumes to authentic uniforms and weaponry for historical re-enactments. He also owned an extensive personal collection of restored artifacts, a moon rock and dinosaur fossils.

Stewart and JJ hoped to rely on his help, for props and costuming. If they required something for a trip to Gettysburg or Pearl Harbor or to witness the signing of the Declaration of Independence, he could supply it.

Adding to his value to the team, Griffiths was a former military intelligence officer who served in Vietnam in the early '60s. He was a passionate and loyal patriot. Now eighty, and still sharp as a tack, he loved history and his family. Having only a daughter, JR became the son he never had. The only negative about involving Griffiths was his failing heart.

But when JJ met with the man, Griffiths waved off their concern and jumped at the chance to, again, help the Armed Forces. He promised to hand-deliver the goods whenever possible, flying them into an executive airport near Andrews, in his private jet. "It'll give me an excuse," he said, "to visit the most important place in my world. And to visit JR more often."

"You understand that BOTM is top-secret," JJ warned. "We can only share details of our missions on a need-to-know basis."

"Major, that goes without saying." Griffiths signed the documents that would protect their secrecy as much as a piece of paper can. "I just wish I could be as much a part of your team as JR."

JJ shook his head and touched the old man on his shoulder. "Not possible. We both know that." He smiled. "But if something special comes along that I can bring you in on—know that I will do that."

To limit exposure to the program, JJ and JR would be his only contacts. Not even the pilots flying his jet or the attractive flight attendants Griffiths employed would know anything about the cargo or the reasons for the trips. The flight crew signed non-disclosure documents. Regardless, as an additional security measure, the Griffith delivery service would always fly in and out at night.

The old man winked at JJ. "Used to like flying First Class, up front in those big spacious airliners, but I can't get my 45 or my pacemaker through the damn x-ray machines. And they stopped letting me hang out in the cockpit."

"Damn terrorists spoiled all the fun," JJ commiserated.

"You said it. Besides, TSA might have an issue with the World War II hand grenades and the other stuff in my carry bag."

Wilson and the other team members were skeptical about dealing with someone outside the military. But they kept their reservations to themselves. If Griffiths shot off his mouth and jeopardized a mission, they wouldn't hesitate to do what was necessary to silence him. Wilson, the deadliest and coldest of the bunch when it came to paybacks, would take out the old man, or anyone else, without a second thought. It was general knowledge that he was always on edge. But most people were smart enough not to ask why.

Finally, it was time for their first mission.

Their first interactive journey would be to New Orleans

on January 25, 1981, to watch the Oakland Raiders beat the Philadelphia Eagles in the Super Bowl. The choice of event was the result of a bet. Oakland-born White won. She proudly pounded the spot on her arm where her Raiders tattoo once was. She beat her Team Leader, JJ, a die-hard, hometown fan of the Eagles, in a best two-out-of-three arm wrestling match.

To General Stewart, going to a football game sounded trivial. But he and JJ talked it over and JJ's enthusiasm won out. Besides which, it was a safe choice for the next step. At least the team would remain in contemporary America, should something go wrong. The game-time fan gear was readily available, and the event celebrated the return of the U.S. hostages that had been held in Iran for over 440 days.

That patriotic twist closed the deal with Stewart. "Test your team," he ordered, "and work through any bugs you foresee. Be ready when we need you."

Moretti wasn't as easy to convince. "It's a dumb idea." She waved it off. "Choose something truly memorable. Stand on the deck of the Titanic. Watch President Lincoln deliver the Gettysburg Address."

But she was overruled. "Kids!" she muttered, shaking her head.

The first trip goes without a hitch, despite Wilson catching Abrams and Richard trying to place bets before the game. For that, they forfeited the post-game Bourbon Street bar hopping that had been planned.

"We'll go back for Mardi Gras if you behave yourselves," Wilson assured them. "You can drink as much as you want and toss beads at some beauties. Just don't toss your necklaces!"

Two weeks later, JJ briefed his team on their first real

time-travel mission. This trip would place lives at risk. Afterward, he took them out for beer at a local bar. Sitting around a table, after too many pitchers and shots to count, JJ asked his team about their religious upbringing and beliefs.

"What's that got to do with anything?" White asked.

"If any of you get nuked on a mission or drink yourselves to death, I'll need to know if I have to bury your butt before sundown, or cremate you and toss your ashes in the Ganges," JJ slurred. "Let's go around the table. Wilson, you're up."

"You know me, JJ. I grew up a Catholic just like you. But in all the time since my father's funeral mass, with the exception of taking my dad's place to walk Michelle down the aisle, I haven't set foot in a church. And let me tell you, I'd like to have a word with God about that. My dad would have wanted to be there for her day." He sighed. "Anyway, with all the shit I've seen in the world, I guess you'd say I'm a bit ambidextrous."

JJ frowned at him, certain he hadn't heard him right. "You're what?"

"I mean I lean toward being an atheist. Hey, if I'm gone you can leave my dead ass wherever it lands. My soul will have to find its way from there." Wilson chugged the mug dry and looked across the table at Christy White. "Your turn."

"I don't believe in anything," she said. "First we're lied to about Santa, then the Easter Bunny, and the God damned tooth fairy! Then we find out in school that Adam and Eve didn't exist, so why should I believe anything I was told about God? Hell, for all we know a bunch of old timers back in the day made it all up to keep people in line. People might be able to beat the law but if they think there's eternal fire waiting for them if they're bad, then that might keep some from breaking a few heads. If God really does exist and I ever get the chance to ask a few things, believe me I'm gonna."

Abrams laughed. "Damn, White. Remind me not to sit next to you in a thunderstorm. I can't believe you don't believe in the frickin' tooth fairy though."

White's eyes laser fixed on the Corpsman. He crossed two fingers to make the sign of a cross. Everyone laughed, but JJ felt for her. The home she grew up in was so very different from everyone else's. It seemed obvious she was still carrying so much of the past with her.

"I was raised in a Muslim household," Sharif began, "but after studying my own faith and all the rest, I am 110% into Karma and nothing else. You reap what you sew, and consequently you deserve what you get. When I die I have no idea what happens or where I'll wind up. It's sort of like hanging out with JR in Tijuana."

That earned a laugh all around.

"Okay, party boy, what about you, JR?" Jackson asked. "Something tells me beer and boobs are what you worship."

JR sighed and looked down into his mug. "Well, my mom raised me as a Catholic and dragged me to mass early every Sunday morning. I know all about God and believe in the basics, but it ends there."

"What's that supposed to mean?" Abrams said. "You believe but I've never seen you go to mass since we've been here."

JR straightened up on his bar stool, his expression now serious. "If God was all-loving like they say, he wouldn't let one man, woman, child, or animal be abused by anyone. Heck, he let some asshole kill something like six-million innocent Jews. I know some of them were probably a pain in the ass, like anybody else, but they were still innocent. Someday, I might get to meet Jesus or the Big Guy, but I'm like White. I'll for sure have some questions for him

"You assume they speak English?" Abrams questioned with a smile.

"I'm sure we'll be able to communicate. I'll take you with me, Abrams. Just in case."

"What about you, boss?" JR asked. "Wilson says your wife is the center of your universe but where are you with the Big Guy?"

"I grew up going to a Catholic Church. I even had an Aunt that was a nun. I went to church until I was old enough to start questioning things that didn't make sense to me. But I believe Jesus walked the planet 2,000 years ago and that there's something out there. It's like electricity. I don't understand it, but it's there."

JJ took the last few sips of his beer and pushed the mug away. "When Abrams and I were stationed in Israel we took a weekend trip to Jerusalem. I visited the Old City and Gethsemane for the first time. The Garden had a deep impact on me because it was a place where Jesus actually walked. That is where he gave sermons and prayed with the Apostles the night before he was betrayed, tortured, and killed on the cross. I know that happened."

"They can say all they want about what took place and where—exactly where he was born, where the cross went in the ground, and where he rose from the dead," Jackson stated soberly. "But standing there in Gethsemane, that is where *The*

Man walked among the olive trees. Over two-thousand years ago, those hills were there and were never torn down or destroyed or moved by all the different armies that raided and rebuilt the city, over and over and over again. Christ walked there! So did I. That is powerful feeling; it really touched me. I've been in the White House, The Vatican, and on Everest, but that place leaves me in awe. That's the shit!"

With that, JJ stood up. "I won't remember what most of you said tonight. But please remember this: I'll never leave you where you fall. We'll get your butts home and then, if we aren't sure, we'll flip a coin on dropping you in a hole or shake-n-bake. See you all at 0800."

The next morning, Team Leader Major Jim Jackson assembled his group at a ready area within a hangar at Andrews. "Glad to see everyone's bright-eyed and bushy-tailed on this fine day. Tomorrow morning we'll meet here at 0400 and activate at 0500. We are going on the first real back-in-time, armed mission. We will have one hour to execute and get back here in one piece. We've all talked as a group, and individually, about the good and the evil we've all seen in the world. Tomorrow morning, the good are going to score one over evil."

Abrams asked, "Where we headed, boss?"

Smiling, Jackson walked to a nearby dressing area and drew back the curtain revealing the uniform of the day. He then pulled away sheets covering items laid out on a massive table. Before them lay a collection of original, finely maintained German Lugar pistols, MP34 and MP40 German assault rifles, a Mauser sniper rifle, six assault knives, ammunition, and a dozen potato-masher type hand grenades.

White, Wilson, and Sharif spread out around the weapons table to inspect the gear. Richard and Abrams walked over to the uniforms and each take one from the rack.

"These are German SS uniforms from World War II," Abrams said with distain. "I can't wear this. Men in these same uniforms killed hundreds of thousands of Jews during the war. I won't wear this!"

Jackson picked up a Lugar from the table and walked toward Abrams. Unlike the pistols of that time, this one had been fitted with a state-of-the-art, modern-day low profile hi-tech silencer.

"We've sworn to not change history, so here's how I see it," JJ said. "Hitler was responsible for the torture and murder of millions of innocent men, women, and children. He was also responsible for the war itself and the incredible loss of life and destruction that resulted from it. Just as the war was ending he hid in a bunker in Berlin with his dog and his new wife. He killed himself and his bride so they wouldn't be taken alive. The few guards that didn't run away when they ran low on ammo, stayed to guard that piece of shit. When they heard the gunshot from his quarters and saw that he had killed himself they burned the bodies so his couldn't be recovered and paraded around with a pole up it's ass. We're not going to *change* history, we're just going to drop in early, under the cover of a moonless night, and deliver some justice. He's still going to be dead and burned to bits, but we're not going to let him take the easy way out and avoid justice. And, Abrams, you're going to pull the trigger on this gun."

"This isn't exactly what the Chiefs had in mind, boss," Sharif said.

JJ turned to him, then looked at each team member. "General Stewart approved it personally, so it's a go. His father was one of the first American soldiers to discover the horror that existed at Dachau, and the general grew up listening to his father's stories. They haunted his father until the day he died. We've all heard the same stories and seen the pictures. Hitler was the ultimate asshole, and he deserves to be executed." There were nods all around. "Remember, we may be adjusting the events in the timeline. But the outcome is the same. Technically, the charter's not violated."

"So, we know the technology works," Wilson said. "And killing bad guys is nothing new to us. But we're testing ourselves for the first time, nearly seventy years back in time, in a foreign location and under dangerous combat conditions."

JJ nodded his head solemnly. "Exactly. If this works, and we get permission to go after the likes of Idi Amin and the shitheads in Darfur, they'll be top of my personal wish list—that is, kill list. But for now, planning ops like that are above my pay grade." He drew a deep breath. "Now *this* entire exercise is to test the process. But it's also to test us under this added element of travelling back in time and the stress."

Without flinching, Abrams ripped the SS jacket from the coat hanger and slipped it on. Jackson extends the Lugar toward him again. This time he took it. Looking around the room at his comrades, he smiled and, in a quick gesture, snaps his right arm straight out, whispering with a grin, "F-him!"

6

Berlin 1945

THE TEAM HAD one hour to travel seventy years back in time, accomplish their mission, and return safely. Jackson and Wilson scouted and planned the action by reading everything they could find to determine what structures existed in and around the bunker back then. They relied on accounts in books and audio interviews of former Nazi soldiers and citizens of Berlin who had any knowledge of the Chancellery and the concrete bunker beneath its grounds.

Jackson was stationed in modern times at the U.S. Embassy in Berlin, right across from the Brandenburg Gate. He had been to Check Point Charlie and the few sections of the Berlin wall that remained, but most were post World War II sites. Berlin had been leveled during the war. And the Russians destroyed the bunker and everything around it when they assaulted Berlin in the last days of the war. So, for the most part, nothing he saw in modern time had existed in 1945. Nothing would seem familiar on the trip back in time. Everyone was anxious.

"You sure you want to do this?" Richard asked the group.

"You got something better to do tonight other than killing Hitler?" JJ asked jokingly.

"Guess not, boss." Richard continued his prep. "Remind me again, what do we do if we get stuck there?"

Their anxiety wasn't anticipation of confrontation with the enemy. They all hoped and prayed that the coordinates programmed by Dr. Moretti would get them to the right spot, not drop them in the middle of a highway in the path of a military convoy, or into a factory or warehouse that was being bombed.

"You must have slept through that part Richard. I'll remind you of the 5-30 protocol if anything happens," Wilson said.

All six members of T1 double-checked that the pulse devices were in place against their chests. White was dressed provocatively, masquerading as a young black *fraulein* Jackson intended to present to Hitler's guards. Her matching garter belt held a Lugar and a large knife. The rest of the team was dressed in black German SS uniforms and carried restored weaponry fueled with state-of-the-art American hollow-point ammunition. Each packed a silencer, a high-tech sound suppressor, either mounted on their weapon or in a pocket for use with a Lugar, if needed.

In addition to the MP40 Richard was holding for White, he carried a K98 Mauser sniper rifle over his right shoulder. Jackson and Wilson had test fired all the weapons during a private test session at Quantico, days earlier. They'd been cleaned, reloaded and were ready for action.

They had German currency in case they needed it, and

Jackson had taught them basic questions and responses in German, should they have to engage anyone. Two of the team wrapped bandages around their necks to make it look like they had injuries that would inhibit their ability to speak if confronted.

Hopefully, White would be distraction enough to get them close to their target. It was risky bringing her along but she wanted in just like everyone else. And, while Black people in Nazi Germany weren't victims of mass extermination, as in the cases of Jews, Romani and Slavs, they were still considered by Hitler to be an inferior race. White was willing to put her life on the line to punish the animals who'd targeted her race, as well as others.

With Moretti's technology, wherever they landed they'd be operating under the same clock. It was 0500 and time to go. The lights were reduced by 95% to simulate the darkness in which they'd arrive. They waited another minute for their eyes to adjust, and then Moretti hit the enter button on her hand-held controller. Within a second of pulse activation, they were standing in the dark, in a Berlin alleyway, at 5:00 a.m. on April 29, 1945.

They hunched down then moved quickly and quietly, spreading single-file along the side of the building.

Abrams whispered to White, "So what if we'd landed on a moving truck?"

White snickered but focused on her surroundings. They assume the standard 180-degree protective semi-circle—a set of eyes and a weapon forming a shield around the group. It was dark, cold, and quiet. The buildings surrounding them looked just as they did in the photos that were taken after the war. Berlin had its butt kicked by Allied bombers and the once-vibrant city was now a shell, a ghost of a town.

"Night goggles would be nice," Wilson muttered.

He and Jackson peered around the corner across from the bunker entrance. There it was, the rear of the Reich Chancellery and the emergency exit of Hitler's Bunker, only twenty yards away. They fanned out and employed stealth techniques to get as close as possible. The intel was dead on. Many buildings had been damaged by the intense and more frequent Allied bombings of Berlin.

Jackson whispered to Wilson, "Is my eyesight screwed or do you see only five guards?"

"Roger that," Wilson responded. "My bet is, with everyone knowing the war's over, most of the Krauts have run off. Only the extreme shit-heads will stay behind to protect the bastard."

JJ nodded. The briefing had also stated that, by now, most of the German military had run out of ammo and headed for the hills.

The five German soldiers huddled around a fire drum to keep warm. The flames' orange light picked out black SS officer's hats and uniforms, red armbands high on their sleeves, holstered Lugers, assault rifles riding shoulder straps. Four black Mercedes Benz sedans, untouched by the destruction around them, were parked nearby. JJ waved up three other T-1's, leaving Corporal Richard to watch their backs.

On the whispered count of three, five German-made rifles, operated by the most elite 21st-century combat fighters on the planet, and modified with state-of-the-art silencers, took out the guards with simultaneous headshots. They rushed toward the bunker door.

Taking the lead, JJ was within five feet of the door when it suddenly swung open. A lone guard, returning with steaming hot coffees in both hands, stared at JJ with more curiosity than shock. Wilson opened fire. The guard took one lunging step then went down hard. JJ winced as the ceramic cups hit the cement and shattered.

But there was nobody around to hear it. Berlin was on its last legs, gasping for air, and the only noise was a dog barking in the distance.

The bodies of the dead SS guards were quickly pulled behind the cars, into the shadows. As Jackson dropped the arms of the guard he'd moved he peeked into a side window for just a second, muttering "Nice ride."

"Goebbels and Goering might still be here, but this late they'll be in drunken comas," Wilson whispered.

Jackson looked at Richard. "Find a jerry can full of gas, not diesel. Remember it will be marked benzin. We'll need it quick." Sticking to plan, Wilson remained outside the entrance to act as the lone guard and watch for trouble while the others moved slowly into the bunker. JJ knew his second in command would rather be headed inside for the action, but the warmth of the burning wood in the drum was, at least, a small consolation. Jackson thought it only fitting that a Jewish-American Navy corpsman and a Black American Marine should be involved in carrying out the execution.

"Whatever you do, don't let a Russian sniper kick your ass before we come back through here," JJ whispered with a smile to his brother-in-law.

"I just realized these uniforms won't do us no favors with them. They're shooting anything in a uniform that isn't theirs. Get moving. I'll be here. Go kick some ass! Remember, no souvenirs."

Through the door and down thirty concrete steps, slowly moving into a dimly lit hallway, they encountered one uniformed clerk. Sharif neutralized him quicker than a sneeze. These silencers were quieter than anything they'd used before. Suddenly, a beautiful young woman, a kitchen worker, stepped into the hallway.

Jackson grabbed her face, covering her mouth, shoved her against the wall. He whispered in her ear, "*Schweigen bitte!*" *Quiet please!* Time was of the essence, as was the element of surprise.

He sensed that she wasn't a threat and definitely had no desire to be a martyr. "*Wer ist hier?" Is anyone else here?*

She nodded 'yes' and whispered, *"Der Führer."*

JJ thought of his wife Michelle, hoping someone would look out for her if she were in harm's way. The woman pointed to the left, toward a door twenty feet away, at the end of the hall. He gently guided the woman back into the dimly lit kitchen with a gloved finger across his lips, urging her to remain silent. She slowly took a seat at the table as a cautious smile crossed her face. JJ took a moment to scan the room and with no other sign of trouble he returned to the hallway. With two Americans on one side of the hall and two on the other, they moved quickly past a stairwell entrance that led down to the lower levels of the bunker. Sharif took position at the top of the stairs and protected their backs as they moved toward their target. The adrenaline rush in Jackson was fiercer than he'd ever experienced.

The door was marked *Lagerraum.*

"Storage room," Jackson whispered. "For assholes, these guys are pretty smart."

Richard arrived with the can of gasoline and, setting it down, looked at JJ for an update. "He's in there?"

Abrams whispered, "It's too quiet. You sure he isn't already dead?"

"If he were dead he'd already have been turned into firewood and the soldiers we nuked would have been long gone. Remember, history says we're here just in time."

Their intel indicated that the bunker extended many floors below ground level and was comprised of dozens of rooms. Their pre-op research indicated that the deeper underground the shelter went, the damper and colder the rooms became.

Now, JJ was surprised by how quickly they'd been able to move from the exit door to the dictator's quarters. Perhaps the Germans would only seek the much deeper quarters if the air raid sirens raised the alarm. Jackson and White took tactical positions at the entry door with Abrams watching down the hallway toward Sharif for any surprises.

JJ could hear soft music playing through the door. He tried the knob and it turned easily but with a squeak. Slowly opening the door, he peered into the dimly lit room. There, just fifteen feet away, sitting together on a large sofa, were a uniformed man and a woman. The distinctive mustache confirmed that they'd found their target and his wife.

Major Jackson pointed his assault weapon directly at their target's head. "Adolph frigging Hitler, live and in person!" he shouted.

Nobody had ever pointed a gun at Hitler before and lived to talk about it. There were a dozen or so attempts on his life with misdirected bombs and airplane sabotage, but this was different. Jackson and his team of four U.S. Marines and Navy corpsman had traveled back in time to deliver justice with a vengeance and they planned on living.

Slowly placing his drink on an end table, Hitler stood up, his hands raised to show he had no weapons. Sergeant White pointed her gun down at Eva Braun, Hitler's new bride, a German Shepard puppy curled up at her side. Despite being only thirty-three years of age, lack of sleep and fear of the unknown made Braun seem old and worn. White gestured for her to stay seated. Braun slowly pushed the puppy away from her and raised her hands.

"*Sprechen zie English, Mein Führer*?" Jackson asked.

Hitler responds in a heavy German accent, "*Ja.* I am very surprised to see an American in my quarters. I am relieved my countrymen have not betrayed me, but it is obvious they have failed me. They have all failed me."

Only five foot, eight inches, the dictator looked smaller than in the photos Jackson had studied. The once fiery Fuhrer seemed broken—defeated. That didn't bother Jackson; it made him feel proud.

Hitler looked from Jackson to White, then to Richard and Abrams in the doorway, and back to Jackson. "You are all Americans, yes? Sent by your crippled Roosevelt to capture me. Here, he would have been thrown in the trash." He paused again for a moment, looking down at Braun. "*Ungeachtet.* Regardless, I accept that the Reich has been defeated and I formally surrender to you."

"Screw your surrender. You're not much of a rock star now, are you?" Jackson taunted. "I wish I had time to ask you a few questions, like why you hurt so many innocent people, so many innocent women and children. But I don't have time for that shit. Satan is waiting for you in hell. That's where you're headed, you piece of shit."

Hitler's eyes sharpened, as if his thoughts were finally clearing. He stood taller. Jackson backed to the doorway and motioned for Abrams to enter and take his place. It took Abrams a long twenty seconds to get hold of his emotions as tears stream down his face. Tears for the people the man in front of him had tortured and killed. Tears of exhilaration that he was now in the same room with the most evil human being known to the modern world. A cruel monster that *he*, a Jewish kid from Brooklyn, was going to put an end to.

With Abrams in his place, Jackson ran down the hallway to check status with Wilson. At the top of the steps, Wilson taps his wrist to show the clock was running. JJ nodded and headed back to the action at the end of the hall.

Abrams was glaring at Hitler, seemed to be in the middle of a prepared speech. "My hatred for you is too great to even express. A big trial and public hanging isn't in your cards, Adolph!"

From the doorway, Jackson said, "We're short on time, guys." He looked at Hitler. "We know your plan is to commit suicide with your bride to avoid capture. We're going to spoil your going-away party. It's time we laid a little American justice on you, courtesy of the United States Marine Corps. You're not a soldier fighting for a noble cause. You're just a sick sadist."

JJ could tell from the way the dictator's eyes darted around the room that his mind was racing. His end was near and he knew it. But it must, just now, be occurring to him that it was impossible for these Americans to have known his plan. He hadn't told anyone, not even Eva.

Standing just three feet from Adolph Hitler, Abrams unbuttoned his uniform, reached inside, and pulled out the gold Star of David medal he'd worn since he was a boy, back in Brooklyn. It hung from the same chain as his pulse device. Hitler's eyes went to it, and widened.

Abrams stepped forward, raised his MP34, and pushed the end of the silencer against Hitler's face, right between the eyes.

Eva screamed and jumped up from the sofa, grabbing for the gun. White slashed her with a short burst and Hitler's mistress dropped to the floor.

Hitler shrank back against a bookshelf in shock. He stared at White, struggling with the realization that a black woman, an American fighter, had killed his bride. He stared down at Eva's body, and then glanced at the little black puppy cowering on the sofa and gave it a slight smile before turning toward Abrams and standing at attention, "Go ahead Juda. I am ready. Go ahead. Shoot!"

Richard, anticipating the end was near, stepped into the room carrying the gas can. But Abrams shook his head. "No. Wait. This isn't enough. Get the chair."

Richard looked puzzled for a moment but then nodded in agreement and quickly pulled a chair from the desk, placing it behind Hitler.

"Schwarz!" Hitler spat at White with disgust.

They searched him, removing the Lugar from his leather holster, and then shoved him down onto the chair. Richard pulled large black zip-ties from his inside jacket pocket, handing two to Abrams. They quickly secured his arms and legs, and gagged him with a napkin from the table.

Jackson stepped further into the room, tapped his watch to show everyone they needed to get moving. He frowned. "What's with the chair and the zip ties?"

Abrams picked up the jerry can and poured gasoline all over Hitler's uniform. The vapors immediately irritating their prisoner's eyes.

"History tells us that you killed yourself and your SS shitheads burned your body so it couldn't be recognized. Some people even think you escaped to Argentina. I doubt you got away, but right now I'm goddamned going to make sure of it. We're not supposed to change history, so we're going to keep it that way. You're going to die here in Berlin—just a little earlier than you planned. A bullet is too good for you. They say hell is full of fire, so we're sending you there the way you deserve to go."

Abrams picked up a lighter from the pipe box on Hitler's desk and prepared to light it."Say 'hi' to your brother the devil when you meet him, you evil bastard!"

7

TWO MUFFLED SHOTS zipped past Abrams and blasted the top of Hitler's head off. Abrams whipped around to see Jackson standing in the doorway, holding his smoking gun.

"We are *not* animals like him," Jackson explained. "We don't torture people. He's now in hell getting what he deserves. Let's move! White, get the dog. Abrams, *now* you can torch his dead ass and you have to burn her, too!" He pointed at Braun's body, crumpled on the floor where White's shots had struck her down.

Abrams picked up the lighter he'd dropped when the shots struck their target. The others were already running up the hallway toward the exit. He looked around quickly. No souvenirs, JJ had said. The heck with that, he thought to himself.

He pulled a military medal from Hitler's uniform. "Nobody will ever know," he muttered. As he stepped back, a drop of blood from Hitler's massive head wound fell on Abrams' hand. In disgust Abrams wiped the blood onto his own uniform and then shoved the medal into his pocket. He pushed the dictator's body over Braun's, sparked the lighter and tossed it. Within seconds both bodies were engulfed, the room quickly filling with smoke. Corpsman Benny Abrams paused to take in the scene, and then pulled the door closed behind him.

Jackson reached the base of the stairway—White, Sharif, and Richard closing in, and Abrams way behind. Suddenly, from the kitchen doorway machine gun fire blasted into the corridor. The young kitchen worker might have appeared harmless, but a guard who must have fallen asleep somewhere, had been awakened by the noise. He wasn't going to let the intruders leave without a fight.

JJ swung around in time to see Richard hit by most of the fire. Sharif returned two quick blasts from his assault rifle. Abrams lobbed a grenade into the kitchen. A fiery blast exploded through the door, adding more smoke to the haze caused by the gunfire. JJ signaled Abrams to clear the kitchen. Through the door, he could see that the guard and the woman were both alive, but seriously hurt. *No prisoners*, he thought, and gave Abrams the nod.

Abrams aimed his assault rifle and delivered two quick bursts. "Clear!" he shouted, then stepped back into the hallway.

JJ stood beside Sharif over Richard's body. No doubt in his mind that JR was dead. Abrams, their medic, checked him to be sure, but the head wound left no doubt he was gone. JJ looked at Abrams as he stood up, and their eyes met. Was Benny thinking the same thing he was? If Benny hadn't taken those extra seconds back in the shelter, doing God knew what, might he have been the one in the sights of that guard?

Wilson ran halfway down the stairway and shouted, "Okay, now *that* was a lot of noise. We need to get out of here right now!" Suddenly he froze, eyes fixed Richard's body. "Oh, Shit."

Stunned, JJ tried to clear his head to evaluate their situation. They were 4,000 miles and seventy years from home. They had a KIA. What now?

Wilson wrenched his gaze away from the body on the floor and stared at JJ. "We don't have time to fuck around here. This sucks, but we need to move. We can't leave him behind. Let's carry him to the rally point. If we hold him upright in the middle of us it will only take a second to engage."

JJ shook his head violently, still desperately trying to process all that had just happened. They'd succeeded in their mission, but made a deadly mistake that cost his team a life.

"JJ, what about Goebbels and Goering?" Wilson gasped.

Right, he thought. They might be somewhere beneath them, hiding further down in the bunker.

White shifted restlessly from foot to foot. "If they're here they'll either engage us real soon. Or they'll hide out and live to tell the story."

JJ's head finally cleared. There was only one thing they could do now. "We're outta here, leaving nothing behind. They won't be able to figure anything out, other than the shithead must have killed himself and someone burned his and Eva's bodies. The Russians who find them won't give a shit. They'll toss their bones in the trash where they belong."

White looked toward the stairs, their only way out. "But we need a sixth pulse. Let's grab a local. When we hit Andrews, we click their clock."

"Are you nuts?" Jackson glared at her. "Where's that puppy? A pulse is a pulse. If that doesn't work we'll grab someone else. Now let's get back to the alley and take our boy home."

They grabbed a tablecloth from the kitchen and covered Richard's head and upper body. JJ and Wilson struggled to carry their fallen comrade up the stairs and through the door. Everything outside the bunker is still, but the sun was starting to rise. Before long it would be daylight, and their chances of escaping without detection would be drastically reduced.

The team headed quickly toward the area where they'd first arrived. Sharif removed Richard's pulse from around the dead man's neck and held it on the pup. JJ rolled out what they'd nicknamed "the flying carpet," and they stepped on. They pinned Richard's body upright, between them.

"Remember, we have to hit all six pulse buttons at the same time," JJ warned. "Ready? 3-2-1." JJ punched his.

Nothing happened.

"Damn it!"

The team stared at Jackson. It didn't take much to read their minds. *Now what, boss?*

JJ hoisted Richard's body over his right shoulder. "Okay, move in tighter. Abrams, you'll have to hit my pulse. Sharif, you have yours and the puppy's. Ready, 3-2-1!"

In an instant they were back at Andrews. Someone on T2 shouted, "Medic!" The members of T1 stepped back from their marks and helped JJ lay Richard down on the floor.

"I *am* a medic," Abrams muttered dejectedly to anyone close enough to hear him.

Whatever excitement and anticipation had existed in the room before their arrival, it now turned to sorrow and disbelief. It struck JJ that, although they'd known there was a risk, none of them had thought this would actually happen.

The support crew relieved the travelers of their assault weapons and other gear. Dr. Moretti had stood up on their return, but now dropped back into her chair. Everyone knew that she cared about every member of T1. But she'd admitted to JJ that, working from the safety of her isolated laboratories for many years, she hadn't seen death in many years. Sadly, everything had just gotten real for her.

In the many battles and covert ops they'd each fought, they'd of course lost team members. Iraq, Afghanistan, Damascus—death was always close at hand. Now, members of T1 and T2 surrounded the fallen Marine and stood silently with their own thoughts for nearly a minute. The only sound was the whimpering of their German souvenir. Jackson ordered them to attention. In unison, they saluted their comrade.

Minutes later, the medical team arrived and prepared to remove the body. Moretti slowly approached Jackson. "What happened?"

JJ knew he'd need to explain events to everyone, but not now. "Listen up T1," he called out, "we'll debrief back here tomorrow. Stow your gear. Go eat, drink, sleep—do whatever you need to do. Just be here sober and cleaned up so we can go over what happened with the doc and T2. Dismissed."

He drew a deep breath and looked to Sharif, a dog lover. "Do you want the pooch? Otherwise I'd like to give it to my wife."

White interrupted. "All due respect, sir, but Richard is dead, and you're thinking about the puppy?"

JJ didn't respond. He took the puppy from Sharif and, holding it close, walked away toward the door.

"You've never been around dogs, I guess," Wilson said to White after their team leader had gone. "That little distraction will allow him to decompress. Get his head straight about what happened tonight."

"Seriously?" She looked unconvinced.

"He used to make friends with stray dogs all over Iraq to stay loose and relax. Plus, it'll piss off my sister. She's only ever had outside dogs, ranch dogs. So, why not back it down a bit. Let's go find some beer and raise a few to JR. He was a damn good Marine."

White looked as though she were biting her tongue.

"Forget the damn dog, White," Wilson advised.

She shook her head. "That's not it, sir. I don't know how to suggest this but, down in the bunker, the Major seemed distracted. In the kitchen, he didn't really check the room, just trusted the German bitch with the pretty face to keep quiet and not interfere."

Wilson was incensed. She had just challenged their commander's decision-making. And yet...he hadn't been there to see it for himself. Had JJ made a mistake in judgment that proved fatal?

"This afternoon, at the briefing, White, bring it up. For now, it's time to wind down."

During the three-minute drive to his on-base

apartment, Jackson returned to his thoughts in the moments after Richard was killed.

What could I have done differently? Was this my fault? Why didn't I clear the Goddamn kitchen?

He wasn't sure whether he should call Chairman Stewart now or wait a few hours. And then there was Bill Griffiths, JR's grandfather, and his mother. It was his duty to inform them that their boy had died for his country during a covert op, overseas. At least that much was the truth.

He pulled up his car in front of his apartment but sat there quietly for a few minutes, replaying what had happened that night. The pup slept beside him on the bench seat. He shook his head in disbelief at everything that had just occurred. He had been face to face with Adolph Hitler. He'd lost a man on the mission of a lifetime. And he couldn't talk to anyone about any of it.

JJ reached down to pet his sleeping souvenir. "Well, pup, let's see how this goes. She'll either love you or kick my ass. But the way things are going, your guess is as good as mine."

Michelle was excited to see her husband home safe, and thrilled with her present. But she also knew him well enough to realize that something had gone wrong. She didn't press him for details. She would offer her open arms or a wide berth, whatever he needed to deal with it.

An hour later, she and her new friend were fast asleep in the bed. JJ lay down quietly beside them, rethinking that night until he was finally able to calm his mind. He'd report in and make the dreaded calls in the morning. Sadly, there was nothing more he could do but try to get some rest.

8

Michelle had known what life with a Marine, a special Marine, would be like. It wouldn't be dinner together every night at six or always having him there to say goodnight. She knew what she'd signed up for. Nevertheless, any other woman might have grown frustrated with this new top-secret assignment. Her husband and her brother were working together. Neither of them could discuss anything about their work with her. Michelle tried not to let it bother her, and, for the most part, succeeded.

Living in an exciting city like the nation's capital, being able to work with children every day, and having an entirely new and different landscape to photograph kept her busy and fulfilled. She shared the same passion as JJ and her brother Tommy for protecting the innocent and their country, so she supported them without question. She once joked with them, "If these kids or either of you ever get on my nerves too much, I just might join the Navy and become a Seal. Why should you boys have all the fun?" Growing up, her father had been away a lot, even though he rarely left the farm. Way before sunrise each morning he was out the door, tending to the cattle or the property before she rose. He was still working hard most nights, even after she went to bed. Her mother was a nurse and drove sixty miles to work the second shift at the regional hospital.

JJ's upbringing was also unconventional. He was raised by a military man, as was his father before him. The adult men who surrounded JJ when he was growing up were also servicemen. It was God and country first, working nights, weekends, and extended periods away from home. His DNA was made up of discipline, history, training to avoid confrontations, and training to wage and win them if they needed to be fought. His father's career in the Air Force, stationed overseas and across the United States, meant JJ wasn't used to staying still or living in one place for very long. Settling down wasn't necessarily what he wanted. He knew nothing about it. His mother died when he was in school, so a traditional home life was foreign to him. Discipline and camaraderie among fighting men was what he knew.

Growing up on a remote ranch south of Helena, Montana, Michelle was accustomed to her father's absence, but also to the peace and quiet the property and the small family that raised her provided. Her mother didn't want her to be a lonely, only child, so when she learned she was unable to have another baby, they adopted Tommy. Tommy and Michelle became closer than many biological siblings.

Tommy loved the ranch, his adopted family, and Montana, but he wanted to explore the world. The Marine Corps caught his eye, and then terrorists attacked the United States and he was gone. The day Tommy returned home, bringing

Jim Jackson along to meet Michelle and his parents, everyone's world changed.

Wilson didn't let on his intentions. He had promised Jackson that he'd love the area and the ranch he grew up on. They'd ride horses and then go down to Yellowstone for a few days. JJ had steered clear of relationships as long as Tommy had known him. It was clear JJ withdrew from attachments and focused on fighting the bad guys. He was angry at life, was taking it out on the terrorists and he was very good at it. Tommy knew exactly what he was doing though. His sister was a very special person and once the two met, JJ was never the same.

She taught him how to ride horses properly and enjoy it, something her brother neglected to show him. Afterwards, they sat in front of a fire as he nursed a sore seat. He explained to her that he was dedicated to the corps and consequently didn't feel it would be right for him to father a child because he was always away on secret missions or fighting wars. He also, reluctantly, offered that he didn't think it would be fair of him to marry someone who needed a conventional husband who'd be home every night and on weekends.

Hearing all this didn't bother her as much as he might have thought. When she was a teenager she had dealt with a pre-cancer that eventually left her unable to bear children. It took a full year for her to be able to discuss that loss with her parents and begin planning a childless life. A month later, the two eloped at a chapel in Las Vegas and headed east to their new home in Quantico, Virginia.

When they moved to Andrews, they got into the habit

of taking his Toyota Pickup across Route 50 to the beach at Ocean City, Maryland, an hour away.

It was there, late one night, that JJ saw his bride in an entirely new light.

Just before they left a marina bar he excused himself to use the bathroom and she waited for him by the exit. Within a few seconds a local with too much to drink walked over to her and whispered something in her ear. She shook her head no and stepped away. He stepped closer, this time with a determined look on his face. He put his hand on her shoulder.

In one swift move she knocked his arm down with one hand while the other struck the side of his neck. When JJ returned two minutes later he found her standing over an unconscious man who was being attended to by security.

"I didn't like his idea of a thrill ride but he couldn't take no for an answer. I figured he'd had enough partying for one night and gave him a little help turning in for the night." She flashed JJ a smug smile. Yes, understood.

JJ decided there was no need for the police. Tommy had taught her well.

9

THE DUST HADN'T yet settled, but as is the case in any combat situation that suffered a KIA, a killed in action, the team would honor the fallen as a group but each of its members would mourn and process the loss in their own way. Then they'd focus on the next mission to keep their minds from dwelling on what had occurred.

The fact that they had traveled back in time and executed Hitler kept them focused. They still felt the rush of adrenaline and exhilaration, knowing that justice had been served. They pushed the reality of what they'd lost deep into their memory banks to deal with at another time.

Team Leader Jackson called General Stewart to report what had happened. He knew Stewart was very disappointed and ready to hang someone over the fiasco. He also expected that much stricter protocols would be implemented going forward.

JJ then made the painful calls to Bill Griffiths and JR's mother, to deliver the news and offer his condolences before the team assembled for their debriefing.

"I always knew this day would come," she told him.

"He loved the Corps and loved living on the edge. At least he was doing good when he died."

With tears in his eyes and a lump in his throat he offered the only words that came to mind. "Yes, ma'am. He did good."

In their meeting, led by Jackson, T1 reviewed what they did right and wrong, discussed what they learned from their costly mistakes, and prepared to move on to the next mission.

"I was the one who eyeballed the kitchen so that's on me," JJ remarked. "I don't know if that bastard was hiding in there all along or got into the room from some secret entry door. I didn't see anything other than a hot coffee pot and a scared cook praying for her life. I should have left someone to watch her." Understanding nods and a full minute of silence followed. There was nothing more anyone needed to say.

At the end of the debrief, they stood up and started out of the meeting room. White intercepted JJ. "How'd Michelle like the pup?"

"It was love at first sight. She's not been feeling all that well so I figured the dog would lift her spirits and it has already. She stepped in shit barefoot three times this morning before her first coffee, so I think it's me who is in the dog house for a few days."

White seemed satisfied that her commanding officer took the blame for the incident but then JJ could never be sure about her. She, like the rest of the team, needed to know that everyone was aware of the mistake and that it would never happen again. He wondered if Wilson also might be thinking more than he was saying. Although no one on the team had challenged his version of what happened, he had a sense that someone was holding back. JJ understood the look on Abrams face. He realized they could be headed for Brooklyn instead of Havasu for a funeral. What he didn't know was that Abrams had broken the rules and taken a souvenir. Worse yet, when he feared being caught with it, he panicked and stuck it in Richard's pocket.

Wilson came up alongside JJ and reminded him that Chairman Stewart was expecting him and T2 leader Scott at the Pentagon shortly. "If I don't get shipped off directly to Who-gives-a-shit-astan," JJ said, "do you want to come over tonight for beer? Your sister misses you."

Wilson smiled and waved his hands to decline. "No way Jose, I know to stay away when she's not feeling good."

Team Leaders Jackson and Scott's ride to the Chairman's office was quick. Military shuttles ran every thirty minutes between Andrews and the Pentagon. They could have hitched a ride on a government helicopter, but they were in no hurry. "This is one time I don't mind sitting in traffic," JJ told the captain. "The Chairman wears a big shoe. I'm pretty sure it won't quite fit where it's going to wind up today."

His attempt at humor received nothing more than a nod from the Army officer. Putting their differences aside, losing a team member was tough and it weighed heavily on everyone.

"Major Jackson," Stewart barked as soon as they walked into the room, "I put my trust in you. General Brooks and the other chiefs are outraged at what happened. I am as well. But, mostly, I'm disappointed in the both of you. You were supposed to see if you could get eyes on Hitler, not shoot him! This could have had unimaginable consequences if things got any worse than they did. If I had carte blanche with a god-damned time machine, I'd have gone to ancient Rome to watch the Gladiators fight elephants and tigers, but you had to do something off-charter and it got someone killed."

Jackson stood at attention and took it.

"You do anything like that again and your God-damned disobeying ass will be on front gate duty guarding the Embassy in friggin' Nigeria!"

After waiting a few moments to let that sink in, Stewart turned to Scott. "I know you were hoping this might mean you'll get an assignment, Captain. Technically you violated your top-secret clearance and also violated the chain of command by contacting General Brooks and relating what happened in the bunker. Don't do that again or your ass will be right alongside the major here, demoted, if not behind bars. Understood, Captain?"

"Yes, General."

"Good. Now give us the room now, Captain."

Scott nodded, saluted, turned stiffly and walked slowly out to the reception area. He looked shocked but also relieved that the briefing had ended so quickly. Stewart's aide acknowledged the general's nod and closed the door to leave the two men in private.

"Okay, now that I got that off my chest, JJ, here's how I really feel. You really put my nuts in a wringer with the other chiefs. Brooks wanted to have you locked up, for Christ's sake. I had to hand out a lot of IOUs to keep you in charge, but you're on a tight leash now. So, going forward, don't do anything like that again."

JJ realized he had put the general in a pinch and swore he'd stay within the limits of their mission from then on.

Knowing Stewart as intimately as he did, JJ spoke from the heart.

"General, you gave me an incredible opportunity. I'll never disappoint you again. If it helps you with the brass, I'll resign. But on a personal note, knowing how you and your father felt about old Adolph, I believed I had to move on him. Shooting that bastard actually felt good. For me, it was like shooting a rabid dog that had attacked someone. I just wish I had done a better job of clearing the kitchen. That's something I'll live with until the day I die.

"You know why I joined the Marines. To kill bad guys. Period. I can teach strategy and do whatever I'm called on to do, but when it comes down to it I'm built to protect and serve. It's what makes me tick. I believe I was put on this earth to fight evil. Rules of engagement sometimes get in the way. There are moments when you just need to take the shot. When I was sure we could pull it off, I took the team on an extraordinary mission...and they executed flawlessly."

Stewart nodded and walked over to Jackson, extending his hand. "You lucky son of a bitch, you got to Berlin during the war and killed the craziest bastard we've ever seen. Semper Fi to you and your crew. Just don't come home with any more body bags! You copy that? Make sure everyone is focused and prepared. And keep an eye on Scott. Someone got the drop on you in Berlin, which is uncharacteristic of you, but this is the last time that can happen."

JJ relaxed and nodded in agreement. "Yes, General."

"Listen, JJ, if your father were here with us right now, you know what he'd say, don't you? He'd say, 'Well that didn't take long. Leave it to our American ass-kickers to break all the rules and do the right thing.'" Both men thought about that for a moment, then smiled at each other.

"Now stay out of trouble, don't go after Genghis Khan or Ho Chi Min or anyone for Christ's sake. Go visit Valley Forge during the Revolutionary War and tell me what it was really like there. I'd love to know. It's the perfect next assignment. It will look like a punishment sending you there in the dead of winter without decent clothes or boots. See how Washington was holding up behind closed doors, then report back."

"And I want you to come over this weekend. Bring Michelle this time. With Mrs. Stewart still AWOL it will be good to have a pretty face in the house again. I heard you brought home a puppy, bring it if you want. While Michelle's chasing the damn dog around the yard you can tell me everything about Germany—the city, the bunker, the bastard, and his bride"

Jackson took two steps back, "Yes, General. Thank You, General." He snapped a salute, turned and left the meeting room.

Putting on a good front for Scott, Jackson rubbed his own rear end and put on a show of misery. "Let's get back to Andrews. We need to plan a proper funeral for Richard and then prep for the next mission."

The remaining five members of T1 asked to accompany Richard's remains back to Havasu for his burial. They would serve as pallbearers in full Marine dress and plan on spending a few days there with his mother and family sharing stories, enjoying beer and barbeque, and coming to terms with their loss. Richard's Uncle Bill flew in on his private jet to Maryland to retrieve the remains and carry him home. Unlike earlier trips, Griffiths wanted answers and asked for his uniforms and guns back. He stayed in D.C. for three days until the body was released into his care.

"You guys go charging off to 1940's European war games, or who knows where else," Griffiths snarled. "And I'm supposed to convince his mom, my sister, that he was KIA somewhere in Afghanistan? She might swallow that bullshit, but *I* want to know what really happened to my grandson. That boy was like a son to me and he's in a box now and I need to know why."

To distract and calm him, Jackson and Wilson took Griffiths on a behind-the-scenes tour of Andrews while they tried to share with him what little information they could. They brought him into the ultra-restricted hangar that housed both Air Force One 747s, but Griffiths was no lightweight and he didn't buy what they were selling.

"Listen, if I wanted to see Air Force One I would have asked the President for another ride in it. We go back a long way. So, don't try to blow smoke over the issue or up my ass." He huffed at them. "I accept that you are restricted in your ability to tell me exactly what happened to the boy, but you have to give me something. You've returned the SS uniforms and pistols, assault weapons, and defused hand grenades. One of those grenades is missing, by the way. Three uniforms have blood on them and one smells like it was soaked in gasoline. Do you know how hard it is to get dried blood out of material like that? I can't return them to the collector in LA. They'll need to be destroyed, and it'll cost about $60,000 to replace them. And I found this German Luftwaffe Medal of Valor in a pocket. I spent the night researching it. I know one thing; only one person was ever photographed wearing this medal and his first name was Adolph. So, tell me, what did you guys do?"

Wilson looked at JJ, his eyes red and teary. "We can't tell you very much, Bill, and I know that's not going to satisfy you. But the long and short of it is—we were on a covert mission to retrieve valuable information and it went bad," Wilson offered. "JJ and I are really surprised to see that medal. We've never seen it before. You sure it didn't come with the uniform?"

Griffith shrugged off the question and headed back to his jet, no doubt wishing this would be his last ever visit to the area. Within an hour, the flag-draped casket was placed aboard the Bombardier jet, and Griffith and T1 were headed west to Havasu.

JJ knew that Griffith wasn't satisfied with the explanation he'd received, but he understood what he'd signed up for. As the flight attendant filled their glasses, the jet rose to 42,000 feet. Griffith raised his and led the team in a toast to the fallen fighter. After that he retreated to the cockpit, as he normally did, to watch the night sky. The other five passengers settled in for the five-hour flight.

The flight attendant served dinner and offered more drinks, but as the cabin lights dimmed, most of the passengers settled into their own thoughts and whatever electronic distractions they found on board.

"I hope he doesn't wander off the reservation and really screw things up," Wilson whispered to JJ. "He's smart enough to know you don't F— with guys like us."

"Yeah, he knows, but if you're in the brig before you get the chance to shut him down, then who was smarter?" JJ responded.

"He's fine for now, but if we start to smell anything we may need to shut him down. Talk about smelling, I can't believe Richard stole that medal. He knew better. We all do. I hope he wasn't planning on giving it to his grandfather."

Wilson nodded, "Well, the old man has it now."

They had just discussed the possibility of a death sentence for the man riding high in the cockpit admiring the stars. Griffiths, gazing into the darkness, was smart enough to know that you don't mess with special ops—especially the elite of the elite. At least, JJ hoped so. He tried not to think about that, and shoved those dark thoughts to the back of his mind.

"Michelle hasn't been feeling well and she's gotten worse since I got home," JJ whispered to Wilson.

"You get my sister pregnant?" Wilson joked, but the look on Jackson's face stopped him in his tracks. "What's wrong with her? Has she been to the doctor?"

Jackson took a long draw from his beer and nodded. "They're going to do more tests, but there's something wrong with her plumbing and I'm not sure she's telling me everything. When we get back I need to push her to get to the bottom of it."

"Well, you know she's as stubborn and mean as a drunk donkey. Whatever it is, she's a fighter so she'll be okay." Wilson added and then sat back in his chair, the start of a tear in his eye.

"What?" JJ asked.

Wilson lifted a shoulder. "I just remember how sick she was as a teenager. I hope the cancer hasn't come back." He turned to gaze out the window at the clear night from nearly eight miles up. JJ wondered if he was praying for his sister.

"Hey boss," Abrams called out, "where'd ya tell Michelle the pup was from? You give it a name yet?"

"We're calling her Bunker because, as the story goes, some Seals rescued her from an ISIS bunker in Syria."

"Sweet. Hey, I was thinking, is there any chance the pup could be carrying any diseases from back then that could get passed on to other dogs around the base?"

"No way Jose, whether she's from Damascus or Deutschland she's fine. I had the vet look at her and give her a bunch of shots. Speaking of which, when we land, the first round is on White and none of that Jaeger shit. Patron this time!"

With the change of topic, and the jokes that ensued, Jackson and Wilson's moods lightened and they refocused on the friend they'd lost.

They buried their fallen comrade, paid the respect due to his family. After two days of storytelling, laughter, and tears, they said their goodbyes to Mrs. Richard and Lake Havasu, and headed home to Andrews. Griffith declined to fly them home on his jet so they rented a van and drove North to Las Vegas, to Nellis AFB, where they hitched a ride on a noisy C-130.

On the flight back east, Jackson and Wilson discussed finding a replacement for Richard and they both opted for Jones. Lieutenant Freddie Jones, second in command on T2, was a perfect fit for the group. He smoked expensive cigars, was a history buff, and like Richard, was one of the top weapons guys they knew.

"You realize Scott is not going to like being passed over," Jackson said with a smile.

"Fuck him." Wilson grinned.

Once back at base, Jackson and Wilson gave Stewart a

call as part of the recently revised protocol. After a short discussion, he approved the transfer. The two argued over who got to tell Scott he'd been passed over for Jones, but they were interrupted by an impatient Stewart.

"I don't care who tells him. Just don't forget, if you go off-plan again you'll be fighting over which one of you takes the transfer back to Embassy security, and this time it'll be in the Congo."

They signed off and, after a coin-flip, Jackson smiled at the chance to deliver the news.

"This is bullshit," Scott shouted as he threw his coffee mug across the room.

"Hey, orders are orders." Jackson shrugged, trying to keep his grin in check.

"One of these days you guys are going to screw something up really bad, and I'm going to be sitting here waiting to not lend a hand," Scott responded. "Jones, get in here," he ordered. "You're with Team 1 now. Watch your ass with these guys and don't forget who your friends are."

Jackson and Wilson welcomed Jones to the group and led the way through the door. To their surprise, Jones muttered, "Thanks guys. He's a POS so it's fitting he's in charge of number two."

JJ counted Valley Forge, located about twenty miles West of Philadelphia, one of the United States' most historic National Parks. It might not offer the elk or grizzlies of Yellowstone or Denali, or the magnificent face of El Capitan in Yosemite, but its geography and topography made it the perfect place for the men fighting for the thirteen original states to shelter and hibernate as best they could.

During the American Revolutionary War, in the winter

of 1777 to 1778, it was home to George Washington's Continental Army. Both civilian and military historians had written volumes about the incredible hardships the troops suffered. The invading, heavily funded British Army bought up, stole, or seized every bit of food, clothing, and warm shelter available in the region. Washington's soldiers were forced to wait out the long, cold winter in small, drafty log cabins without sufficient food, blankets, or even basic winter gear like gloves or socks. With only a few huts built before winter set in, the war weary soldiers had to cut down trees and build quarters for themselves. Dozens of letters to Congress, asking for money and supplies were ignored.

"That's our next mission," Jackson announced to the team. "We're going to Valley Forge, 1778, to see the conditions for ourselves. We've all been trained to survive extreme heat, cold, and lack of food and water so let's see what it was really like back then. We can't help anyone but we may learn a few things. Congress didn't believe conditions were as dire as Washington reported, so they finally sent representatives to tour the area and see for themselves. That will be our cover, if needed."

"Maybe old GW will come by on that big white horse of his," Abrams said.

JJ recalled history books showing the general on that very same horse.

"I'd have eaten that friggin' horse," Sharif joked. "I've had worse."

The team asked Griffiths for Continental Army style officer's uniforms from 1777 and the rifles and pistols to go with it. Reluctantly he obliged, but it was clear his enthusiasm for the covert missions was waning, along with his health.

They read as much as they could about Valley Forge, George Washington, and the history of that deadly winter. They determined that the best time to visit was late in the afternoon of February 23, 1778. That was the day Baron von Steuben arrived to aid Washington. He was an experienced military instructor and strategist from Europe, recommended by Benjamin Franklin. Von Steuben was a badass character who appealed to JJ.

It would get dark quickly. The plan was to get in and move around under cover of the fading light.

"I spent some time at the park when I was growing up in Philly," Jackson said. "It hasn't changed much since I was there, but, according to everything I've read, there were many more houses and structures surrounding the house Washington rented. In the two-hundred plus years since then, most of those fell apart and weren't restored. We can plan on landing behind the old mill that sat across from GW's HQ, and move on from there. If something goes wrong, the mill's on the river's edge so we'll have an escape route and the cover of darkness if needed."

"We going to have to deal with the Secret Service if we want to eyeball the old man?" White asked.

"Nope," Abrams volunteered. "The Secret Service didn't exist until 1865, same year Lincoln was killed. Washington did have what he called lifeguards to protect him, his family, property, and papers. They had to be native-born Americans. He figured they would have a real interest in the success of the war. These were the same boys who made up the

Third United States Infantry. They're the ones who stand guard up at Arlington over the Tomb of the Unknown."

"What's with the frickin' history lesson, Abrams?" Jones chimed in. "His guards might be the tough guys of their time, but if we have to engage them for some reason I'll just lay some ninja stuff on them and that'll be it."

"And you picked this guy over the cute one on T2?" White said.

JJ shrugged. "Let's just remember. We're to act like we know where we are headed, observe on the move, resist contact. And, whatever happens, don't anyone yell, "Hey, GW!"

JJ decided it made sense for four of the team to make the short trip up I-95 to Philadelphia and scout Valley Forge before the mission. They'd bring their Colonial Army uniforms with them and participate in a military re-enactment to get a better sense of what life in the military was like back then.

"Makes sense," Jones agreed. "Besides, if we show up in 1778 looking like we just left the dry cleaner's we're going to attract suspicion. Let's rough this stuff up a bit and then check out Independence Hall and some Philly bars."

"And we need to take those muskets out somewhere and shoot them before we go," Sharif added. "I heard they didn't target past 20 feet worth a crap."

"Yeah," Wilson says, "the barrels clogged a lot so they used smaller balls, which spun like curve balls when they left the barrel. That's why they shot so many friggin' volleys back then. They figured if you threw fifty projectiles at the enemy, something had to score."

A week later at 13:00 they arrived at the range at Quantico for target practice. JJ drove the Suburban right up to the shooting stations and quickly organized the unloading. "Okay, it was tough to get this range time, but everyone's headed for the mess so let's get moving. We've got thirty minutes at best. Do what you have to do, and let's get out of here."

The team familiarized themselves with their weapons, regarded as state-of-the-art during the Revolutionary War. They'd learned everything they could from the articles they'd read about the antiquated arms. Now they had to load, fire, master the art of a quick re-load, and then fire again and again as if they were on the battlefield.

Not ten minutes into their range time and their secrecy was blown. "Attention!" Wilson proclaimed as the Quantico Base Commander and three members of his support team approached the staging area. The T1 team snapped to attention. They exchanged salutes, received an "at ease," and spent fifteen seconds on small talk. With little time for distractions or smokescreens the Commander got right to it.

"So, what have we here? You Marines practicing for a Civil War re-enactment?" Sharif stepped forward, presented his 1776-era American Musket to the Commander for inspection. "Tell me about it, Marine."

"Sir, this Musket weighs just short of ten pounds, is nearly five feet in length, and is ready to fire a .78 caliber lead ball. It incorporates a paper cartridge reloaded with black powder and the projectile."

Three others had the same type of weapon. White demonstrated loading her 39" Blunderbuss. Wilson held a Fowler. The Blunderbuss was for close-up engagements only, never long-range shooting. It had a remarkable 1-foot, 5/8-inch bore. The Fowler was just that—a bird gun. Once

Wilson got to the targets, he would quickly learn its value as a sniper rifle.

"Sir, these are weapons from the Valley Forge era back in the late 1700's," Sharif explained.

JJ almost choked. "Sir, a collector got hold of these for us. He's trying to get us involved in some events out near Mount Vernon."

The Commander looked puzzled. "So why would you need to roll right up to my range to play with these toys? Sounds to me as if you're dicking around with a hobby on government time."

JJ was usually quick with a comeback, and he didn't fail his team now. "Birding, that's what this is about. We're supposed to provide these to members of the Joint Chiefs, who are going to try their luck competing against weapons of different periods. Sort of an off-the-books inter-agency contest."

Wilson, ever the good wing man, jumped in. "Sir, it was my request to have a quick session while everyone else was at lunch. We didn't want these weapons to turn the place into an all-day show-and-tell and competition against other Marines. Plus, these are authentic, battle-used weapons. They are older than dirt. If everyone wanted a turn blowing up targets, these old things wouldn't survive."

White stepped forward, offering her Blunderbuss to the Commander. "Go on, sir, give it a go. We've got a bottle of twelve-year-old Scotch on the line for the best first shot of each weapon today."

The Commander wanted to, everyone could tell, but he was short on time and the weather was moving in. "I wish I could, Marine. Thank you though. I have to get up to the Pentagon, and this weather is going to screw up I-95 big time. Captain Jackson, I remember you. You were moved over to some Pentagon program, correct?"

"Yes, sir. I was here at Quantico some time ago teaching strategy, but we never met."

The Commander's expression showed that he expected further elaboration, but he got none.

JJ said, "My assignment is classified, sir, as is the case for these Marines." The Commander must have known there was more to this, but realized that if a higher up had pulled this team into something special he had no choice but to move on, offer his support, and get out of the rain.

Still, he seemed reluctant to let it go. "Reports came to me about a group out here a short time ago, playing with what looked to be World War II German machine guns and pistols. Was that your group, too, Captain?"

JJ hesitated for a beat. "Yes, sir, it was."

Now the man looked truly annoyed. "Well, I can't comment on the priorities of whoever you report to, but it would seem to me you should be practicing with Ak-47's and more sophisticated weaponry being used in our war on terrorism. But that's not my call. Very well. Carry on. We'll need to get this range open now, especially in the weather. Anyone can shoot straight. I love to see Marines who can display excellence regardless of the conditions. If you need anything more from me or from this facility, send your request straight to me and I'll green light it. But let's not waste assets and time. By the way, I prefer German beer to scotch. May the best Marine win. Good luck, oh, and Corporal, unless you're hunting a Goddamned ostrich you might want to leave that Blunderbuss at home."

The team saluted the Commander. Within two minutes

they were back in action, on the clock and firing away. "Remind me to get him a case of Paulaner, the real stuff. I'm sure you can get it at one of the beer stores off base." JJ and Wilson both looked to Sharif.

"Valley Forge era?" JJ asked sternly.

"You forget about 'speak only when spoken to' Marine?" Wilson asked.

"Won't happen again, sir." By the time the other shooters arrived at the range, T1 had finished, packed up, and headed for the liquor store to pick up a bottle of scotch for White.

At 19:00 they met as planned in the briefing room at Andrews. Wilson led the meeting, going over the map of Valley Forge, reviewing phrases the locals used back then, double checking that everyone had their uniforms and equipment ready to go, and that nobody was carrying anything that, if taken or left behind, could cause an issue.

"Where's JJ?" someone asked.

"He's running late. His wife had a doctor's appointment that ran long, but he'll be here at any minute. We are a go at 17:00 sharp."

At the top of the hour, led by Jackson and Wilson, they formed their circle under the watchful eye of Dr. Moretti. The men were fully dressed as officers in the Continental Army. White wore a maid's clothes—the plan for her, to follow the officers as they toured the grounds. She was the only operative without a weapon of some kind. The lights were dimmed to resemble late dusk and they waited a full minute for their eyes to adjust. Then, following Team Leader Jackson's familiar 3-2-1 count, they engaged their pulse devices. In an instant, they were transported just over 100 miles North and 238 years back in time to the Keystone State.

They found themselves standing in eight inches of snow, behind a mill building on the edge of Schuylkill River. They quickly assumed the standard defensive 180-degree tactical stance and familiarized themselves with their immediate surroundings.

"I know it's not any colder here than what we left in Maryland, but these uniforms aren't worth a damn," Sharif whispered to Jackson.

"Yeah, the boots aren't worth shit either, but we'll be back home and out of them before you know it. These poor guys will freeze their feet off for another month or more."

As planned, Group One, consisting of Jackson, Abrams, and White, walked off from the east side of the mill. Two minutes later, Wilson set out from the west side. A minute after that, Group Two, consisting of Jones and Sharif, stepped out from behind the east side. They planned to move in a block pattern, one group clockwise the other two counterclockwise, winding up back where they'd started. They all want to get into a hut and see, first hand, how bad the conditions really were for the troops. But all six were also determined to get a glance at George Washington and the Baron they had read about. Maybe the two men would return for dinner to the house he'd rented, after visiting the troops.

"From the outside, the house looks just like it did when I took the tour," JJ said. "I want to peek in through those windows and see how good the historians really were in restoring things."

"Some of GW's lifeguards will be with him—some in the house and the rest in their huts up on that hill."

"You do realize if any of us are caught they're for sure going to think we're British spies. We'll get our asses kicked and then put in front of a firing squad," White whispered.

"Well, at least they haven't invented water boarding yet," Abrams said with a grin.

"Well actually, they used that during the Spanish Inquisition in the 1500's, so yeah, they might know a thing or two about it," JJ responded.

Group One started their walkabout, following the path up the hill toward the lifeguard's huts. As far as they could see, soldiers had lit fires to provide light and heat, and to cook whatever they could. Ventilation in most of the quickly built wood huts was so poor that many men choose to huddle outside around the flames and only go inside when the wind blew hardest.

Within minutes, a group of eight uniformed officers approached JJ's group. They were sixty feet away and sharing the same path cut out of the deep snow. If JJ and the others diverted off the path, or turned around, it would be obvious they were outsiders, and the battle they didn't want to fight would be on.

As the group of Continental soldiers drew closer, Jackson swallowed hard. He whispered to Abrams on his right, "Look how tall two of those fuckers are. They have to be six-three, maybe six-four!" Washington and von Steuben were that tall and always stood out. "It's the Old Man and the Baron. Holy Shit!"

Walking straight toward them, General Washington and von Steuben were engaged in conversation and seemed unaware of the three time-travelers until the two groups were nearly face-to-face. But JJ noticed the wary expressions of the guards, preceding Washington. Had they noticed how clean and healthy the three of them looked, compared to the ragged, half-starved men in their army? They must have suspected something wasn't quite right.

Wilson was on a path on the other side of Washington's house and had lost sight of Group One, but Group Two could see them. Jones and Sharif had managed to get much farther ahead and crossed in front of the lifeguard's huts. Jones was the first one to realize that JJ's group was on a collision course with the Continentals. But before he could say anything he was distracted by three men standing around a small fire.

They could only be Colonial Army soldiers. Their clothes were worn and dirty. Without gloves, they could only thrust cloth-wrapped hands into thin pockets. Scarves and more cloth strips wound around their heads in place of the warm hats they should have worn as they stood in the snow.

One man coughed harshly, clearly in poor health. Jones looked back to Wilson and raised his left hand to his ear, signaling him to catch up; two men were tailing him, and Jones sensed trouble around the corner. Wilson glanced behind him and picked up his pace.

JJ and his group moved into single file to pass Washington and his group. Now they were within two feet of the man who would soon become the first President of the United States. Eyes forward, salutes as they passed. White let out an audible sigh of relief as she cleared the last man in the group. JJ let out a held breath.

"Soldier," von Steuben called out.

JJ froze and did an immediate about face, his heart racing in his chest.

"Is that the way you salute your General and his staff?" von Steuben said in a heavy German accent.

JJ snapped to attention. "Sir, we saw that you were engaged in conversation and did not wish to interrupt you and the general." Out of the corner of his eye, he could see that the guards had spread out, weapons at the ready.

Washington stared at JJ, then Abrams, and finally White. "Men, I have not seen you here before. And you have a slave woman with you." It was growing darker and the low light from the fading sunset and few fires burning nearby were making it harder to see anyone's face. Two of Washington's aides approached with oil lamps to light the path to his headquarters.

"General Washington, sir, we just arrived and were going to report to you in the morning." JJ clung to the hope the explanation he was about to give would make sense to the general. "We have been sent by Congress to obtain more information about the conditions of the encampment here. We had thought it would be easy to find accommodations on our arrival, but we got here later than expected. Clearly, conditions are even worse than any of us had thought. We brought this woman with us to attend to our needs and in hopes she could lend a hand to Mrs. Washington while we are here. I understand she has enlisted the help of as many women as possible to sew socks for the troops. This woman turns a mean stitch. Look at how well she has kept us."

From twenty feet away, Wilson signaled Jones and

Sharif that he saw what was happening in the path below them. The three of them watched the faceoff with George Washington, but were unable to hear the conversation for the shrieking wind.

One of the soldiers following Wilson called out, "Stop." Wilson kept moving, wanting to get closer to JJ in case he needed help. "Stop now or be shot," the soldier shouted again.

Heads turned at the challenge. The weary soldiers sitting around their fires stared. Men in Washington's group looked suddenly alert. Wilson stopped and turned around to find a pistol pointed at his chest. Washington's guards lifted their muskets and aimed at the three time-travelers standing at attention in front of them.

"You have an interesting accent, soldier," von Steuben said to Jackson. "What is your name, where are your orders, and where were you born?"

JJ's mind whirred with possible responses—none of them right.

It was then that Jones and Sharif made their move.

While everyone's attention was on Group One and Wilson, Jones had crept closer to the fire nearest Washington. And Sharif had moved toward Wilson. In unison, they tossed high-tech concussion grenades into the fires. Soldiers fighting the British in the late 1700's were accustomed to cannon fire, but the detonation of modern concussion grenades dropped them on their backs and left them momentarily dazed, although injured. The diversion gave T1 just long enough for an escape at full run toward the old mill.

Muskets and pistol shots rang out. Two-dozen Colonial Army officers, soldiers, and lifeguards rushed out of their huts and the headquarters. Some raced toward Washington. Others ran after the suspected British spies, toward the river.

As soon as the team arrived back at the spot where they landed, Jackson threw his hat onto the riverbank and Wilson tossed his into the river to send their pursuers across the water on a wild goose chase. Sharif pulled the travel mat out from under the snow. They stepped on, reaching through their buttoned uniforms to push their pulse devices close to their chests.

"Hurry up, they're almost on us," Abrams shouted.

"3-2-1!" came JJ's command.

And they were gone.

Three members of T2 and Dr. Moretti stared at the returning team. "Is everyone all right?" Moretti asked.

JJ caught his breath. "Other than losing two Colonial Army hats and being half frozen, we're fine." He turned to face Jones and Sharif. "Grenades? You brought grenades with you?"

"No worries, JJ," Jones responded with a smile, "they were free-range grenades—one hundred percent biodegradable. There won't be anything left of them."

As they headed back to the prep room to change out of what White called their Halloween costumes, she remarked, "Thank God those muskets shoot like shit, or we'd have been screwed. For a recon mission that got a bit hairy."

After changing their clothes the team members log on to their laptops and did a series of extensive Internet and government intranet searches. They found no reports of attempts on Washington's life at Valley Forge.

"It would have been demoralizing if word got out that

strangers were able to get that close to the Old Man," Wilson said, matter-of-factly. "Just like today, I guess the higher ups decided to keep it quiet."

JJ stood near the doorway deep in thought. "One last thing. When I say don't bring *anything* I mean just that. The grenades did cause the diversion we needed, but what would have happened if Washington's men had captured us and found them on you?"

Everyone looked at Jones and Sharif, who seemed hopeful of another diversion. "JJ, they were pretty primitive," Jones said by way of an excuse. "Probably would have looked to them like nothing more than gun powder wrapped in cloth. He glanced at Wilson for help but got nothing more than a sheepish look.

The room remained silent for a moment. But, at last, JJ gave a nod. "Well done then, Marines." And he turned to leave the room. What was done, was done. There was nothing he could do about it now. He needed to get home to Michelle. She would have the test results back by now.

10

Rome, Italy

"THIS ISN'T POSSIBLE, Michelle," JJ said. He turned away from her and threw his coffee mug against the kitchen wall. Bunker barked and then retreated to the living room but stood watching through the doorway.

Michelle didn't flinch. She sat at the table, staring at her hands. He couldn't understand how she could be so calm.

"Uterine cancer runs in the family. My mom survived her chemo okay," she said quietly. "But hers hadn't spread to other organs and bones like mine has."

JJ walked over to her and went down on one knee, wrapping his arms around her. "Maybe we need to take you to another hospital, get a second opinion. Or go to Mexico or Europe. Try some of the new drug treatments the wealthy bastards can afford."

They held each other for a minute. Michelle sighed. "I never smoked a day in my life, and here I am with lung cancer." As if hoping to lighten the mood she said, "I always wanted to try pot. At least now I'll finally get a taste of the medical kind. It's supposed to make the chemo more tolerable."

She gently moved JJ's head away from hers and peered up into his eyes. "Look, mister. I'm not going anywhere. I've asked enough questions and done enough research to know chemo is the way to go. I also have faith that I'm not supposed to die until I'm old and gray. We're going to beat this, but I don't need you stomping around here breaking all the dishes." She smiled at him, and it nearly broke his heart. "I want to sleep for a while. Why don't you take Bunker for a walk and then get your butt to work. Sitting around here staring at me won't do either of us any good. We'll take this one day at a time."

JJ held her close for another minute, then kissed her cheek and stood up. "Sir, yes sir." He helped her to the sofa and kissed her again. He knew there was no sense arguing with her. She needed to rest and he needed to try to process what was ahead.

That afternoon, Chairman Stewart summoned Team Leader Jackson to his office at the Pentagon. After what had taken place in Berlin, Stewart now required a briefing after each mission.

"JJ, my schedule is very full this morning, so I will get right to it. The inauguration is coming up, and the Navy commander has been sounding off in the news, calling the President-elect inept. We all know the new POTUS is a—well, let's just say he's not a meat eater. I hope I can keep my opinions to myself, or I'll be out of a job, too. We know the commander will be forced to resign on January 20, and we have no idea who will be chosen to replace him. On top of that, General Shields might be filing his retirement papers within the next thirty days. He wants no part of this new President's administration either. There's as much political bullshit going on in this building as there is up at the Capitol or the White House. There's posturing, backstabbing, and brown nosing. It's impressive to watch, but at the same time very disappointing. So, what I am telling you, confidentially, is that we aren't quite sure what's coming with regard to the country…but also how it may affect BOTM."

"I appreciate your confiding in me, sir," JJ said.

"At the last meeting of the Joint Chiefs, with everyone realizing that soon there will be a new sheriff in town, some of the commanders started asking about stepping it up and proactively using BOTM to our current-day advantage. That can be trouble for us."

JJ nodded. He could foresee all sorts of complications if they moved too quickly, without adequate testing.

Stewart continued. "General Shields was the biggest advocate for the program and, for that matter, it's based on Air Force turf at Andrews. If he retires that's a game changer, depending on who the President appoints. If they aren't one of us, then we may have to rethink a few things, including the possibility of putting the program in mothballs or moving it out West."

Stewart went on to explain that, while the Chiefs had all agreed to the original charter, Army General Brooks now seemed to have issues with some elements of it. "The short story is—he thinks we should send the team to take out some of the Chinese and other Asian leaders who started their countries down the anti-American road. Prevent them from growing their economies and their armed forces in ways they could use them against us."

"But, sir, that would be changing history, and we all agreed that's dangerous and—"

"I know, I know. Everyone has agreed to table the discussion and conduct more research into the question. We're to reconvene in three weeks. Between that discussion and the possibility of a Shields retirement, it is going to be a busy time at the Pentagon." The general brushed a hand across his forehead. "Enough of that crap. I want to talk to you about the Valley Forge mission. You said that you got to see the old man. Was he as impressive in person as he looks in all those portraits?"

"Yes, it was incredible to see him so close. We even got to speak with him, but we were only in contact for maybe a minute before things got dicey. Von Steuben did most of the talking" JJ thought for a moment. "I find that each time I meet a historical figure the thrill doesn't live up to the experience before that one. I guess it's like meeting a President. After a few times, you realize he's just another guy in a suit."

"Interesting," Stewart responded. "So, before long, if you get to meet Lincoln it may feel as though you're talking to me or any other ranking officer. That might be helpful. Who knows, though, with the way things are going you might be back at Quantico studying tactics again."

JJ laughed, but brought up another question. "Does it make sense for us to go back to Valley Forge knowing what we know now? All we'd need to do is land about five minutes earlier. We'd be able to avoid the confrontation and would get to see more of the place before having to bail."

Stewart shook his head no. "Let's keep moving forward.

You learned what you could under the circumstances." With a wink, he patted JJ on the shoulder. "Don't you know, you can't change the past?"

Jackson nodded in agreement but went on to ask his dear friend a tough question. "General Stewart, Stew, we have an incredible capability at our disposal. Have you ever considered trying to see Mathew again—seeing him before we lost him?"

The suggestion seemed to take the general by surprise. He took a moment before responding in a firm voice. "No, I don't want to go back. Why should I have that privilege? If I got to do that with the son I lost, then every parent who has lost a child in war should be given the same opportunity. No, JJ, this is the hand that God dealt me and Elizabeth, and that's the one I will hold."

The two stood silently for a while, each in his own thoughts. JJ had once thought about the possibility of seeing his parents again, if only for a moment. He he'd decided against it. He agreed with his mentor, his friend.

Stewart's tone softened. "There is something else I wanted to address with you, JJ. I understand your wife is not in good health. It's a personal matter so I'm not going to ask for details. What I am going to suggest is that you either send Scott from T2 in your place on the next mission so you can stay home with her, or you take her to Italy with you. Whatever care she is receiving at Bethesda, she can get at our facilities in Naples. Spending time together there, in that environment, might do you both good."

JJ considered this then smiled. "General, I appreciate the thought. But there's no way I'd put Scott in charge of anything other than latrine duty, and Michelle is doing okay. You know, you were with me back in 2001. I really didn't think I would ever open my heart up again. I didn't want to feel that hurt ever again. I was good with what the Marines and the world had to offer me. I had free room and board, and got to blow up shit and kill bad guys. I figured I'd put in my years and then retire to a beach house somewhere and grow old counting beer bottles."

"And then Michelle came along." The older man smiled knowingly at him.

"Right. The day I met Michelle everything changed. She hooked me and I haven't looked back. The walls I'd put up since I lost my parents were shot to shit. Now, no matter what happens, I am so happy I met her." He thought for a minute before continuing. He admitted to himself that he was more concerned for her health than he was letting on. "The thing is, she hates to travel and she's used to my being away. Her mother will probably come in from Montana to stay with her. She'll be okay, but thank you."

With that, the meeting ended. Stewart wished Jackson and the team good luck.

An hour later, the T1 team was assembled in the briefing room at Andrews.

JJ got right to the point. "Our next mission will take a month to prep for. No haircuts as of today. Grow out your beards if you want. No more manicures or pedicures. You hear me Jones?" The group laughed. "White, you'll have to research whether you're going to have to stop shaving. And here's something we all forgot about. Everyone will need to visit the dentist. There can be no silver fillings. They need to be replaced with natural looking fillings. If you have anything like dentures or a bridge, it will come out and stay out for this next mission. Where we're going, if you had a bad tooth they just yanked it and left a space."

"Oh, man," someone groaned.

JJ ignored the murmured complaints around the table. "Now, I know some of you have expressed the opinion that the missions we've gone on have been bullshit— sightseeing, Disneyland stuff. Let me remind you that we lost a man on one of these. You may think that if we aren't going to change history, take out some bad guys, then we might as well be tourists. But we went to Germany to lay some vengeance on that asshole on behalf of every innocent he hurt. We didn't change history, but we got our vengeance, justice. Anyone feel differently?"

The room was silent.

"Not all missions will be peaceful ones, or at least attempts at peaceful ones, like with GW. But we will engage whenever possible if that gives any of you some hope. The point of doing these missions is to work through a multitude of operational and psychological tests. We need to exist in the past as if we are from that time and place. Look at it as a casting call, if you need to. Who are our best actors? We need Marines who not only fight the best, but who can act the best. We don't want the brass to force any CIA performers on us, now do we? We're also witnessing fighters and military leaders in all kinds of situations. The better we get at this, the more we can explore. The more time we spend traveling, the more we meat eaters can push for chances to engage."

So far, everything Jackson had said seemed to have hit

home. They got it. "You're a carnivore, JJ. We saw that in Berlin" someone said.

"This is a top-secret developmental program with an unlimited budget. If the government will spend $200 for a $5 toilet seat, then nobody gives a crap about what we're doing or what we're spending. We are government employees so we're supposed to waste time and money. We've been given an all-expense-paid, all-access pass to history. If you aren't interested or aren't curious and don't want to ride this out with the rest of us, let me know now and we'll get you back out in the field pronto. Any takers?"

Again, the room was silent. "You can count us all in, JJ," White responded for the group.

"Good. We aren't like any other unit on the planet. We're Marines and a Navy doc testing a time machine. You can't make this shit up!" Jackson paused for a moment, gathering his thoughts. "Oh yes, boys and girl, another thing—some of you seem to have forgotten the No Scent rule. You can't soap, shampoo, shave, douche, or roll on anything with a scent of any kind. Sharif I know the douche will be an issue for you, but deal with it."

Everyone laughed and then in unison responded, "Sir, yes sir!"

Jackson's expression turned serious now. "Anyone still need to question what we are doing or why?" Silence. "Good. Now let's get to it."

"Where we goin' boss?" asked Sharif.

JJ drew a deep breath. "Just a minute. First, effective immediately, drop the 'sir' and the 'boss' too. Get used to not using them. I know it's been beaten into your heads from the day your first Gunny popped your cherries, but no more. A slip like that can get us killed. Now as for the mission, I know you've all seen that gladiator movie with Russell Crowe. Well, guess what? We're going to Rome, 82 AD, to witness the circus first hand. We're going to the Coliseum!"

Team members exchanged high fives, laughs, jokes, and enthusiastic shouts.

"Don't get too excited," Wilson says. "The Rome you're going to is ancient, barbaric. This will be the farthest back we've gone so far. Intel, maps and such are sketchy at best. The plan is to drop into the center ring of the Coliseum in the middle of the night when it's deserted."

"We'll move from there," JJ added, "and lay low in the outskirts of the city until the crowd starts heading in for the day's events. We can blend in with the people as long as Sharif doesn't draw any flies."

Sharif groaned and rolled his eyes.

Wilson continued. "So here are a few things to think about. In addition to growing out your hair and beards, you'll need to bulk up a bit and also get some local skin tone so we look like we're naturally tanned from the Mediterranean sun."

"And," JJ cut in, "we're going to have to learn some sword play and other Roman fighting styles, just in case we need to engage a bit there.

"Right," Wilson said. "Monday at 0600 we'll leave for Naples, Italy. We'll spend a month there training, sunning, and learning some Latin. So, pack up and be ready to roll. Enjoy your weekend. I'm hangin' at the Olive Garden tonight if anyone wants to join me. Might as well get used to wine, bread, and olive oil."

Abrams said, "You're just there to see your favorite waitress, the one with the great cleavage. Count me in."

With the briefing concluded, the group dispersed. Wilson came up to JJ afterward. "JJ, that was the quickest briefing I've ever seen. I thought we were going to fill them in on a few more details. You all right? You seemed distracted."

JJ shrugged. "There's a lot going on at the Pentagon. I'll tell you about that later, but I need to tell you this now. Michelle is sick. She got test results late yesterday, and they weren't good. They say it's cancer and it's metastasized into one of her lungs."

Wilson stared at him, stunned. "JJ, that doesn't make any sense. She's can't have lung cancer. She's too young. That's the stupidest thing I've ever heard."

The two men looked at each other in disbelief. "We'll get a second opinion," JJ said. "I thought it was bullshit too, so I insisted on more tests. I took her to Johns Hopkins in Baltimore last week. Her insides are a mess."

Wilson punched the wall, attracting the attention of Dr. Moretti and others in the time travel team.

JJ put an arm around his shoulder. "Let's get out of here and go see your sister."

Moments later they were in their cars headed to the apartment. JJ found Michelle resting on the sofa and greeted her with a kiss while Wilson dealt with an excited Bunker at the door. Then JJ turned around, it was to see Wilson looking across the room at Michelle, tears streaming down his face.

He and his sister had gone through a lot in recent years.

They had watched their mother struggle through cancer treatments and get better only to lose their father to a heart attack days before Michelle's wedding. But this was the only time JJ had ever seen his friend cry. Now it was his sister's turn to stare death in the eye.

JJ held Michelle for a moment. "Listen, I'll take Bunker out for a walk. You two spend some time together."

He put the dog on his leash. When he looked back before stepping out the door, Wilson had sat down beside Michelle on the sofa and wrapped his arms around her. His friend looked crushed.

Fifteen minutes later when JJ returned, he could hear Michelle talking in the living room. "Okay, baby brother, let's knock this stuff off. Daddy didn't raise a couple of cry-babies. Time to shut off the faucets."

His brother-in-law sat back and, wiping the tears from his face, he laughed. "Yeah, he'd be pissed, wouldn't he?" Michelle smiled at her brother. JJ thought of his own father. He never had much time for tears either.

Moments later, all three were laughing hysterically as they retold stories about their parents and growing up in Montana. At last, Michelle took charge, as she always did, and got the immediate future organized. "All right, I have treatments scheduled, and I'll need to stock up on medical marijuana. But in the meantime, Anne is coming over from next door to have dinner with us. She ordered pizza. She's volunteered to look after me while you guys continue to do whatever it is you do over in that hangar." She looked at her brother. "You know Anne likes you, so be nice!"

"But she has cats," he protested. She gave him one of her looks that meant he'd better shape up. "Yes, ma'am."

After more stories, laughter, and tears Wilson fell asleep on the floor in front of the television and Michelle remained where she is most comfortable, on the sofa under a comforter that had been one of their wedding presents.

In the morning, JJ made coffee and heated up leftover pizza for breakfast. The two men talked with her again about treatments, travel, and their wish to remain by her side at Andrews as she went through her journey.

Michelle insisted JJ and her brother go on their mission to Italy so she could begin her chemotherapy without them fussing over her and treating her differently. "I'm not going anywhere, boys. You go do whatever it is you're supposed to do in Italy. I'll be here with Bunker, getting better and waiting for you to come back in thirty days. Anne's a great neighbor and she'll look after me. Mom wanted to come, but you know she's scared to fly and she's not getting any younger."

"Michelle," JJ began.

"No," she said firmly. "You can take me to the Vatican and Positano next spring, as a make-good for me missing this trip." Case closed, the men knew when their girl's mind was made up.

Before leaving for Naples, JJ reached out to Bill Griffiths in California. He called him one afternoon and put in his request. The team needed cloth tunics and togas, linen robes, leather sandals, knives, and whatever other accessories the average spectator at the Coliseum in 82 AD might wear. Their outfits would be of materials used back in that time, hand-sewn using the same stitching styles and thread from that period.

"JJ, I would like to help you, but I'm not sure I can, at least from my local sources. I took care of you pretty easily with the Continental Army gear. Thank you for getting most of the gear back to me all in one piece. I explained the missing hats as being damaged in a film production accident." He paused, as if working something out in his mind before speaking. "I know some people in the film industry in Italy and Greece who might be able to help. Give me a few days. I'll get back to you."

"Thanks, Bill. How is your daughter doing?"

"As well as can be expected under the circumstances."

From the man's tone, JJ had the sense that his enthusiasm for life was waning. "And you, Bill?"

"I'm still pissed off and frustrated. That comes with age, disease, and a broken heart. Losing that boy took it all out of me."

JJ understood. Michelle's battle with cancer weighed so heavily on him, he'd neglected to properly acknowledge Griffiths' contribution to BOTM. "Bill, you've supported us and your country since before I was born. We have something planned for you in about sixty days. Your grandson and I discussed this when we first formed T1. He might have teased you about it without filling in any details. He was supposed to be a part of what we had planned, but I think it's fitting we carry on. I know that's what he would have wanted. I need you to hang in there. Stay healthy."

JJ and Wilson had discussed the serious issue of what to do about Griffiths if he threatened to leak news of the project. To his immense relief, the old man had kept his mouth shut. Now, he thought it only right that they take him on a mission, somewhere that would mean the world to him in the last years of his life.

JJ said, "For this other event, we'll need U.S. Navy uniforms, dress whites, and daily gear for our five male team members and the same for you. All I can say at this point is they should be World War II style. If you feel up to it in sixty days, plan on bringing them with you to Andrews. And make sure you bring enough of your heart medicine to last a week."

On the other end of the call, Griffiths was silent.

"You still there, Bill?"

"Yeah. Just thinking about JR. Fine. If I can make it to Andrews you guys can take me wherever you want, long as you promise it's not to the deck of the Arizona on December 7, 1941."

JJ laughed. "You're getting warm, but we would never put you in harm's way. I promise you that."

The call ended and JJ went to find Wilson. "I just shot my mouth off and bought us some time with Griffiths. If he's healthy enough for the trip I think I've come up with something that will seal our secrecy with him forever."

Wilson considered this then sighed. "One thing we never discussed was the possibility he might write his memoirs, to be published after his death. We could all be in them. That would put us in deep shit."

"He's not a dummy. My bet is he'll keep his mouth and pen quiet. Like we said on that ride to Havasu, he knows not to screw with us."

A week later the team was in Naples, getting used to their new quarters and studying for the mission.

"I found some really interesting intel on Roman history," White offers. "Sounds like things didn't go down the way we've seen in the movies. Turns out not all the fighting at the Coliseum was warrior versus slave, or animal versus slave. And not everyone died at the end."

White explained that there were hundreds of professional fighters who traveled all over the region battling for gold coins and fame. If a good fighter was injured they would be given time to mend and then they got back into the action, fighting at another sporting venue. Not every thumbs-down given by an Emperor or local dignitary meant death. It could simply mean he was removed from the contest.

"I read there were female gladiators who fought in the Coliseum and other events," Wilson added. "This is starting to sound more like professional wrestling. They put on a show for the crowd. I guess they got tired of watching the big guys or tigers slaughter worn-out slaves and petty criminals. Inject some well-tuned women into the mix and I'd pay to see that." And that was exactly what was in store for them.

The team trained in Naples with short swords, tridents, scimitars, chains, shields and other types of weapons used in gladiator fights at the Coliseum almost 2,000 years ago. Griffiths' contacts in the film industry had delivered clothing, armor and weapons. Their cover? They were participating in a documentary tracing the evolution of hand-to-hand combat. Before long, they were ready to return to Andrews and step back in time.

The effects of chemotherapy had left Michelle stretched on the sofa with Bunker at her side. JJ was prepared to hand off his spot on the mission to anyone from T2, except Scott, whom he still didn't trust.

Michelle wouldn't hear of it. "I'm not going to lie here trying to get better while you sit and stare at me or the TV. Get your ass in gear, go on your mission, take care of my brother, and you will be back in no time," she barked.

"Sir, yes sir," JJ responded. He knew she was right. He'd have driven her crazy, sitting around and fussing over her. If peace and quiet was what she wanted and needed, then that's what she'd have.

A few days later, as Dr. Moretti and the T2 team watched, T1 dressed for their mission and did a final review of the plan.

"Sharif, did you have to eat a pound of garlic before we got here tonight?" Abrams joked. "This close-quarter ring is tight and your breath is like dog ass."

Wilson quickly chimed in, "Abrams, don't even think about offering him gum. I've told you a thousand times, no gum. Hey White, nice pits. Okay girls, let's saddle up. Dr. Moretti, please kill the lights so we can adjust. JJ, it's all yours."

Moments later they were standing in the dark in the middle of the Roman Coliseum. It was a moonless night and that allowed them to move ahead with their plan quickly.

"What the fuck was that?" Jones whispered to Wilson. "Sounds like a God-damned Tiger!"

"It's down below us in a cage or crate," White said. "They kept all the animals in warrens beneath ground level and let them loose at show time. Let's keep moving."

Undetected by anyone, except for the big cat, the team

was able to move quickly away from the arena. Within minutes they found their way to the banks of the Tiber River where they would rest until morning. A few campfires burned, set by the many other travelers who had come to Rome to witness the exhibitions.

"We'll do without a fire," JJ said, opting to direct the team to an unoccupied spot where they sat, huddled in a tight circle. "Remember, above all, don't engage anyone. Not a vendor or a competitor or a guard, especially the Pretorian Guard. They're the Roman badasses who protect the Emperors. Their experience and fighting skills with swords and other weapons might give them a tremendous edge over us in hand-to-hand combat."

"JJ," Jones said, "White and I took a tour of Rome when we were on leave from Naples. These were the same guards who looked the other way when Brutus killed Julius Caesar. The tour took us to the spot where that happened. Pretty cool. I'm glad you guys moved me up to T1. The things we're seeing and doing are unbelievable. Any chance we can go to the Moon and watch those guys land and walk around?"

JJ and Wilson shook their heads.

Abrams said, "No way Jose, one look out the LEM window at a bunch of galactic sightseers in spacesuits and Houston would *really* have a problem."

Wilson said to the group, "This will be our third mission, and I'm happy to see all of you are getting along and swapping spit. Now how about a lot less talk and we all get some sleep? I'll take first watch."

Someone whispered "Goodnight, John Boy," as others chuckled before they all went quiet.

When the sun rose, they found themselves among many other road-weary travelers who had slept by the river for the night. While the team had studied Latin and worked with a language specialist in Naples, they intended to avoid speaking to each other or locals. People of all kinds, from all parts of Europe, came to Rome. It was the center of the universe during that period. Different cultures, languages, styles of dress, and appearances were commonplace. This allowed the team to blend in.

They breakfasted on something that resembled water and bread purchased from a local vendor using the gold coins made available to them by Griffiths' contacts at the Italian film industry and historical society. By mid-morning large crowds moved toward the Coliseum. The team soon found itself inside the entrance, marveling at their surroundings. "I could hardly see anything last night, but today it looks just like it does in the movies," Abrams murmured.

"Yeah, this is the most famous arena ever built," White added. "You could fit it inside the Silverdome or the LA Coliseum, but it's the shit now and in the future."

They continued to walk the property and take in all they could see. "Notice anything in particular?" JJ whispered as they circled around him. "None of the statues are stained with centuries of air pollution." Everyone acknowledged the observation, but then quickly continued their tour.

Wild animals in crates were on display to the public and to participants who would soon be fighting for their lives. White winked at the lone tiger that heard them the night before. Access to view the professional fighters, the gladiators, while they prepared came at a cost. JJ, Wilson, and

White paid their way while Sharif, Jones, and Abrams opted to stay out in the open, keeping an eye out for trouble.

"This frickin' flying carpet is hotter than hell under this robe," Sharif whispered.

"Yeah, the pulse device really feels great stuck in my ancient underwear too. Let's get some wine."

"Quiet. Stop bitching," Abrams warned. "We're on a mission and you guys know better."

"Okay, Mom," Sharif and Jones responded.

The three checking out the preparation rooms under the Coliseum were furious. They passed the cells where the slaves and criminals awaited their slaughter. Wounds hadn't been treated. None appeared to have seen a good meal, fresh water, or a place to clean themselves for days. Then the three passed by the fighters who appeared to be well-trained specimens in great physical shape. Many bore the scars of past battles.

"Nothing like a fair fight," Wilson whispered to JJ.

When they came to the female gladiators' area one of the women took notice of White and whispered something unintelligible to her. Within a minute the two were nose-to-nose, exchanging insults in very basic Latin. It was clear to JJ that he needed to step in or there was going to be bloodshed.

JJ clamped his hand on White's shoulder. "Relinque eum." *Leave it!*

White's training kicked in. She backed away from the fighter. As they walked away the Roman fighter hurled insults at White's back.

"How do you say pussy in Latin?" Wilson asked JJ.

Almost forgetting rank, White slowed down. JJ wasn't

sure whether she was about to challenge Wilson or go after the female gladiator.

"Just kidding, White. Keep moving," Wilson whispered with a smile.

The two groups reunited and made their way to seats that gave them a good view of the action, but were also close to the exits.

Before long, as the sun stood high above them, the horns played, Emperor Domitian, the self-proclaimed "Lord and God," entered and took his place in a lavishly adorned area. The crowds cheered. The Emperor used the entertainment at the Coliseum to remain in favor with the citizens. Free admission and free food and drink for anyone who wanted to watch the show. Feed them and they will follow was his approach, much like another famous leader they'd already dealt with on an earlier mission. But they weren't here to go after the Emperor. They were in Rome to watch and learn. To fine tune the time travel program and its participants.

Halfway through the afternoon's events the female warriors entered the arena. "There's that bitch," White whispered to Jones. "I've been waiting for this!"

Just as they had witnessed throughout the day, the fighters in the best shape were chained at the ankles to their inevitable victims, the weaker or injured who stood twenty feet from them.

"This is bullshit," White said louder than she should. Luckily the people sitting around them were more interested in the fighting and the free wine, and ignored her strange sounding outburst.

JJ gave her a look and then Wilson. She acknowledged

her mistake with a nod and ran her finger across her lips to signify they were sealed from now on.

The team watched in amazement as the gladiator who had tried to pick a fight with White attacked the first victim she was paired with. It was more like a cat playing with a captured mouse. She used her sword surgically to slow her poor victim down. First, slicing at one knee, then her other leg, and finally her throat.

Her victims were given smaller swords to defend themselves, but they were useless against her onslaught. She went on to kill the next and then the next, picking up a discarded axe or a barbed hook to bring her victims lives to a miserable end. JJ's modern-day warriors had seen evil before, but not like this, and not from a woman.

After her final match, the fighter surveyed the crowd, her gaze fixing on White. It was then JJ realized something wasn't right—although he couldn't have said what it might be.

Hours later, after watching more violence than they cared to, they made their way back toward their resting spot near the Tiber. "It's one thing to watch a bad guy's head get shot off. It's another to watch the untrained try to defend themselves against a professional killer," Abrams said to the group as they walked.

"It's worse when a woman's doing it," Sharif says with a nod.

Everyone felt the same way. They would wait until nightfall and then return to Andrews under the cover of darkness.

They were halfway back to the Tiber when Wilson said, "I think we're being followed."

"Keep walking, everyone," JJ said. He cautiously looked back over his shoulder.

The female gladiator and two of other women, who might be maids, were close behind. The gladiator was no longer in fighting gear; she wore a plain white robe. He wondered if her interest in White might be more due to curiosity, rather than an intent on violence. One of her maids was carrying a basket with wine and bread. Okay, what now? JJ thought to himself.

When they reached the river, the gladiator approached White. While she seemed to have designs on her the feeling was far from mutual. To keep the peace and buy time until nightfall White sat with the woman, communicating with signs rather than words, pretending she didn't understand the language, which seemed to intrigue the Roman even more. Still, it was safer than trying to talk and risk alerting everyone that something wasn't right with these travelers. Jones and Wilson managed to do the same with the two maids. JJ and Abrams moved away from the couples to observe the situation. Sharif took the first watch.

"What do you think, JJ? How do you want to play this?" Abrams asked.

"Not sure. But we can't make a hasty retreat with all these locals around us. They'd be telling stories about the six gods that disappeared into the air. I'd rather we wait until dark. Maybe the two boys can enjoy a taste of Italy and White can put her new girlfriend in a sleeper hold when the time is right."

After sitting for a while, Abrams had a question. "JJ, in all the times we've hung out together, I don't think I ever asked you why you joined the Corps. Why'd you sign up?"

JJ was surprised by the question. "You know I grew up in Philly, right? Well, when I was in college I got a night job as a security guard at the seminary there. It was a lot of fun. They gave us a radio and a nightstick, and that was it. They had a lot of valuable art in those buildings and all they gave us was a nightstick. Luckily, I never had to deal with armed shitheads because that stick would have wound up in my ass. I had seen enough sick stuff by the time I got the job, and the darkness of the world was really bothering me. I decided to challenge one of the seminarians one night. I asked him how an all loving, all knowing God could let some of the sick shit that goes on in the world happen. How could he let a bad guy live while he let a good man die."

"Word got back to one of the professors there, a priest of course, and he came out one night to walk rounds with me and talk about it. He said there was good and evil in the world. Hell, we all know that. But he told me to consider that maybe when one miracle happens good won out and when bad things happen evil might have won that one. It made sense to me then, it was like a light bulb went off. I had sat through too many sermons where the priests threatened us with hell, asked for money, told us God loved us, and then threatened us with hell again. I had stopped listening. For some reason, maybe it was timing, what this guy said registered."

Abrams continued to keep an eye on White and her guest. JJ stopped long enough to glance in the direction of Wilson and Jones.

"It was right then and there," JJ continued, "that I started to grasp what was really going on. That there truly was an evil in the world. Once 9/11 happened, I saw a tangible evil I could go after, and that's when I signed up."

Abrams smiled, "You saw evil today, for sure."

JJ shook his head in frustration. "Yeah, and it killed me that we couldn't do anything to nuke some of the assholes that enjoyed being cruel to the poor shits they were chained to. Maybe someday we can come back here with about 100 Raiders and kick the crap out of the bad guys." Abrams laughed. "Let's bring some Seals, too."

A minute or so went by before JJ added, "I'm just thinking back to that conversation with the priest. I remember telling him that I had questions for God that I hoped to be able to ask him if we ever met at the pearly gates." Abrams' expression told JJ he wanted to hear more. "No, I'm not sharing any of them with you. If you want to hear them you'll just have to show up the same time I do."

They both laughed and then went back to watching the sky. "Abrams, I'm not going to ask you why you joined. I know you'd do anything for a free meal." Abrams started to protest. "I'm kidding, Benny. I know why you joined up. You're into killing bad guys just like the rest of us. I just hope someday we can use this technology to really shake things up. I'd roll the dice and hope for the best if we could just go back and kill assholes. I already have a list started."

Abrams smiled. "Me too, JJ."

As the night progressed and the wine worked its magic, the men enjoyed the intimate companionship of their newfound friends. In the darkness, neither of the maids realized the pulse devices they came across weren't jewelry from their time. One mistakenly thought Jones was giving it to her as a gift, but that was corrected quickly.

White was able to keep the fighter interested, but at arm's length. White hadn't forgotten the viciousness with which the fighter maimed and killed her opponents in the ring that day. She also remembered the hatred in the fighter's eyes during their confrontation in the preparation room. She played along and slowly gave in to the other woman's advances until the time was right. The team exchanged glances and JJ gave a signal for two minutes to liftoff. She also acknowledged the sleeper-hold signal that JJ sent her.

The men slowly gathered in one spot. Sharif lay out the travel mat as each man reached for his pulse device. JJ looked toward White. She was holding the Roman fighter close. A few seconds later, White removed her arm from around the fighter's neck, stood and joined the rest of the team on the mat.

"Bitch tried to steal my necklace! She's going to sleep a really long time now."

The maids, seeing their mistress lying where White had left her, ran to her.

Okay, 3-2-1," JJ counted down.

By the time the two servants looked up from the dead woman, the strangers were gone.

11

Within an hour of standing on the banks of the Tiber River in Ancient Rome, JJ was back at his on-base apartment. He curled up on the sofa next to Michelle, who was in a deep sleep. The chemotherapy had taken its toll on her, but she clearly was comforted when she felt him close to her.

The rest of the team opted to get cleaned up and head to one of the local bars that stayed open until 4:00 a.m.

"White," Wilson said after his fifth beer, "I have some bad news for you."

She put down her beer and listened attentively. Abrams, Sharif, and Jones decided it was a good time to head for the exit because they knew what was coming.

"What, they've stuck me with the check again?" White laughed.

Wilson asked the waitress for another two beers, two shots of Patron, and the check. "No, I got this. I also drew the short straw on having to tell you that you're going to sit out the next mission."

White sat quietly for the first thirty seconds of his explanation. "Hold it right there. 'Nough said, I'm fine with it. I hate Navy whites and while you, JJ, and the other girls are doing all your research and getting your 1945 haircuts, I'll request some leave time. There's a YMCA in Bethesda that's giving woman's self-defense training and they've asked for guest instructors. Anytime I can help a girl put a thug in his place I'm on it. Okay with you or do I need to ask JJ?"

Wilson was surprised she'd taken it so easy. He was equally surprised to hear that White wanted to give back to the community. Normally, she was strictly a kick-ass, lookin' out for number one kinda girl.

"Don't think I'm getting soft, sir," she said, taking a sober tone. "I've always wanted to help people who get picked on or bullied. I saw it a lot growing up in Oakland. Whatever I can do to help, I'm in."

Wilson was impressed. "That's cool. Permission granted, White."

She took a long swallow of her beer. "Can I ask how Michelle's doing?"

"Chemo. My mom went through it and survived. I'm going to go see Michelle in the morning. You should call over there and stop by. The one thing she doesn't want is for people to avoid her because they don't know how to act or what to say. She'll be fine. She's one tough lady."

Wilson looked down at the table, shook his head then knocked back his shot, and settled the tab. They finished their last beer and headed off to their apartments for some sleep and a few days off. Everyone but White would be preparing to time travel to Tokyo, Japan, on September 2, 1945.

The trip to Rome 82 A.D. had been the team's longest mission to date. Berlin lasted a few hours and, unfortunately, Valley Forge lasted only a matter of minutes. The adventure to the Coliseum was nearly twenty hours and, aside from the history lesson, the team learned a lot. They had to deal with the mat and the pulse devices in a situation where it wasn't easy to hide things. This meant they needed to ask Dr. Moretti for smaller equipment, if possible. When the request was made, she claimed there wasn't anything she could do to upgrade them and they'd just have to live with what they already had. Since she maintained control of the devices it was impossible for anyone else to examine them and try to improve on them. In his briefing to Chairman Stewart, JJ shared his concerns. He wondered if her age limited her drive to innovate.

"On another topic," JJ said, "we were concerned someone might bring back a disease that our modern day world wouldn't be able to deal with. One of the team got what we think is herpes, but the doctors said they've never seen a strain like this."

"You have to be kidding me." Stewart glared at him in disgust.

"No, seriously. We also had an enemy KIA. A female gladiator tried to steal White's necklace and she was forced to put her down. We were out of there before anyone knew what happened. Nobody will believe the servant girls who will say we disappeared into thin air, so the history books are safe."

"Very good." Stewart studied JJ's face for a moment before asking, "How is your wife?"

"Sleeping most of the time. The chemo has taken some of her hair and her body is weak. Still, she intends to get better and wants to get back to taking walks with our dog before long. The doctors have a different take on it, so we will see. We aren't the most religious people around, but if I thought I could find a miracle worker somewhere I'd get her there."

"I'm sorry she has to go through this. Please, let her know I'm thinking of her." JJ nodded. Stewart poured him a cup of coffee and waited a full minute before changing the subject. "What else you got?"

JJ related his conversation with Griffiths and asked if the next mission could be a more modern-day military exercise.

"General, he has served his country well for his entire adult life. His father was killed in the Pacific early in World War II. With your permission, I'd like to take him to Tokyo Bay 1945 and watch the Japanese surrender to MacArthur on the deck of the U.S.S. Missouri. He's already arranged for the uniforms we'll need and, although his health is failing, I think we can pull it off. The plan would be to get him there in a boat as close to the Missouri as possible. The story would be that this Marine veteran lost his son in the Pacific and we brought him there to watch the war come to an end. We considered going in, getting fake passes to the deck, and walking right on board, but that's pushing it."

Stewart sat down behind his desk and looked out his window for a minute. "You might not know this, JJ, but my grandfather was killed in the Pacific, too. He was a Marine sergeant and died on one of those tiny islands the Japs and the Americans paid such heavy prices fighting over."

JJ remained silent and watched Stewart consider the mission he'd proposed.

"Permission granted," Stewart stated at last. "We'll look

at this as a goodwill mission, but I disagree with sitting in a boat watching from afar. Get the passes, get the right uniforms, and get him on board to watch. Keep him safe and bring him back alive." Stewart paused for a moment. "You're sure this guy isn't writing any of this down? If he dies and then some notes or a book goes public we're all in extremely hot water."

JJ nodded. "We have this covered, General."

The meeting ended with a salute and wishes for a safe mission. As JJ headed for the shuttle from the Pentagon back to Andrews he ran into T2 Team Leader Scott. "What brings you up here?' JJ asked.

"Just visiting old friends. Rumor has it there are two chiefs retiring after the first of the year. I know both of their expected replacements so I'm just paying my respects."

With that, JJ jumped into the front seat of a black government Suburban and Scott continued on to his meetings inside.

Once back at Andrews, JJ told Wilson, "We've got a problem brewing with Scott. As I was leaving my briefing with Stewart, Scott was arriving for some meetings with—what he said were—his buddies, the next Joint Chiefs."

"Fuck him, JJ," Wilson snapped. "I told you one of our contingency trips would be for you to stay home with Michelle and send Scott in your place. We'll take him to check out Lewis and Clark in the Rockies, maybe show him the Little Falls at Yellowstone, and that prick will never make it back. I know all the places up there where it's easy for someone to get hurt."

"We know he's a mole for Brooks. Stewart told me at the onset that adding an Army Ranger of Brooks' choosing was the only way he'd endorse the program. Not sure throwing him off a mountain is the way to go quite yet. There are other ways to cook a mole. Let me think about it for a few days. They've confirmed Jones has some strain of a venereal disease, so they might quarantine his ass. That would mean you'd need to take a replacement for me and for him."

Wilson considered this. "We'll need three. I don't see a black woman roaming around the mountains in 1806 with a bunch of white explorers."

The two men discussed the situation for another ten minutes and decided that both JJ and Jones would go. White could remain behind, as originally planned, and Scott go in her place. "Jones will be ok. It's just a cold sore."

"We need to make sure he's the one that gets left behind out there—not you or me," JJ said firmly. "We can do this as a team-building, mountain-climbing, high-elevation wilderness test." JJ hesitated before going on. He'd given this next conversation a lot of thought, and wasn't sure how his friend would take it. "Listen, I've also been thinking a lot about what we talked about a long time ago. About you being adopted. The clock is ticking so we need to move quickly. I want you to think about this for a bit. Don't take your eye off the ball in Japan or Yellowstone, but when we get back, if Michelle's okay and you're up for it, I'd like to go back to the week before you were born."

"Seriously? Why?"

"Let's see if we can find your biological mother. Michelle has a copy of your original birth certificate. Your mom had it. We know the when, where, and who to look for."

Wilson looked stunned. JJ knew he'd always wanted to see his mother's face. "I would give anything to know why she gave me up for adoption," Wilson had once told him. If he had a chance to see who his father was that would make the journey even more unbelievable.

"JJ, I don't—" he cleared his throat "I just don't think I can process this right now. You're right, I've always wanted to meet them and find out more about them, but the flip side is— sometimes you're better off leaving things alone. If I'm the product of a rape, for instance, I'd rather not know. It's a grand and generous gesture and a great idea, but let me think about it for a bit."

JJ patted Tommy Wilson on the shoulder. "Whatever you want to do, bro. Michelle told me this is something you've talked about since you were a kid. You might never get another shot. Just give it some thought."

With that, they were both off to prepare for their next mission. They had a few days to double-check earlier intel about their destination. Then they'd head off to World War II Japan.

Griffiths' jet arrived in the early morning hours at Andrews and taxied into the BOTM hanger. When he and JJ met at the foot of the plane's stairway, he said he'd slept well on the flight. "But now I'm anxious to find out what this big mystery is all about, Major."

JJ was shocked to see how much their guest had aged in the few months since he'd last seen him in Havasu. "Well, the wait's over. I hope you're ready for what we've prepared for you, Bill."

"I most definitely am and stop looking at me that way, JJ," Griffiths admonished him. "I might be old and worn out, but I can still do whatever needs doing—unless it involves sex, drugs, or rock and roll." The two shook hands then JJ escorted his guest to the briefing room.

The team was already assembled and exchanged pleasantries. Doctor Moretti walked in and spoke briefly with Bill Griffiths. "I'm sorry I did not make the trip to Arizona to attend Richard's burial. Please accept my belated condolences." Minutes later, the conversation had become much more relaxed. She jokingly asked if any good cigars accompanied Griffiths on his trip East.

"Come on, you two," JJ admonished, "no contraband allowed. If either of you want Cubans, I can have them here on the next plane coming in from Guantanamo, no problem."

Griffiths laughed. "I have my own sources, JJ. Your buddy Scott already sent me some two weeks ago."

JJ smiled, but abruptly changed the subject and ordered the team to take their seats for the briefing.

Doctor Moretti turned to leave but almost immediately swung back around to face Griffiths. "When you are finished, please let's sit and talk about the good old days. There's nobody I can talk with around here who's over forty."

Griffiths smiled and gave Moretti a wink as she left the briefing room.

After the dress whites and the other uniforms JJ had requested were moved from the jet to the staging area of the briefing room, JJ instructed T1 and its special guest to change into the outfit of the day.

"I haven't worn dress whites since graduation, JJ." Sharif said. "Where we going, boss?"

JJ shook his head. "Still with the 'boss' I see?"

"Sir, yes sir." Sharif grinned at him.

As soon as everyone was fully dressed and lined up for inspection, JJ delivered the news. "Gentlemen, we have done some extraordinary things since joining the Marines. Bill Griffiths, our guest today, has served his country both in and out of the military. He lost his father in the Pacific during World War II, served during wartime in Vietnam, and has supported us without question in our covert missions. We were all there when Bill's grandson was KIA overseas. He's known a lot of heartache. Today we're going to take him on a journey that is meant to show the thanks of a grateful nation, as well as this special operations team and the Joint Chiefs of Staff."

Griffiths stood at attention, a proud smile on his face as tears welled up in his eyes.

"Bill, I have to remind you that everything you know and everything you are about to hear and experience over the next few hours is top secret."

Griffiths acknowledged this with a respectful "Sir, yes sir."

"Gentlemen, in a few minutes we are going to form our circle and travel back in time to the deck of the U.S.S. Missouri. We are going to arrive there on the morning of September 2, 1945. The ship will be anchored in Tokyo Bay, and General Douglas MacArthur will represent the United States in accepting Japan's surrender. We have the proper military ID's in case anyone checks. Retired Colonel Bill Griffiths is our guest. The story, if anyone asks, will be that we were all at Pearl Harbor the day it was attacked and we're lucky enough to be present for Japan's surrender and to watch the war come to an end. We'll land in one of the engine equipment storage rooms deep inside the ship and make our way up to the deck. Any questions?"

Griffiths looked stunned. "Damn it, God damn it! I knew it! You sons of bitches figured out a way to travel through time! I have a thousand questions I want to ask, but since this is my first time at this amusement park I'll hold on and see what happens."

Wilson stepped up beside the older man and touched his arm. "Are you okay with this, Bill? You don't have to do this if you're not up to it."

"Son, I am elated. I'm excited, that's all."

The team members congratulated Griffiths, patting him on the back, shaking his hand, thanking him for his service, reminding him that they miss JR and share in his mourning.

"Thank you, all. JJ, I have one question. Is this what you planned for dress of the day on the Missouri?" JJ nodded, hoping they'd got it right. Griffiths grimaced. "Well, we're going to stick out like Thanksgiving turkeys. MacArthur limited the pomp and circumstance to the point that there really wasn't any. Every Marine and Army officer and enlisted man on the U.S. side wore their everyday khakis, no dress uniforms. Only a few of the Navy sailors wore their whites."

JJ stared at him. "Really? How could we have missed that?" *God damn it!* This was the second time he'd messed up because he wasn't at 110%. His wife's waning health and the guilt he was beginning to feel for not being there were costing him his focus. The first time might have cost a man's life. And now this. A monumental mistake if Griffith hadn't caught it.

JJ looked around the room at his team. "Well, I feel like

the guy who tells everyone it's a costume party but when they show up it isn't. Luckily, being prepared is what we're all about. I also had Bill acquire khaki uniforms. Heck, since the Marines got rid of dress whites a few years back there's a chance some of you may never have worn them. Guess you won't now. Let's get dressed and then get some protein bars and Gatorade in us before we blast off."

Thirty minutes later, Wilson placed a pulse device necklace over Griffith's head as the rest put theirs into place. "Best you leave behind that Rolex, Bill. It'll be a dead give-away. Now, just relax and place your right hand against this device, holding it over your heart as JJ does a 3-2-1 count-down and you'll be fine." Wilson looked across the room and smiled. "Still can't believe the Doc smokes cigars. She's awesome."

Griffiths took White's spot in the circle. As Doctor Moretti gave an approving nod at Griffiths from the control room window, JJ called out the familiar countdown.

Within seconds the six were standing in the bowels of one of the biggest battleships the U.S. Navy had ever put to sea. It took a moment for their guest's eyes to adjust to the poor lighting. The smell of grease and hydraulic fluid hung heavy in the air. Sharif and Abrams gave each other the same look.

JJ thought they were probably glad they didn't have to work in these conditions. He couldn't help thinking about the many sailors who had been deep in the belly of ships like this one, at Pearl Harbor that morning and during World War II. He looked across at Griffiths who appeared concerned about the steep stairs they'd need to climb to get out of there and up to the main deck. He hoped the man's heart and legs were up to the task. They'd carry him up if needed.

"Let your adrenaline kick in, Bill. It'll help," JJ said. "We'll get you up top after we conclude your tour of the ship. That's why we're down here—if anyone asks."

Within twenty minutes they were stepping out into the sunlight. Hundreds of men in khaki uniforms lined every deck of the ship. Sailors sat on the long barrels of mighty guns that had helped bring the war to an end. Less than a month earlier, just a few hundred miles to the South, the U.S. had dropped an atomic bomb on Hiroshima and another on Nagasaki, forcing the Japanese surrender. To the east, a few thousand miles away, the U.S. continued to deal with the consequences of Japan's attack on Pearl Harbor, in Hawaii. After being attacked on December 7, 1941, a ship similar to the Missouri, the Arizona, sank beneath the harbor water, with many brave souls still aboard.

"Look at the size of those sixteen-inch guns," Abrams said in amazement.

"Yeah, Big Mo could kick the crap out of just about anything with those suckers." Griffiths gazed at the nearest gun with obvious pride. "This ship took a kamikaze strike at sea and kept on kicking ass. She's a very special ship!" He gazed out across the bay. "My father was killed by a kamikaze strike. Who would have thought that, so many years later, terrorists would commit such atrocities in the same way, in New York City and DC."

JJ broke off scouting the deck on hearing the last sentence. "I can tell you this, Bill. I can tell all of you this. General Stewart and I have been discussing future missions, and I think you will see a hell of a lot of target practice on terrorists in the very near future. Let's leave that for later and watch history being made."

The mood on the ship was mixed but focused. Some Americans still wanted vengeance and watched with hatred for the enemy while others were starting to process the losses they and their country had suffered since the war in the Pacific started.

At 0900 Tokyo time, representatives of the Japanese government and military boarded the Missouri and proceeded to sign the formal surrender documents to end the war. MacArthur had ordered that no side arms or weapons be worn or displayed by the US or the Japanese. There were no holstered .45's or Thompson machine guns with the Americans. No Arisaka rifles, Nambu pistols or swords with the Japanese. The leader of the Japanese party used a walking stick; he had lost a leg in the war.

Everyone's attention was on General MacArthur and the Japanese officials. The ship was silent as the Japanese first approached their side of the table and marked each of the many pages. JJ and the team had been able to secure a good vantage point and witnessed the entire event. Not one person asked them a question or gave them a second look, so intent were they on the event unfolding before them.

MacArthur, and the other military leaders who fought with the U.S., signed from their side of the table. The U.K., Canada, France, New Zealand, the Netherlands, even China, and Russia were on the U.S. side of the table.

"Who would have thought today's enemies were yesterday's allies," Jones whispered. "You guys notice how things have changed? Today, everyone sits shoulder to shoulder for the photo ops. Here, the U.S. won't even share the table with the Japs."

"I like it this way," Wilson responded.

MacArthur's prepared remarks were short, but included the words, "The issues involving divergent ideals and ideologies have been determined on the battlefield of the world and hence not for our discussion or debate."

"Hey, what's that? I think I can smell Hiroshima from here," Wilson muttered.

Once the documents were signed, the defeated left the ship as quickly as they had arrived, and the Marines, Army, Air Force, and Navy personnel aboard the Missouri looked forward to getting as far away from Japan, and back home, as quickly as possible. JJ felt it best to get Griffith and the team inside the ship and out of sight so they too could return home.

Given the large number of crewmen, officers, and guests that were aboard, and the time necessary for everyone to disperse, Griffiths had a chance to move to the side of the ship and look out over the bay. He turned to JJ. "Thank you, Major. I thought I had figured out what you were doing, but I had no idea what the actual experience itself might be like. Young people today say things are amazing or awesome, but this truly is. Seeing the bastards who orchestrated this war with their heads bowed in shame and surrender allows me to finally let go of some of the hatred I have carried for these people since they killed my father. Thank you for this. This is a profound moment for me."

JJ saluted Griffiths, and the salute was returned. Then Bill Griffiths stepped closer to JJ and whispered, "I know where this came from." He pulled a ribbon and medal from his pants pocket. "I've carried it with me since the day my grandson died. It's time this was laid to rest too."

Before JJ could respond, Griffiths threw the medal into Tokyo Bay. The medal Hitler wore at the time of his death in the Berlin bunker, the only souvenir any team member had ever brought back, was gone forever.

JJ watched the medal splash into the water, only then realizing that man who had thrown it was falling backward.

"Abrams!" Wilson called out.

Within seconds, the team's medic had Griffiths lying down on the deck of the Missouri. The team had managed to make it through the historic ceremony only to become the center of attention now as a man in uniform was down.

"We need to get him to sick bay STAT, JJ." Abrams said. "He's having a heart attack. He's still breathing but he needs oxygen and whatever meds they have for this."

JJ searched Griffiths' pockets for any medication he might carry with him, but he found nothing.

Sailors lifted the fallen man and carried him to the medical facility on board.

"You guys stay together up here and start developing Plan B, C and D," JJ told Wilson and the team. "I'll go with him."

Abrams grabbed JJ's arm as he stepped inside the ship to follow them and whispered, "JJ, he's got a pacemaker. They didn't have them in 1945, so be prepared for anything."

Wilson frowned, exchanging looks with JJ. "Just go. We'll be close if you need us."

Ten minutes later, after the Navy medical team had tried their best, Bill Griffiths was gone. Oxygen and an adrenaline syringe were the extent of what they could do for him.

"What was someone his age doing on board?" the doctor demanded.

JJ told him the cover story, which seemed to appease him. The orderlies asked JJ for vital statistics and contact information while they prepared to cover the body and move it to the ship's morgue. "May I have a few minutes with him, please?" JJ asked.

The doctor agreed and left with the two orderlies. *Okay, now what, JJ?* He stepped out into the hallway to see Wilson and the rest of T1 standing at alert.

"The doc told us he didn't make it," Wilson said quickly. "Here's what we came up with."

They shared the intel the group had gathered while they were waiting. They knew they needed to get Griffiths' body back to Andrews. They couldn't leave his daughter in limbo and they couldn't leave him and the pacemaker behind.

"This ship has dozens of severely wounded on board. They're here because they are too sick to move. One orderly told us they are all terminal. We found one poor son of a bitch who is badly burned and they have no idea who he is. His dog tags were lost in battle and nobody can ID him. I say we grab him for the pulse and take him and Griffiths back to Andrews with us."

"Are you guys on crack? There's no way we can do that, no way. It's inhumane. We're not monsters!" JJ protested.

But now wasn't the time to debate the morality or come up with an alternative plan. The hallway wasn't very wide, and there was a constant flow of officers and sailors passing through their group. Wilson stepped inside the small trauma room, and the rest quickly followed him in.

"So, what do we do with the poor guy once we're home?" JJ asked the group.

"He's not going to last the night they say, so he probably won't be with us for long," Jones said. "We take him back and care for him the best we can and, when he dies, we get someone at the Pentagon to pull strings and we bury him with full honors, privately, as an unknown at Arlington."

Sharif nodded. "That's more than he'll get if he dies here, JJ. He's saving our lives, and it's a sure thing that he is going to die for his country. We need to do this for him and for us."

Abrams grabbed a vial of morphine and a syringe. They weren't touching this unknown hero until additional pain-killer had been administered. "This will slow his heart even more. Might even stop it, but that's the only way I'm in. He gets the shot and we roll the dice!" JJ and Wilson nodded their approval and Abrams was on his way.

Within seconds they were able to move the burn patient, along with his medical chart, into the trauma room with Griffiths' body. "Careful, guys, careful!" Wilson cautioned. They needed to move quickly, but had to care for the poor man as best they could.

Two orderlies attending the terminal patients rushed down the hallway toward the team. "Whoa, wait, wait! What are you guys doing with him?"

Abrams beckoned to them to follow him into the room. Wilson came along behind and closed the door even as one of them shouted for security. They had no time for lengthy explanations, even if they could have explained. Wilson knocked one of the men out with a sleeper hold. Sharif and Jones stepped in and used their Special Ops training to render the second orderly unconscious without making a sound or leaving a mark.

"Give them both a dose of anesthesia gas, and do it quick," JJ shouted to Abrams. "Heavy. They'll be confused and puking for a few hours, but they'll be okay. I doubt they'll remember any of this."

Wilson said, "We could pull the alarm as a diversion and drive everyone into a state of panic."

JJ scowled. "No friggin' way! The wounded have been through enough. So have the crew. This mission ends here and now. Drop the mat and let's go home!"

"If it turns out they do remember, we can come back and execute a better plan," Sharif offered. It was a possibility they hadn't tested before—trying a redo. This wasn't the time to discuss that option. It was time go home.

As they'd done in Berlin, Valley Forge, Rome, and now aboard the Missouri in Tokyo Bay, the team stepped onto the travel mat and prepared for a quick departure.

Wilson removed the pulse device from Griffiths' body and placed it over the head of the semi-conscious sailor. Jones held the sailor upright in his arms.

JJ could hear the wounded man release a faint groan. Knowing he must be in agony, JJ was crushed to think they were causing him even more pain. He reached across the six-man circle and held the pulse against their hero's heart. But Sharif was struggling with Griffith's body, and they needed to move. Now!

JJ counted the familiar 3-2-1 just as someone banged on the locked medical room door.

The team reappeared at Andrews. JJ looked around to see T2 and the support team staring in astonishment at the returned travelers, plus one. Jones was struggling to hold up a wounded stranger. "Need some help here!" he called out.

Wilson and Abrams immediately came to his aid. Sharif couldn't hold Griffiths' any longer. JJ and T2 leader Scott helped him lower the body to the floor as respectfully as possible.

"What the fuck, JJ, you brought *two* KIA's back this time?" Scott railed.

"Griffith suffered a fatal heart attack. And our hero isn't dead yet, but he is going to die."

"He's gone, JJ," Abrams whispered as he stood up from checking the patient's pulse.

Doctor Moretti stood over Griffiths' body. JJ wondered if seeing the passing of this man she'd liked and considered a friend reminded her that her time also was short. But she managed a smile as she leaned down and gently touched the top of his head. "At least he died seeing something that meant the world to him," she whispered. "Rest peacefully, Bill."

The quickest way to bring everyone back to center was to order a command to attention. JJ issued the order and saluted the fallen, lying before them. The rest of T1 and T2 snapped to attention, saluting. As JJ lowered his right hand back down to his side he directed the team to take the sailor's body to the small medical unit within the hangar. If they took him to the base morgue, questions would be asked and names recorded.

"Abrams," JJ commanded, "get Mr. Griffiths over to the base medical center to be pronounced. I hate this, but you will have to change him back into his street clothes first. Make sure his ID is on him. You found him slumped in his chair, here in the briefing room; he had come to visit at my invitation."

"Right, boss."

"You and Sharif place him in a Suburban and take him to their ER."

What had started out as an incredible journey back in time to a significant moment in American history had turned into one of the most difficult and heart wrenching missions his men had experienced. JJ was sure that everyone on the team was thinking about what had happened that day. For some, perhaps, it was time to let someone else take their place.

But before JJ had a chance to follow up on that thought, Josh Scott lunged toward him.

"Nice job, JJ," Scott sneered.

Neither of them saw the punch coming. Wilson leveled the captain with one blow of his fist to the side of the man's head.

12

The morning after T1's return from Japan, Chairman Stewart asked Army General Brooks to join him for the debrief. T1 leader Jackson and T2 leader Scott along with T1 second-in-command Wilson were summoned to the Pentagon. Chairman Stewart directed Jackson to describe the trip in its entirety to the group.

"So, let me get this straight, Major Jackson," Brooks said, his voice stern. "You messed up on the dress of the day, witnessed one of the American military's proudest moments, brought back the remains of one of the President's friends, as well as a badly burned unidentified sailor who died on arrival. We need to arrange for a secret burial, a hero's burial at Arlington and, at the conclusion of the mission, your second in command sucker punched a team leader." He glared at JJ. "Did I miss anything, Major?"

"General, no you did not."

Brooks looked across the meeting room to Chairman Stewart. "We can discuss the nuts and bolts of this afterward, Stew. For now, I want to know what we're going to do with Wilson here and whether T1's next mission should be to the brig or guard duty in Bangladesh!"

Scott spoke up before Stewart had a chance to respond. "General Brooks, sir, Wilson was acting in defense of his Team Leader. What I said was out of line. I deserved what I got."

JJ and Wilson exchanged surprised glances. But, as soon as their eyes met, they realized he was just kissing up to the brass.

Brooks asked, "So, Captain Scott, you're okay with getting knocked on your ass by a Marine?"

Scott responded immediately. "General, that's a negative. An Army officer should never yield to a Marine or anyone else. I was caught off guard. It was a sucker punch, and—" he stared directly at Wilson "—it will never happen again, sir."

The room fell quiet while everyone considered the remarks.

General Stewart broke the silence. "Okay, so here's what I want to propose. Before they went off to Japan, Major Jackson suggested that T1 finally take Captain Scott on a trip with them. I think it was suggested that some winter trek, some high-altitude excursion might be a good test. Wilson grew up near Yellowstone, so the original thought was that you all go there, back to the early 1800s, to see if you can connect with the Lewis and Clark expedition as they make their way across the region."

Neither JJ nor Wilson trusted or liked Scott, but if the Chiefs were going to let the water run under the bridge and send them to Yellowstone that was fine by them.

"Now we have the issue—no, the honor—of burying an

unknown at Arlington. All things considered, I should make you two go out there in the rain some night and dig a six-foot hole by hand, but this poor soul deserves better than that. Give me a day or two and we'll arrange for a service at dusk after the tours are gone and gates closed." Stewart wasn't pleased that things had turned out as they did, but now his focus was on taking care of a hero who died for his country. "General Brooks, unless you have anything more for these men, I suggest we dismiss them so we can discuss the rest of our agenda."

Brooks agreed and, after salutes were exchanged, the time travelers left the room and headed back to Andrews.

"Don't think that cold cock is behind us, Wilson," Scott muttered as they approached the shuttle. "An eye for an eye is what you have coming. One of these days we're going to be even."

Wilson looked at JJ and then to Scott. "Sounds fair."

While they waited for their ride back to base they talked about the mountain ranges they'd climbed and the parks they'd visited.

"Never been to Yellowstone so I'm looking forward to it," Scott said. "Never saw a grizzly in the wild either, so I hope you guys have done your homework and we can get on this ASAP."

"I grew up in that park," Wilson said. "You're going to be in awe of that place by the time we get done." He shot JJ a quick look. "It's your turn to tell White she's not going on another mission."

As they climbed inside the shuttle Scott turned to JJ. "Hey, I know your wife is real sick. I only met her once. That time at the bar, I made an ass of myself. I hope she gets better. Seriously."

Scott rode shotgun in the front while the two Marines filled the second row of seats. JJ turned toward Wilson and mouthed: "asshole." Wilson smiled and made a stroking gesture with his hand. Sentiment not accepted.

Back at the Pentagon, Brooks and Stewart sat down to discuss the most recent BOTM excursion, JJ's fitness for duty under the circumstances, plans to elevate the program to a full-on seek and destroy program, the upcoming retirements of two chiefs, and relations with the President.

Two days later, as taps played and the honor guard fired their rounds, the unidentified from the Missouri was laid to rest in a grave at Arlington National Cemetery. The Joint Chiefs and twelve that made up T1 and T2 saluted the fallen as the American flag was folded by the honor guard. Rivalries and agendas aside, these representatives of the Army, Navy, Air Force, Marines and National Guard stood as one, acknowledging the ultimate sacrifice this lone hero had made. Sadly, with no family or friends in attendance, the flag would be transferred to the Capitol where it would be flown the next day, and then given away.

Before leaving the cemetery, Stewart approached JJ. "Brooks is going to push his agenda to the rest of the chiefs. He wants to make some bold moves before the new President is sworn in and replaces our retirees. Watch your back with Scott. We all know he's a mole. You and your team do what you must with that prick while you're in Yellowstone. Once you get back, the sightseeing part of the BOTM testing might be behind you." His voice turned even more grave. "Be careful out there. Whatever you do, JJ, make sure everyone comes back alive!"

On the ride back to Andrews, the T1 team was unusually silent. JJ and Wilson were deep in their own thoughts. JJ prayed this would be the only funeral he'd have to attend for a very long time. Wilson visualized watching Scott getting stomped into the snow by a raging bull moose at Yellowstone.

"I still wish we had pulled DNA before we buried that poor guy," Abrams said to anyone who might be listening.

"I get it," JJ responded after clearing his thoughts, "but, like I said before, if that guy has parents, or a wife, or siblings, they're all dead or almost there. There's no reason to upset his survivors even if we were able to find them. If he had kids, they'll have lived seventy years without him, so same deal." The van was quiet, but only for a moment.

"There's something to be said for closure, JJ," White offered. "If he did leave anyone behind all they know is that they sent him off on a mission and he never came back. No news, no body to bury, nothing. At least we could send them his flag."

Wilson balled his fists in his lap. "Life's a bitch and then you die! Let's move on. Whoever he left behind had to move on. Why not pull DNA from all the unknowns buried there? What would that accomplish? Leave the dead to rest in peace." And that seemed to settle the issue.

Back at base, JJ and Wilson took a moment away from the team to discuss their next mission. "As much as I hate to say it," JJ said, "with all that's happened, we're going to have to make sure Scott comes back without a scratch on him."

Wilson shook his head in frustration. "I was thinking

the same thing. Too bad. All eyes are on us now, and I know we can't lay a hand on him. But I just know that jerk is up to no good. Brooks would have our butts for sure. And if we cancel the trip they'll figure we had something planned for him."

The two turned to watch as Air Force One came into sight and began its approach for landing.

"Just once I want to party on that bird," Wilson joked.

"Okay, back to Yellowstone," JJ said. "Going in winter would be a bitch. Since we no longer intend to put anyone in danger, like making Scott climb the Little Falls in the ice and snow, let's reset the destination date so we get there in the summer. We can try to intercept Lewis and Clark on their way back from the Pacific."

Wilson nodded with a smile. "My man, anything to stay out of the cold. I was there once when it was twenty-seven below. I'll double check the dates and get with the doc in the morning."

"Good. And, Tommy, why don't you stop by to visit Michelle later today. We'll have a beer."

"Nope, I've got some calls to make first. I have to track down some 1800s Montana summer gear. I'll get there after supper." He paused for a moment. His eyes welled up as he shook his head in disbelief. He cleared his throat and said, "I'll be there."

JJ gave him a thumbs-up as they headed for their cars.

Back at their apartment, JJ and Michelle sat together on the sofa. Michelle's chemotherapy treatments were continuing to take their toll. Luckily the side effects weren't as bad as she had heard, thanks to the medical marijuana.

"You do know you're going to make me flunk a pee test, young lady," JJ said jokingly. "Secondhand smoke." They shared a laugh. "Look at Bunker," JJ added, "the stuff's even got her chillin'."

They laughed even more. Laughter was a constant in their home—it helped break the tension, relieved stress, and relaxed both of them.

"I'll be away for just a few days and then done for a while," JJ told her.

"That's fine. Go do what you have to do. I'm not going anywhere."

Days later, T1, with T2 team leader Scott replacing White for this mission, stepped on the travel mat and prepared for JJ's count down.

With Griffiths gone, the team had to find other connections to get the proper gear and guns for future missions. For this adventure, a trip to Yellowstone in early August 1806, it was easy. Having grown up near there, and with the help of his survivalist buddies in the region and in Alaska, Wilson was able to acquire whatever they needed. Clothes made from animal skins and all the supporting elements were in good supply. The standard weaponry of the period was also easy, but JJ wanted one item in particular and knew it would be a big request.

"Did you get me a Girandoni?" he asked.

"Sorry," Wilson said. "Unless you want me to break into a museum, that's not going to happen."

"Damn. To think Lewis and Clark took an *air* rifle on their trek across that undiscovered wilderness is amazing. The damn thing was state of the art at the time and could fire forty consecutive round balls before needing to be pumped back up. Those were .46 caliber shots. If the damn thing didn't take something like 1,000 hand pumps to get fully charged it would have been the shit." Some of the team had heard of the rifle, but were still amazed by its features.

Scott said, "Some Italian guy, guess it was Ghiradelli, made it for the Austrians who needed something special to fight Napoleon. Eventually a few of them wound up in Lewis and Clarks' hands."

Wilson was laughing. "It's not Ghiradelli—that's chocolate!—it's Girandoni, city boy."

JJ asked Wilson how White took the news that she wasn't going on this trip. "She's fine. She's actually involved with some pretty cool stuff off-base. She's also not into bears, elk, and wolves. You just better hope she never finds out about Sacagawea. I told her it wouldn't be fit to have a woman with five other guys walking around Yellowstone back in the day. Sacagawea was the Indian woman who helped get Lewis and Clark from North Dakota to the Pacific."

Jones laughed. "She was hot. At least that's the way Disney made her in Night at the Museum."

"So, Wilson, you sure these long rifles and knives will be all we need out there?" Jones asked.

Wilson nodded in the affirmative. "I really wanted to get hold of that air rifle. Can you imagine dropping a Grizzly or a Buffalo with an air rifle? Impressive!"

"Guys, I just realized something. If we need a sixth pulse we've always been able to adapt—we could grab a dog, grab a guy right out of his hospital bed, whatever—but out there in the wilderness, extra heartbeats aren't that easy to come across if we need one," Sharif pointed out.

"Hell, we'll just set some traps and latch onto a wolverine or something. You can hold it. Dr. Moretti would get a kick out of it if we brought one back." Wilson laughed at what he'd just said and they all joined in. But JJ was already counting.

"3-2-1!"

They landed within the sound of rushing water from the Little Falls in Yellowstone National Park in Northwestern Wyoming. It was 09:00, August 1806. Within a few days they hoped to cross paths with the Lewis and Clark expedition as they traversed the Yellowstone.

"Thank God they didn't come through here in winter. That would have sucked," Scott said as the six stepped away from the travel mat and took in the beautiful landscape around them. "Listen, you can hear the— Oh shit!"

They all spun around at the sound of rustling grasses and thundering hooves. A huge brown buffalo, head down, was charging the group. It brushed past Sharif toward its target. Weighing 2,000 pounds and able to reach forty miles per hour, its huge head bulldozed into Scott, throwing him ten feet into the air and hard against a tree. It took a second for others in the team to react. The buffalo turned and came back at them on a second charge.

JJ could feel the ground tremble beneath him. JJ, Wilson, Sharif, and Jones aimed their rifles and fired at the charging animal. It went down with a thud, let out a last gasp and died, its eyes wide open. JJ looked around at his men, still trying to catch his breath. His team was used to confronting terrorists and attacking enemy combatants at close range. But they'd never had to bring down anything this immense before now—and never with guns that lacked full auto and large ammo mags.

Abrams was already down on his knees attending to Scott. "This isn't good," he muttered to himself, as he gently probed the downed man.

"I think my ribs are broken," Scott gasped, before losing consciousness.

"A fucking Buffalo! What the fuck!" Jones shouted. The men quickly reloaded and formed a perimeter ring around their wounded comrade. Buffalo usually run in herds so others should be close by.

"You think we scared the son of a bitch or what?" Sharif asked.

"Probably," Wilson responded. "We might be the first people that thing ever saw. Since we popped up so close to it, we gave it no choice. Our gunfire would have run off anything else that was close to us. I think we're okay."

"Scott's pretty beat up, boss," Abrams said, looking up at JJ. "I think he's got a punctured lung. Breathing's labored. Means it's probably filling with blood. We need to get him back to medical STAT."

"Mother F-ing God damn stinky-assed buffalo," JJ shouted at the carcass. "This isn't good. It's going to look like we f'd him up ourselves."

Jones said, "Wilson tried to push Scott out of the way. We all saw that. We'll just tell the truth. That's all we can do."

Wilson walked over to the fallen Buffalo and cut off its right ear. "We've been gone ten minutes and come back with a messed-up team member. I'm bringing this along for proof."

They quickly re-assembled on the mat. Still unconscious, Scott was struggling to breathe as Jones and Sharif held him upright. Even as JJ started the count down, Josh Scott's color worsened.

"Shit, his necklace is gone!" Abrams shouted. "JJ, the pulse device is missing."

The group quickly stepped off the mat and Scott was laid back down on the ground.

"The hit from the Buffalo could have sent it flying anywhere," Wilson groaned.

Abrams checked inside the patient's shirt. "It's not there."

The team broke up and spread out to scour the landscape. JJ was sure that Scott was near death and it seemed there was nothing Abrams could do for him. The best they could hope for was to find the pulse fast and get back to Andrews where a medical team would take over.

"It's not here, JJ," Jones shouted, his eyes wide with panic. "It's not anywhere!"

Sharif stopped short. He looked down at the buffalo carcass and then at Wilson. "Think it's under him?"

"You kidding? That beast is too heavy to roll," Wilson shouted.

"We're losing him, JJ!" Abrams called out.

"Wilson, grab that tree limb," JJ shouted. "We can use it as a lever to roll this monster over." Wilson walked as if in a trance toward the limb. "Hurry the fuck up, Tommy!" JJ shouted.

Wilson looked startled but picked up the pace. He shoved the limb under the Buffalo's side. Jones and JJ joined him to push. Nothing. Abrams jumped up and leaned in to add his weight.

And there it was—stuck to the underside of the animal. JJ threw the necklace over Scott's head, and they got him back on his feet, propped between them. With a hasty countdown, they were back at base.

"A frickin' buffalo rammed his ass!" Abrams shouted to his counterpart. "I think he slammed his head on a tree when he landed."

T2 Corpsman Devine took over, quickly checking the injured man's his vitals. The Captain's airway was partially obstructed, his blood pressure dangerously low. With no time to spare, they intubated Scott, placed him on a stretcher, and shoved him into the back of a Suburban. JJ could only stand back and watch them do their jobs. The two medics would continue to work on him until they arrived at the trauma center for x-rays and emergency care. He watched them drive away, his heart heavy.

"This isn't going to go over well with Brooks or Stewart," he said to Wilson. "We're back early, so here's the plan: get changed into the same khakis we all wore on the Missouri. They're in the dressing room, all dry cleaned and ready to go." The rest of the team clustered around him, listening in. "Get hold of White, eat some food, and be ready for another mission within an hour," JJ said. "I'm going to Dr. Moretti's control room to talk with her in private. Wilson, here comes the rest of T2. Head them off. Tell them there was a training accident. Nothing more."

Ten minutes later, JJ was back in their hangar with his team. "Brooks is going to shut us down when he finds out about his bitch, so we need to move fast. Tommy, I told you that I wanted to help you find your biological mother, so that's what we're going to do. Everyone on T1, including White, is in agreement on this. Doc Moretti has all the info she needs. She'll be here any minute. I did the necessary intel so we can move on the ground there. Let's get changed, steal some of that pizza, and get ready to roll."

Tommy Wilson looked excited but nervous. "JJ, you don't have to do this, especially not now. It'll look like we injured him intentionally and then ran. If he wakes up and tells the truth we'll be better off if we're still on base. I don't want to run from a fight, especially when we're right."

JJ thought about Wilson's statement but shook his head 'no'. "We're going. I want you to experience this once and for all so you can move on. We might never be able to take a trip again if they take us off the project, so let's do this. We just have to hope we can get there and back before Brooks, or anyone else, pulls the plug and leaves us there!"

Within the hour, T1 was dressed and ready to roll. White had returned to base and dressed in an early 80's top, jeans, and sneakers. JJ had told her weeks earlier that this might be on the itinerary. Finding the clothes in a nearby vintage clothing store was easy.

Abrams updated the team on Scott's condition. "He's a tough son of a bitch, I'll give him that. He'll recover okay, but he's going to be sore for a really long time."

Dr. Moretti was given their destination: August 1, 1981, at dusk, in Cut Bank, Montana, six hours North of Yellowstone and a short drive south of the Canadian border.

"I still can't believe that Army asshole got rammed by a buffalo." White laughed.

"Yeah, there's like a million square miles of nothing out

there. And don't you know we land right in front of that critter," Jones responded.

JJ looked at his group. "Enough of that. Let's concentrate." He gave them a minute to settle themselves. "This will be the trip closest to our current time. We'll be in the good old USA, so we'll all be able to talk normally and fit in pretty easily. I had to use up a few favors with some guys I know over at Treasury to get hold of a bunch of twenties and a few hundreds that were in circulation back then, but other than that we should be good to go. Just remember, think late 70's for news and music. Bee Gees, Genesis, Earth Wind & Fire, the Steelers won the Super Bowl, *Apocalypse Now* and *Kramer vs. Kramer* were the big movies. Got it?" Everyone laughed but answered in the affirmative.

Before long, they were standing behind an old airport hangar just outside of town. Cut Bank was home to bomber training during World War II. Once the war ended the military pulled out and the town got smaller and smaller. They walked the half-mile to the town center and went into a diner for food and to get their bearings.

Wilson checked the phone book in a booth at the back of the diner. There it was. Robert Monroe's name, address, and phone number. JJ's research told him that Robert Monroe and Mary Monroe lived at the same address from 1979 to August 1981. Robert was an auto mechanic in town. Mary worked at the school.

Wilson returned to the table. "Found them, JJ."

"Okay now what?" White asked.

Wilson sat down for a moment, head in his hands. Everyone waited. At last he said, "I want to go right to their front door and knock on it. I want to see what my mother looked like before she had me. See my father's face. I'll just say my car broke down and ask if he can take a look at it in the morning."

The waitress brought their dinners and everyone ate except for Wilson. He said he couldn't. He was nervous, excited, scared, angry, forgiving, and curious all at the same time. He rehearsed the scene in his mind over and over. Would they be home? Would they invite this unknown traveler in? Would they be happy about getting ready for the new baby to arrive? The questions were endless.

Abruptly he stood up and headed for the door. "I can't wait, guys. I'll go do this and be back before long."

The rest of the team remained seated except for JJ. "You sure you want to do it this way? I can come with you."

Wilson shook his head. "You got me this far, JJ, the rest is on me." With that, he was out the door, headed to the address in the phone book.

Five minutes later, Wilson was standing in front of a small house on Lookout Road under the dim glow of streetlights, as the moonless night grew darker. The lights were on in the front room—someone must be home. He took another minute to gather his thoughts, and courage. He'd been picturing this moment as far back as he could remember. Finally, he knocked on the door.

"Who the hell is banging on my door at this hour?" a shout came through the front window.

Wilson was taken aback. The door swung open and he was standing in front of his biological father. The stench of whisky, a lot of whisky, wafted off the man. Wilson's training kicked in; he was prepared to handle whatever happened next.

"Sir, I was told down at the diner that you work on cars. Mine broke down over by the airport and I was wondering if you could take a look at it in the morning?" Wilson looked past his father and saw a woman walking into the room and toward them.

"Who is it, Bobby?" she asked.

The man turned and shouted at her. "I told you to make me something better for dinner. Get your fat butt back in there and get cooking."

Wilson could see the woman, dressed in a summer robe, had been crying. She also was very pregnant. "I told you I wasn't feeling good. I can't stand up to cook."

Wilson called out, "You okay, ma'am?"

"Who the hell do you think you're talking to?" the man growled at Wilson. "And you, get back in there and make my dinner!"

Wilson charged through the screen door and knocked the man to the ground. He looked up at his mother and saw that he'd scared her. He also noticed a bruise on her left cheek. "It's okay, ma'am."

Wilson ignored the brute on the floor and approached his mother, hoping to reassure her. He sensed movement behind him. When he turned back, his father was reaching for a hammer on a table near the door. With two swift moves Wilson delivered a savage blow to the man's neck and another to his throat. The woman screamed. The man fell to the floor.

Wilson stood over him, then looked at his mother. "He'll never lay a hand on you again."

She must have been terrified and confused. He watched her brush a hand across watery eyes, her knees wobbled. She quickly sat on the sofa. Wilson bent down on one knee in front of her. "Everything will be okay. Please believe me, I'm not here to harm you."

She stared at him, as if trying to process what had just happened. Her gaze slipped away to the man who had abused her, now unmoving on the floor. Did she know he was dead? Wilson had no doubt. But suddenly he knew everything. He knew how it had been between them. She was carrying that man's baby not out of joy but as a result of a forced encounter during one of his drinking binges. The bastard had claimed her, and she'd had no way out…and now, what had happened here, was too much for her to comprehend.

"I-I think I need to go to the hospital," she whimpered. She was staring at him, and he could see a flash of something. Not recognition, which would have been impossible. But something that confused her even more. She seemed fascinated by his eyes.

Before he could say another word, she passed out.

Wilson picked up the touchtone phone and dialed 911. Nothing happened. He then dialed zero and, after a few seconds, an operator responded.

"There's a pregnant woman here who needs immediate attention." He gave the street address and asked the operator to please hurry. "She's lost consciousness and it's clear her water has broken."

The screen door opened just as Wilson hung up the phone.

"What the fuck?" JJ shouted as he walked into the

room. Abrams and the rest of the team followed close behind him. Abrams assessed the situation and immediately attended to the patient lying on the couch.

"That drunk piece of shit sperm donor is dead," Wilson screamed. "Dead. And I don't give a damn. He's never going to hurt her again."

"All right…all right. Listen, there's no way we can stay here with her," JJ said. "You know that, don't you, Tommy? We have to get the hell out of here. Now! There's a dead guy on the floor, and none of us are born yet. You can't explain us to the local sheriff."

Wilson looked at his unconscious mother on the sofa, and his dead father on the floor. "I need to see what happens to her, JJ. We can leave when the ambulance gets close, but I need to see that she's safe."

"Wilson, that's *you* inside her," White says softly as she points to the woman's belly. "You know that you make it, so she must, too."

A siren in the distance was growing louder. They remained at the woman's side until flashing red lights stopped in front of the house. Jones grabbed a napkin from the kitchen table to avoid leaving fingerprints and placed the hammer in the dead man's hand. Seconds later, as the ambulance driver and the sheriff ran in through the front door, the last of the team was closing the kitchen door behind them.

They stood and watched from a distance as the ambulance pulled away from the house. As it disappeared into the night, they started walking.

There was a small motel on the outskirts of town near the airport. They headed there as they discussed what had just happened and what their next move should be. Wilson remained silent. He wanted to be left to his thoughts.

JJ understood. He checked them into the three available motel rooms to lay low for the night. "No drinking tonight," he cautioned them. They sat outside their rooms, enjoying the night air and quietly considering the situation. To everyone's surprise, Wilson fell asleep first. Two of his teammates led him to his bed where he'd sleep through to morning.

"God, talk about a parallel universe!" Abrams muttered.

"Yeah that scene was pretty screwed up." JJ sighed.

Jones looked at JJ, "You sure about the no drinking policy tonight, JJ? It's a really short walk over to the motel bar. Doesn't look like much, but they've got beer." The idea was appealing to everyone sitting there. It had been a wild ride so far, with back-to-back missions placing a heavy emotional weight on the team.

"I vote it's best to leave things just as they are. Pretend we're in Saudi," White suggested. "If they catch you with alcohol they'll cut off your dick." She grinned at them then turned serious. "We've been rolling the dice a hell of a lot since we all got to Andrews. But, with the exception of losing Richard, we've been pretty lucky."

JJ let out a long breath. "Jeez, now the inmates are running the asylum. Let's be cool and stick to Diet Cokes and Hershey bars tonight. At sunrise, I'll call the hospital to see how she's doing." They all agreed. He continued, "We're strangers without a car, out in the middle of nowhere Montana. There's a dead guy lying in his house just down the road from here, so it won't be long before someone starts asking questions. Get some sleep and we'll move out at dawn." With that, the team headed off to their rooms for a few hours sleep.

"White, no snoring," Jones called out as the doors closed.

*

"She's dead," JJ whispered as he shook Abrams and Sharif awake.

"Wait, what?" Sharif blinked up at him from the bed.

"I called the hospital. They told me Wilson's mother delivered a few hours ago but there were complications and she died while giving birth." The three men looked at one another, shaking their heads in disbelief. Within a few minutes Jones came into the room and then White joined them. They were planning their next move when Wilson walked in.

"Where's the coffee?" he asked while rubbing the sleep from his face.

Wilson glanced at JJ, saw his expression, and saved him the speech he knew must be coming. "It's okay, JJ. I know what happened. I called the hospital myself a few hours ago. I get it." He looked down at his hands, folded in front of him. "The reason I was adopted was because she died while giving birth to me. At the end of the day, she was going to die regardless of whether we showed up last night or not. It was meant to be. But at least I laid some vengeance on her behalf on the shithead. And I got to see her. I saw how pretty she was. And I when she looked into my eyes, I knew she felt something for me. I'm good."

"Wilson," JJ began, "I—"

"Seriously, I'm fine. Anyway, there's a family I happen to know who have been trying to adopt a little boy for some time. Their little girl, Michelle, needs a baby brother. I think they're in luck now. Time to go home, guys."

The team assembled in their tight time-travel circle. "This might be the last time we get to do this," Abrams said. "Let's rock-n-roll!"

Scott was alive, but didn't remember much of the incident at Yellowstone. He had six broken ribs, a punctured lung, and a concussion. Brooks was furious.

Stewart told JJ, "I don't think I can protect the program or you and Wilson any longer. The two of you have been summoned to the Pentagon. You have no choice but to go."

They opted to stop by and see Scott at Walter Reed in Bethesda on the way. Some of Scott's army buddies were there, keeping him company. It was clear the Marines weren't welcome. They said their "get-wells" and moved on quickly.

Stewart was waiting for them when they arrived at the Pentagon. "Gentlemen, I can't tell you how surprised I was to hear about the cluster fuck of a mission you just pulled. Of everything that could possibly have happened out there, how the hell could you have allowed Scott of all people to get hurt?"

JJ opened his mouth to respond, but was waived off by Stewart before he could speak.

"It doesn't matter that it was a freak accident, *if* it was a freak accident. The optics are very bad for Brooks and the rest of the Chiefs for that matter. I've had to keep them in the loop since the election, and they've all started to wonder what the hell is going on – a God-damned Marine Hell Week or what!" Stewart shook his head in disappointment and delivered the news. "Effective immediately, the BOTM program is shut down. Everyone on both teams will take two weeks off, and then we'll either reassign or keep some of you at Andrews through the end of January."

JJ and Wilson looked at each other, unsure what to say next. Try to again explain what happened? Ask to present to the Chiefs?

"Whatever happens, men, the BOTM for the new year and the new administration in the Pentagon and at the White House will most definitely move forward. It will most probably be an ass-kicking, intel-retrieving unit. You've all proven it can work. It's just a shame all these changes are taking place at this time. I would have liked to have done more, learned more, maybe even have gone on a trip myself. Maybe listened in while Lincoln gave the Gettysburg Address."

The room was quiet for nearly a minute. Then JJ spoke up. "What will happen to Dr. Moretti?" JJ asked. "I don't think she has anywhere to go. This project was her life."

"I know." Stewart frowned. "Maybe we could take her away somewhere special, somewhere she could rest, relax. I don't think she'd enjoy a C-130 back to Italy and I know she's not using a pulse. I've got a meeting with the President at the White House in the morning. After that, I'll come down to the base, visit with her and talk through some of this. Colonel Petty brought her to us, so I will confer with him beforehand. For now, put everything on hold and go spend some time with Michelle."

With that, the meeting was over. It was clear to JJ that there was nothing he could say or do to change things. With salutes and an about face, the two men headed back to Andrews.

JJ found himself sitting in his apartment doing his best to keep Michelle company and make her as comfortable as possible. Bunker sat on the floor in front of her, standing guard. Michelle was getting weaker and weaker. JJ had been grateful being away on missions. It was easier than watching her dying. He had already watched his parents lose their battles. Now he had no choice. There was no escape.

Michelle often asked JJ to read to her. Anything would do. *People* magazine, the *Washington Post*, even *Soldier of Fortune*—which, she knew, gave JJ something to hold his attention. The doctors told them that the cancer was progressing and that this type of lung cancer, typically moved swiftly. It was time to consider hospice care.

"No way," JJ insisted. "We can move a hospital bed into our apartment if needed." Her mother wasn't well enough to fly in from Montana, but Anne, Michelle's brother, and JJ could take shifts watching over her and doing what needed to be done for her. If this really was going to happen then all he wanted was help from her doctors to make her as comfortable as possible.

Michelle understood that her death was imminent. Bored with television, the news, and the gossip magazines—all she wanted was for JJ to sit with her when she was awake. The pain medication made her groggy most of the time, even when she wasn't asleep.

"JJ, read to me," she whispered to him one afternoon.

"I thought you were done with all the political bull in the newspapers and the Hollywood crap, sweetie."

She smiled and said, "I am. Reach into my night table drawer. I'd like you to read from my Bible."

JJ hadn't held a Bible in a very long time, but he knew how special this one was. Michelle's late father had given it to her as a present for her First Communion, when she was a little girl. After her father died, she insisted that the priest at their wedding use it to marry her and JJ.

"Whatever you want," JJ said.

He was about to ask her if she wanted him to read any particular passage when he realized she'd gone back to sleep. He sat there looking at her, holding her Bible. With tears running down his face, he suddenly knew what he needed to do. He kissed her on the forehead, wiped away his tears, pulled her blanket up close, and laid her Bible beside her on the bed.

Anne arrived minutes after he'd called her to take over for him. Then he was on the phone to Wilson. "We have one more mission."

"Huh? The general changed his mind?"

"Just get everyone from T1 and Dr. Moretti to the hangar immediately. We have an emergency trip. Top secret, and there's no time to waste."

"If you say so, boss."

"And one more thing. Despite protocol, T2 is not to be called in."

13

"Michelle is going to die. As you know, she has cancer and the doctors say there's nothing they can do to help her," JJ said to his team, his tight-knit group.

They had become family to him and Michelle. She had been a mother, sister, best friend, or conscience to each of them. She'd fed them, coached them, yelled at them about their dating choices, laughed, and cried with them.

"Life isn't fair—we all know that—but, in this case, it just plain sucks," JJ continued. "I haven't been the greatest husband to her. Since we married, I've been away thirty days for every one I've been home. I feel compelled to do everything I possibly can to save her. At this point, there is only one more thing I can come up with. I need to either take her back in time to meet Jesus Christ and beg for a miracle, or I need to go get him and bring him to her bedside."

The team members looked at each other, some with a matter-of-fact, okay-makes-sense-to-me look, while others stared in disbelief. "In reality, she's too weak to travel, and there's no way we could consider taking him back with us. So, all I can do, all I intend to do, is ask for his prayers."

"JJ, that's the wildest thing I've ever heard you come up with," Wilson said. "But I love my sister more than anything, so count me in. What's the worst that could happen? I'll do whatever it takes. What's the plan?"

JJ laid out the mission. They travel back in time to Jerusalem. JJ had already been there a few times. He was stationed at the US embassy there for one tour. The embassy is located a few minutes from the walled Old City and beyond those holy sites is the Garden of Gethsemane. It was there, on a hillside among the olive trees, that Christ delivered sermons on the mound. It was there that Judas betrayed Christ and the Roman soldiers then arrested him, and took him to be judged and sentenced to die on the cross.

"I've been to the Garden. We can get there the night before he is taken. I did a lot of historical research on that area when I was stationed there. We can show up late in the night, find him and, if we can approach him while he's praying and the rest of them are sleeping, I have my shot. I can ask for his help. I can beg for his help."

"JJ, with all due respect, are you nuts?" Abrams asked. "First off, yes, we've both been to the garden so all the recon is taken care of, but you are talking about walking up to a man, *The Man*, the Son of God. If what the Bible says is true, he knows right now what we are talking about doing. You're suggesting that you ass-kicking Marines from 2,000 years in the future, stroll on up and say something like, 'Hi, Jesus, I know you're busy getting ready to be crucified, and there are plenty of people hurting in the world, past and present, but can you take a minute and cure my—'"

JJ's reaction to Abrams attempt at lightening things up

didn't go over well. The look JJ gave his friend stopped him cold. "Sorry," Abrams mumbled.

"Okay, okay," JJ said. "I get that, in a way, I'm being a selfish son of a bitch in suggesting we do this, but Michelle is the only person all of us are intimately connected to. If there is anyone alive on earth today that we all want to help, it's her. Am I right?"

Their answers came without hesitation: "Of course."

"Sure."

"Absolutely, JJ."

Wilson looked at JJ and asked, "You sure we can target the right day, time, and place that far back?"

JJ nodded in the affirmative. "It's the best place and time to find him. We know he will be there. All we can do is approach him, ask him to help, and then leave him to his fate. That's something we cannot interfere with."

"Let's think through this a bit further, boss," White suggested. "I don't even believe in God so let's assume a few things. I know Jesus Christ existed and was crucified, but beyond that I'm not sure about him or anyone else being the Son of God. So, let's say that he was, does that mean he knows what we are talking about now in the present? Let's say we can go back there and meet him. Can he read our minds? Will he know who we really are and what we do for a living? He might just tell you to pray more. He might refuse to help. What then, JJ? Will you be able to accept that decision and say adios?"

Everyone took a minute to digest what White had said. This time travel capability was giving them the chance of a lifetime, regardless of the mission's goal. They looked around the briefing room at one another.

"I hear ya," JJ said to White, "but this is the mission. I need to do this. I'm asking you to help Michelle. This is her only chance. There's no way I can just sit here and accept that she is going to die without trying to do something. I had to do that for my Mom and Dad. Thanks to Doctor Moretti, there *is* something I can do this time. I will never ask any of you to do anything like this again. Think about it, though. How many people would say yes if given the chance to stand in the presence of Jesus Christ? Think about the most important person you've ever had in your life. Would you take this trip to save them? If you don't want to go, now's the time to say so. I can grab someone from T2 or go down to the bar and drag a handful of drunks off their stools if I have to."

A long moment of silence followed. JJ understood what they must have been thinking. Adding to the complexity of this unofficial mission was its basis in pure emotion, without team research, tactical assignments, or contingency plans. Aside from that, for all purposes, they'd been removed from the project's duty roster. General Stewart was in the process of reassigning them. T1 no longer existed.

"We should wait twenty-four hours. This is moving too quickly," Abrams said.

"Your wife is really sick, but she's not at a point where we might lose her at any moment," White added. "There's time, JJ, and we need to talk this through."

"What are you going to do if we encounter the Romans who are coming for him?" Jones asked. "What will any of us do if he gets pissed and says you aren't supposed to play with history? Will we have to interact with his followers? What will we tell them—that we're not a threat, we just need him to perform a miracle, and then he's all yours? Are you sure you can communicate with him? Abrams knows Hebrew, but if I remember correctly Jesus spoke Aramaic. You good with that Abrams?"

JJ looked at Abrams, who gave him a thumbs-up.

"I think he will know us. He will know why we are there, and I think he will have to say something to us. At least, I hope so. If not, we'll just have to come home empty-handed," JJ responded. "If Michelle dies because we waited, I won't be able to deal with it."

Wilson looked around the group. The expression on his face said it all: *me neither.*

They hadn't yet agreed to participate; the tension in the room was incredible. But the thought of seeing Christ in person, regardless of the possible consequences, slowly sank in. The adrenaline ratcheted up despite common sense warning them to slow down and take any more time to consider the consequences or personal cost.

"You need to know, there is more going on than I've let on," JJ said. "Doctor Moretti is growing frailer and more confused every day. We all see it. There's also been added pressure from some of the Joint Chiefs to expand the time-travel program, to alter history and put the teams on seek-and-destroy missions to eliminate history's bad guys. Brooks is pushing hard for this, according the General Stewart."

"But there's no telling how that would mess with history," Wilson said. "Are they crazy?"

JJ shrugged. "I don't know what's going on in their heads. But when Scott got his ass kicked at Yellowstone, many of the other Chiefs wondered just what the hell General Stewart and the rest of us were up to. I'm told that

Stewart may hand in his resignation at any time. Who knows what will happen if he leaves." His throat felt raw and tight—the words coming harder now. "Michelle may die at any time. Her heart rate has been slowing, day by day. Probably due to the morphine they're giving her for the pain, but also because her organs are failing. "With the inevitable changes in the BOTM program, none of us will likely be allowed a role in it. Hell, it may not even exist a few months from now. If we're going to save my wife, Wilson's sister, save this beautiful friend to all of you—we need to move tonight. You're in or you're out!"

One at a time, team members confirmed their willingness to be part of the team, one more time.

"So, how soon do we leave?" White asked.

"In an hour." JJ said. I should have the rest of our gear by then.

T1 surrounded the gear table. There was nothing but robes and sandals. No guns, no sunglasses, no tactical gear. Not even a water bottle.

"I kept everything we used for the Coliseum trip. We're in and out at night so we should be okay with what we have," JJ assured them.

As they changed into their robes, JJ thought about the journey ahead. It would be the first time they'd attempt to bring someone with them to the future and then return them to the past. But their secret was safe, JJ figured, with Jesus Christ.

"We need to slow down a minute. I'm not sure I can deal with this," Jones said. "I watched all the classic movies—*The Robe*, *Spartacus*, and I remember *The Passion of the Christ* vividly. We've all seen the shit people can do to each other and, in this case— especially in this case—I'm not sure I can walk away. Can any of you leave him to be tortured and killed on the cross?"

"If you believe in everything you were taught, growing up, then you know he has to die," Jones continued. "And I'm not screwing with the Big Guy who made that decision. If we stop the crucifixion on that day, I don't want to even consider what might happen to us. I can see us on a chariot of fire sent straight to hell. If we went there with full gear and annihilated the Roman guards and took him into protective custody, do you know how crazy that would seem to the locals and his followers? We'd have the entire Roman army up our butts in no time. That would change history forever, and people would be writing about it for ages. This crucifixion, having his own son die for us, is part of God's master plan and nobody should screw with that. We can't change history. He has to die there on the cross. His death is what saved all of us. We are only changing the present and the future for us—we are going on a mission that will change our lives forever."

"He's right," Sharif added. "Christ knows what fate awaits him. He's the only one who does. Come with us and meet the Man. It'll enrich your life."

The rules had always been that nothing out of the ordinary, nothing that wouldn't exist in the period the team is traveling to, could be taken along. In every other mission, they'd had a weapon of some kind to protect themselves and fulfill the requirements of the mission. This time was different.

Wilson reminded everyone of the rule and then gave JJ

a questioning look. "You've always got a knife hidden on you somewhere. You sure you want to take that along on this one?" They were all combat killing machines, extremely well trained in hand-to-hand combat, but sometimes a knife came in handy.

Everyone smiled as they looked to their team leader. He grinned. "My dad gave it to me years and years ago. He told me, 'Don't leave home without it,' so I never have. He also said, 'Do as I say not do as I do,' so let's change the subject."

Wilson smiled. "Roger that."

They reviewed the plan one last time before doing a final check to make sure they were only taking what they should and nothing more. Some needed to take a quick shower to remove their modern-day scents or smells. "Hydrate. It's going to be hot there," Wilson called out.

Jackson and Abrams would take the lead and approach their target while Wilson, White, Sharif, and Jones discreetly followed, watching the margins for trouble.

So, will he read my mind or will I need to speak to him? JJ thought to himself. He'd talked to Washington at Valley Forge, watched gladiators fight in the Coliseum and been just about everywhere. He'd even sent Hitler to meet his maker. But now he was preparing to meet the most powerful, most influential, most historic, most famous, holiest person ever to have walked the earth – the Son of God, his Maker—and his emotions were on overload.

One at a time, they took sandals from the table and pulled a robe from the closet. Some exchanged a fist bump while others gave a pat on the back or a high five. They hoped to do the same when they'd returned safely.

"Fuck it, boss, let's go!" said White.

"Easy on the F-bombs, please," Jones added, "or you'll have to go to confession when you get back. I'm in!"

JJ and Wilson looked at each other, and then into the eyes of each of the other four team members. Just as they had been on the battlefield, on covert ops, or standing over the fallen, they were united and ready for action.

JJ murmured, "Thank you, team."

"Yes, thank you," Wilson seconded. He turned to Abrams and shook his head in mild disapproval. "Dude, how many times do we have to remind you? No frickin' gum. Chew on some olives when we get there, if you have to!"

Abrams spit the gum with sniper precision straight into a trashcan.

"Mount up, ladies" JJ declared.

They took their places in the six-person ring. Doctor Moretti was watching through the observation window from the next room as always. Typically, members of the second team were there to support the primary group, but this mission was clearly off the books. Moretti alone would know where they were.

"Hey JJ," Abrams called out. "You remember the last time we went to Gethsemane? You hailed a cab. Turned out it had an Arab driver. We must have got pulled over by the Israeli military four times before we got out of there. Holiest place on the planet, and they're still trying to kill each other."

"Yeah, all that and the Garden was closed for the day. This time we're bypassing the front door."

The pulse rings were activated. JJ counted down "3-2-1" and, within a breath, they were standing on the famous hillside covered with olive trees. The sun was almost gone and a warm breeze blew across the olive grove. They quickly moved behind the trees for cover.

"We're here, this is Gethsemane," JJ whispered.

They took a few minutes to eyeball the area. It seemed peaceful, not a soul in sight. Oil lamps burned in windows of houses in the distance, the houses of Jerusalem. As the sun set deeper in the West, the glow from a fire, 200 feet from them, became more visible.

"That must be them," Wilson said.

This was where Jesus Christ met with his closest companions, his Apostles.

JJ looked at Wilson. The cure for their Michelle was close by. JJ felt a surge of adrenaline through his veins, and nervous anticipation of what they were about to do.

Abrams signaled the group that someone was coming. They quickly moved deeper into the cover of the olive trees. Abrams plucked an olive from a branch and popped it into his mouth but quickly spit it out.

Jones whispered, "They aren't ready until they've fallen to the ground or at least that's what I remember from Rome. Shhh."

A shepherd leading eight goats passed by. They started walking toward the glow of the fire. JJ could see a man approaching them on a path.

"You see any weapons?" White whispered.

"You expecting an AK?" Sharif joked in a whisper.

The figure stopped ten feet in front of them, his face shrouded by the hood of his robe. "Are you looking for me?" the man asked.

"That's English! He's speaking English!" JJ whispered to Abrams.

Abrams looked dumbfounded. He slowly stepped out from behind the tree and onto a rock, almost losing his footing. In Aramaic, he said to the man, "We are searching for Jesus of Nazareth."

First in Aramaic and then in English, the man responded, "You have found me."

Every member of T1 stopped dead. This was it. Christian, Jew, or Atheist—it didn't matter. There, standing in front of them, was the man many people regarded as the most important person to ever have walked the earth. He was something beyond human, a being that existed in the universe—not just on earth. For the first time for many of them, they were speechless. Not one wisecrack, not one sound broke the tension.

"We mean you no harm. If you know we were looking for you then you know where we are from and why we are here," JJ said softly.

"Yes," the man responded. "I am here, living in this time and place to do as my Father has asked of me. I have left my disciples back at the fire so they can rest and I can spend my time here in prayer. What is to happen here cannot be changed."

Sharif and Jones hadn't uttered a word since the man approached them. Wilson and White continued to watch the perimeter, but before long they turned as if unable to stop from staring at the man. There was an unusual stillness in the air around them. The magnitude of this moment, the man they were in the presence of, was beyond anything they had felt or encountered before.

"This is beyond trippy," Jones said.

JJ felt suddenly conflicted. Here was Jesus Christ, the Son of God, seeking peace and quiet so he could prepare for the horror that was to come. *What was I thinking*? He looked at Wilson and then back to Christ.

"I can't do this," he said, dropping to one knee. "With the weight of the world on your shoulders, with what you know is coming, I cannot ask anything of you. I need to ask you what I can do. What *we* can do for you?"

His team closed in around them, in solidarity.

JJ felt close to weeping he was so moved by the man's presence. "Lord, I have done many bad things and I feel so selfish. I can't ask you to do anything for me, for us—for Michelle. Forgive me. Forgive us. Please forgive us for our sins. Please forgive us for coming here and disturbing your peace."

Jesus responded, "We, as humans, are all selfish. Soon, here in this garden, I will ask my Father to relieve me of the agony and death I am to suffer, but I know His will must be done. To save others, I will do as he asks. For you, I will pray for Michelle."

Abrams was just taking it all in.

White spoke up, "I wish we had found you sooner. I would spend a year following you, asking you questions, and learning about faith."

"Then you should have. People often wait until the end to learn what is most important," he said.

White was speechless. Tears streamed down her cheeks, but she ignored them. JJ was pretty sure she was an atheist no more.

Jesus looked into each of their faces, into their eyes.

When JJ's gaze connected with his, he felt an emotional rush over and above anything he'd ever experienced.

Here they stood, nearly 2,000 years back in time, in the presence of the Son of God, looking into his eyes, and speaking with him, hours before he was to be taken away and crucified.

Without saying another word, Christ turned and continued his walk away from the fire's glow, in search of peace and prayer before Judas betrayed him and he carried the cross to his death. The team stood frozen, speechless, watching as he continued his journey.

Jesus looked over his shoulder at JJ, "Protect the innocent and those who cannot protect themselves, but remember—vengeance is mine." And then he moved off and away into the darkness. Within a minute he was gone from sight.

For the first time, the team disregarded their years of training by completely ignoring their surroundings. They silently looked at each other, in shared awe of what had just occurred. "Back home they use *amazing* to describe every little thing," Wilson murmured. "I don't know any word that can express what just happened. Did we really do what I think we just did?"

"That was surreal," Sharif breathed, "totally surreal."

"We need to go. Huddle up," JJ commanded. He kicked away a few small stones and laid the mat down. Jones was slow to move, as if he wasn't sure he wanted to go. He finally stepped on.

JJ looked up at the stars and then at the fire's glow in the distance. Still deeply moved by the presence of Jesus, he closed his eyes and counted. "3-2-1."

Nothing happened.

"Check your pulses, ladies," Wilson quietly commanded.

JJ counted again. Nothing. A third time. Nothing again. They were still standing in tight formation in the dark in 33 AD in the Garden of Gethsemane, in Jerusalem.

JJ signaled everyone to step back under the cover of the olive trees.

"I hope this isn't karma biting us in the ass," Wilson said. "I'm thinking this can only mean one thing."

"Dr. Moretti might have had an issue," Abrams suggested.

"I'll bet that asshole Scott and his butthead buddies got wind that we'd disobeyed orders and gone off on our own. I'll bet they shut us down," Wilson said to JJ. "Those Army guys never liked us being the lead."

"It could just be a glitch," Sharif said hopefully.

"I shouldn't have left her there alone," JJ said with regret.

They decided to wait thirty minutes before trying again. They remained on full alert, watching for trouble from all sides. JJ felt their anxiety. They all wanted to go home, of course, but no one more than him. Michelle. Was she still alive? And if she was, how much longer would she be?

"Maybe when I get home," JJ said, "Michelle will be out of bed, playing with the dog. I just hope I can get there to see it." If Jesus himself prayed for her, did that automatically mean she'd be well again? He just didn't know.

"Maybe we pushed it too far, coming here and interfering in his life," Abrams said. "Maybe this is our punishment."

"When we signed up to fight, we all knew there was always a chance we wouldn't come home from a mission."

Wilson looked at JJ. "There was always the chance of getting killed in action. But getting stuck somewhere in time never occurred to me. I could have dealt with getting stuck in Valley Forge. But this is pretty fucked up."

"You just met the Man and you're cursing here, in this place?" Sharif asked.

Wilson fell quiet for several minutes, then, "Maybe this is what was meant to be. Maybe we were sent here to do something else."

"Like what?" Jones asked.

"I don't know. Part of me wants to walk down that path and stay at his side until the end. Other than my sister and my mom back in Montana, there's nothing for me back home. Maybe I'm meant to just stay here and see what kind of trouble I can get into or what good I can do. Or it's meant to be my penance, my fate. Who knows?"

The six of them sat beneath the olive trees and continued to watch for trouble.

"You know, if we do get stuck here, even if it's for a week, we'll need food," White pointed out. "Unless we want olive breath, like Abrams, we might have to start stealing from the locals. We're going to have to figure out quite a few things."

"We need to consider what we should do, could do, if we wind up stuck here whether it's for a day or a month or forever," Jones said.

JJ shook his head. "This is unbelievable. Michelle may get better and we might not be there to see it. If you want to stay here, Tommy, I disagree, but I'll accept it. The rest of us want to get home. Anyway, we need to be figuring out what went wrong. Any ideas, anyone?"

"If the problem is on their end. Maybe they'll send someone for us once it's fixed?" Abrams suggested.

Jones made an impatient sound in his throat. "My bet is we're dead to them. We disobeyed orders and went rogue. If Stewart retired like we thought then Brooks may have taken his place. If that's the case we're screwed. If we *are* busted then the Joint Chiefs may just leave us in this purgatory as punishment. That, or Moretti had a stroke or something. Case closed. She's the only one who knows where we are. We're all KIAs, bodies never recovered."

"I can see it now." Wilson frowned into the dark. "Brooks, or one of his henchmen, is leaning on the old girl. They're probably back at Andrews doing everything they can to get the doc to say where we went and how the device works."

"Knowing that prick," Jones muttered, "he'll water board the ninety-year-old. I wouldn't put it past him."

"I can tell you this," Abrams said, "Doc Moretti's heart is very weak. She's had a pacemaker for years. If anyone roughs her up she'll crash hard. She could be dead right now, regardless of whether Scott or Brooks got to her."

"She has *two* pacemakers so don't write her off that easily," White said. "I was helping her out of her ride one day and saw bumps on both sides of her chest."

"No way," Abrams said. "You don't think I'd have noticed? I'm the guy with the medical background."

Sharif looked at Wilson. "Bingo!"

"Bingo?" Wilson looked lost.

"What are you talking about?" JJ asked. "Nobody needs two pacemakers."

"That's it. That's how this works." Sharif looked pleased

with himself. "Moretti has a seventh pulse; it's in her chest. She always said, whatever was needed to make it all work, she kept inside. We all thought she was talking about her head."

Wilson waved him off. "You may be on to something, but that's not going to help us now. We need to focus on our present situation."

JJ had been sitting on the ground, arms wrapped around his knees, taking in the conversation. Now he stood up and walked twenty feet away from the group. He looked down the hill onto Jerusalem, over to the glow from the nearby fire, and then, slowly, back at his team. He spent another five minutes alone before returning to them.

"I can't tell you how bad I feel about this. I talked you guys into helping me and Michelle—and this is where you wind up. I'm sorry I ever—"

Sharif interrupted him, "I think I speak for the rest of us in saying you chose us for a once-in-a-lifetime mission when you picked us for BOTM. I doubt any of us regret the experiences we've had on T1."

Wilson looked at JJ, and finally said, "Hopefully, Michelle's going to live a long life, thanks to the very special prayers from a very special man. If we play our cards right we might too. Let's say you and I head on down and lend some security to Peter and the rest of those Apostles. Bring that knife along. Maybe one of us can be the guy that takes the ear off one of the Roman guards that comes after Jesus."

"I'm in," offered Abrams.

Sharif stepped forward. "Me too. We can follow Peter all the way to Rome if he'll let us. Come on, boss, you know you want to."

JJ gave him a sad smile. "Sure. But I'm not ready to give up yet. We need to try a few more times to get back home before we go running off to Rome, or wherever. Let's see what we can see while we're here and then try the pulse again tomorrow night. If it doesn't work then, we'll start a five-day, thirty-day protocol—except, we'll make it seven days, if necessary. We need to meet back here every night. If nothing happens after thirty days from today, we discuss Plan B."

Everyone seemed to agree that this made sense. But they wanted to talk about their options if it they couldn't get back.

Jones started. "If the protocol doesn't work and we're stuck here, I'd like to head to Rome and watch them build that Coliseum. Between the women, the food, and the climate, I really like Italy. If I can figure out the timing, maybe I'll stop off in Naples and watch Vesuvius pop her cork. And if you guys make it to Rome with Peter or do it on your own I will hope to see you there. Starting one year from now, I'll be at that spot where we sat on the Tiber's bank every Sunday at noon watching for you."

JJ nodded, "It'll be fifty years before it's built, so you're going to have a long wait. Not sure any of us will ever make it there but it would be a special moment. What about you, White?"

She thought for a bit and then offered, "I'm going with Jones, if he's cool with it. Something tells me I can make some real money fighting in smaller venues until the Coliseum is ready for me. But if not, maybe I can figure out a way to help people. Start teaching women how to defend themselves when their men don't treat them right. I liked Italy too, but with fifty years to kill I might try to get to Greece first." She smiled at Jones. "I heard Mykonos is nice this time of year. We could sail there from here and then on to Italy. I've come a long way from Oakland. I'll go with Jones and meet you all at the Tiber in a few years, if it's meant to be."

"I can see it now, an eighty-year-old, ass-kicking female gladiator in Rome. That will be worth the price of admission," JJ said with a smile. "We'll see you in Rome."

"So, this is really it?" Abrams asked, looking nervous. "If we follow the protocol and the pulses still don't work we're going to split up and roll the dice?"

"Sounds like the plan," Wilson admitted.

"We need to get down to that fire and be there when the Romans come for him," JJ said. "As Marines, we are all used to sacrifice, putting ourselves in harm's way to protect others and seeing people we care about pay the ultimate price. That's exactly what we are going to witness here. We'll all have to figure out quite a lot over the next few days, but if we are stuck here then maybe we need to realize we're actually not stuck at all. Keep the faith that, somehow, we'll get back home. In the meantime, let's continue this mission, this adventure." He paused for a moment. "No offense, Jones, but I wish Richard had been able to be a part of all the crazy stuff we've done. This area looks a lot like where he grew up. And meeting who we just met would have knocked his socks off."

Remembering their fallen team member, someone they all really liked, brought up mixed emotions for many of them.

"None taken. I get it."

"Okay, snap out of it, boys and girl. I've got an idea." Wilson looked at the group for a moment and suggested, "maybe we can lend that POS Judas a hand a little later with his rope."

JJ shook his head. "We're still not going to change history. And didn't you hear what Christ said about vengeance? It's his, not ours."

Wilson smiled. "I heard him, all right. I just want to make sure that traitor hangs himself right the first time. Semper Fi!" As the team members exchanged fist bumps and high-fives, they all respond with, "Oorah!"

Northwestern Montana, Current Time

"It's been a year since they went on that mission and General Stewart hasn't been able to give me one bit of information about what happened to Tommy and JJ," Michelle complained to her mother with frustration. "He's retiring soon, and now I'll have to rely on Colonel Scott for updates. JJ hated that guy."

Mrs. Wilson's health had been failing in recent years. After it had become clear that their men might not be coming back, Michelle packed up Bunker and her belongings and moved from Maryland back to the ranch where she and her adopted brother grew up.

"Stewart is a good man, Michelle, or else he wouldn't come out here every month to check on us. He can't work forever."

Michelle, looking fit and able to take care of the dogs and the horses on the family's 100-acre ranch slowly shook her head in disbelief. "Mom, I'm not saying Stewart isn't, but all he can tell us is that they are missing in action after participating in a highly classified mission that saved someone's life! Six Marines have been missing a year now, and nobody can even say where they were."

The two women sat quietly at the kitchen table for a few minutes until Bunker started scratching at the door to come inside.

"You know, Michelle, whether it's a year from now or ten years from now, I'm not going to be here forever. At some point, you may need to come to terms with the fact that they might never come back."

Michelle stood up quickly. "Stop!" she choked out the word. "Please, I don't want you to talk like this."

"Michelle, nobody knows why things happen. You had a miraculous recovery from cancer only to have your husband and brother go missing right around the same time. Those boys knew the risks they were taking, going on all those secret missions. They loved their country and they loved you."

"Love!" Michelle shouted.

"Okay, they love you, dear." Her mother went on, "But this ranch is no place for a young woman to be on her own. I know you find great comfort in that Bible you keep so close, but you need more than that. They wouldn't want you out here on your own and neither do I. 'You're tough as nails,' your Daddy used to say, and that's true, but we all *love* you and just want you to be safe and to be happy."

Michelle shrugged her shoulders and walked over to let Bunker in. "I know they are out there somewhere, Mom. I know they are." She looked out the door toward the sunset. "You've said it yourself, often enough—God works in mysterious ways."

14

It was late in the day, a week after the crucifixion. The team had returned to the safe place they'd found, a short walk from the city. Here, they planned to camp out and continue laying low to avoid being noticed.

JJ had been deep in thought as the sun fell below the horizon leaving a fading glow in the desert sky. He looked around for his team. Wilson and Abrams were playing hangman in the sand by their fire. Sharif was eating nuts and dates they'd bought earlier at the market.

"Where are White and Jones?" he asked.

Wilson shrugged.

"Don't know, boss," Abrams said.

Sharif looked away from him.

"Sharif?"

"I'm not sure. But I think." He sighed. "Maybe we should just give them another hour before… Don't look at me that way, JJ. They were just talking. I don't know what they were planning to do."

"Do about what?" JJ narrowed his eyes at the man. He'd heard several of the team grousing about punishment owed the soldiers who had tortured Jesus. But he'd thought they'd settled down after he warned them that there was nothing they could do. "Tell me. Now! Where are they?"

Before Sharif could answer, White staggered into their shelter, half dragging, half carrying Jones. The front of his robe was dripping blood.

JJ leaped to his feet. "What the hell happened?"

Abrams helped her lower Jones to the ground and immediately loosened the collar of his robe and felt for a pulse. "He's dead."

Christy White stared in horror at the body of the friend at her feet. "Oh, God. It wasn't supposed to be—"

JJ lunged forward, knocking her back on her heels. "What happened, Sergeant?"

"Jones said we had to do something. Had to make things right—punish the bastards for what they did to Jesus. He got angry, and there was no reasoning with him. I had never seen that side of him before. I said I'd go with him. He figured we could take one or two of them by surprise, when they were alone…" She shook her head violently. "Before we found the ones we were after, a Roman soldier stopped us in the marketplace. Instead of trying to pretend we didn't understand, like we'd planned—" A sob escaped her throat. "I mean, Jones was so charged up for vengeance. He went wild. Threw himself at the soldier. The Roman wasn't able to draw his sword but I never saw the knife, JJ. It just appeared from under the guy's cloak. He stuck Jones in the gut, and he went down."

"But the soldier didn't attack you?" JJ asked. He couldn't wrap his mind about this latest disaster. It had been so foolish, so unnecessary.

"Dressed like this, as a female slave? I don't think it occurred to the soldier at that moment. And Jones just screamed at me, 'Go!' A dozen or more soldiers were rushing at us. I didn't have a weapon. The odds sucked. I was able to blend into the crowd and get out of there. It was either come back for you guys or try to neutralize them myself."

"But you didn't come back here." JJ stared at her. It must have just about killed her to walk away, natural fighter that she was.

"It would have taken too long. I stole a dagger from a market stall, turned around and went back for him. By the time I got to him, they'd beaten him, stuck him again…and left him bleeding in the street."

She looked pleadingly at JJ. "I'm so, so sorry. I should have said…I just didn't want to rat on him, you know. I thought he would have been cooler and quieter. I had no idea he was that enraged by what he saw them do to Christ."

JJ closed his eyes and fisted his hands. Another KIA. Was this the way they would all end up? One after another, they'd all die in battle. Suddenly, home seemed even farther away.

"Are you sure nobody followed you here?" Wilson said without taking his eyes off the horizon.

"I'm sure." She paused. "There's…there's one more thing," White forced out, blotting her eyes with the sleeve of her robe.

JJ just looked at her. Surely it couldn't get any worse.

"The pulse. It was gone when I went back for him. One of them must have taken it as a trophy."

It didn't take long for them to get moving. There was no way they could be sure White hadn't been followed or that some local may have seen something they shouldn't have. They did what they could to bury Jones under the shelter they had been using. There was no time for words. Within a few minutes, what was left of T1 disappeared into the desert night. They spent an hour getting as far from what they had called home and resettled to regroup and plan their next move.

"Okay, so the way Wilson and I see it," JJ said, "we have to find the assholes that killed Jones, recover the pulse, and then get as far away from here as we can. You can't just kill Roman guards and hang out. If we are able to grab what we need, with or without knocking off any guards, we'll leave the area for three weeks and then come back to the Garden for the next step in the recovery protocol."

Everyone seemed to agree. "We're on the same page JJ," Wilson said. "We may need to pick up a goat somewhere along the way." They all laughed. Even in the midst of this most recent tragedy, they all appreciated the perfectly timed one-liner that gave them a moment to escape the battle. The truth was—they'd have to find another heartbeat to get them back to 2016. But first, they had to recover Jones' pulse device.

The team knew where the guards were headquartered. Jones and White had followed them there after the crucifixion and saw that the barracks were right next to the area where Pilate condemned Christ to his death. But, if the guard who took the pulse was there, would he still have the device? A superior officer would surely take away anything that appeared valuable. Or he could have used it to barter for women, or lost it in whatever betting game soldiers in that era played.

T1 surveyed the area for two days, learning that the guards were consistent in their movements and often drunk after dusk.

"There he is," White signaled JJ and Wilson.

After discussing every possible move and contingency and anticipating the Roman guard's countermoves, the plans were set. They'd make their move late that night. Sharif and Abrams sneaked onto an artisan's property and made off with two small knives and a hammer-like club, much like the one used to drive the nails into Christ's hands and feet.

They would hide the weapons inside their robes and put them to quick use if needed. Hours later, when the team estimated it was 23:00, most of the guards were asleep in their barracks. Those on duty were sure to have sat down at their posts for some shut-eye. The team moved in. White and Abrams were in place to watch for trouble. JJ, Wilson, and Sharif moved quietly through the narrow walkways. Upon reaching the first guard, they acted quickly.

Wilson hit the guard over the head with the club. JJ grabbed the man's sword and they disappeared into the barracks, leaving the unconscious guard just as they found him, sitting on a stool, leaning against the building, his Roman helmet at his side. The only light inside the came from a lantern near the doorway.

"I'd give my left nut for night vision," JJ whispered. This was going to be a tough find. Wilson took the lantern as they started to walk through the rooms. The only sounds were a dozen different types of snoring from sleeping men.

"I can't see shit," Sharif whispered to Wilson. After two minutes, JJ gave the signal to abort. Without light, there was no way their plan could work. As they left, White signaled the coast was clear. JJ replaced the sword and, as quickly as they'd arrived, they disappeared into the darkness.

The next night it was time for Plan B: Operation White. "White, I know you don't like the idea of being bait, so look at this more as being a distraction," JJ told her. "We took you to Berlin all dressed up nice. Plan A didn't work so we need you to do the same now."

She listened and nodded in agreement before JJ finished his sentence. "I'm in, JJ. I'll do whatever it takes to complete the mission, but I also want to kill the bastard who killed my friend."

Abrams whispered to Sharif, "Yeah, that whole 'vengeance is mine' thing lasted about as long as stuffing at Thanksgiving."

White heard him and took a moment to check her emotions. "You're right, Abrams," she said smiling. "From now on I'm only going to kill Romans if it's self-defense."

Half laughing with tears forming in her eyes she continued, "Jones said he wasn't going to watch the crucifixion. I believed him. After we broke into twos and spread out in the area we did snoop around the city to see what we could see, but I had no idea what he had in mind. I couldn't bear to watch, but he just stood there staring at Christ and glaring at the guards. I should have said something then."

JJ got up and walked over to her. He sat down and put his arm around her. "He did what he felt he had to do. I get it. It's nobody's fault but his own that he's dead."

Wilson was growing frustrated with the conversation. "Jesus Christ!" He looked at the rest of the team as he shook his head in disbelief. "I can't believe I just said that." He paused for another moment and went on. "Look, he decided to watch. He saw how the soldier's mistreated Christ as he hung up there dying. I get it. But what he did was suicide, and his decision may have stuck us here forever."

"We're a diverse bunch of highly skilled, incredibly talented, ass-kicking Marines stuck in a desert, 2,000 years from home with only the clothes on our backs, these smelly sandals, the knife JJ snuck aboard, and the few things we were able to steal. If we do this right, we should be able to overcome the challenge. We're going up against the Roman guard. They're fully armed with swords, spears, battle armor, and horses. No biggie, right? We're United States Marines so it sounds like a level playing field to me." Everyone broke out in laughter.

Abrams added, "Don't forget, I'm Navy!"

After a moment, Abrams said he needed to confess something to his commanding officer and the team before they went any farther. "JJ, I stole a medal from Hitler's uniform that night in the bunker. I meant to keep it and give it to you when you retired from the Corps. But when JR was killed I panicked and stuck it in one of his pockets so I wouldn't get caught with it. I know it was a stupid thing to do, first stealing it and then sticking it on poor JR, but I didn't want you to ever think he disobeyed orders."

Wilson laughed, looked at JJ, and then made a confession of his own. "I saw Abrams put something in JR's pocket but didn't think twice about it until Bill Griffiths turned up with something extraordinary that he shouldn't have had, at Andrews."

Abrams was speechless. He looked at Jackson for some sign of anger or forgiveness, but Wilson spoke up again. "Hell, we're all just pissed you didn't grab one for each of us!

Don't worry about it, Benny. Griffiths brought it with him to the Missouri. Just like that old broad tossed the necklace in the Titanic movie, he tossed Hitler's medal into Tokyo Bay, and that's where it'll stay forever. We're cool. JJ's just busting on you for the hell of it. He's not pissed. Just don't do it again."

JJ winked at Abrams and then commended Wilson and the team. "Good. Glad we got that out of the way and I'm proud to see everyone hasn't forgotten who the hell we are or what we are capable of! All the locals, at least those who believed in Jesus, are walking around here like they're in shock. I think we have been, too. We all keep talking about Christ and the crucifixion like we can't believe what just happened, but it did. So now we need work on the mission."

"Right," Wilson said. "So, listen up, all. We have to focus on getting you guys home."

JJ continued, "I know all of us are going to process what we've seen here in our own ways. The magnitude of what happened here, who we were in the presence of, is something nobody walking the planet in the modern day has ever done or could ever imagine doing. But I, for one, want to get home and drink a toast with Doc Moretti to our final mission."

"Wilson, you said 'getting you guys home,'" White pointed out. "That sounds like you're not coming with us."

"I've had a lot to think about in the last week. Like I said before, other than my sister and my Mom, there's nothing back there I'm interested in seeing again. Everything is overcrowded and moving too fast. I thought a lot about Jones' words, before he went off track. He liked Italy. It's a lot warmer than Montana. The sea, the women, the food really appealed to him. It wasn't until now that I realized how much I liked it, too. If we get this thing fixed, then maybe I'll pass on the return flight and hope you guys can come check on me in a few years."

"You're not going soft on us now, are you Wilson?" White asked, only half joking.

"Nope. I may have found a place where I could see myself spending the rest of my life. Other than not having any beer around here, I can deal with it. I still might track down Peter and see if I can follow him to Rome. Maybe I can work security."

They all laughed. "Hey Wilson, any interest in checking out Mykonos and Capri with me, if we wind up with a lot of time to kill?" White said with a wink.

"Sergeant White, are you coming on to a superior officer?" JJ asked with a laugh.

Night fell as they discussed final plans for their next attempt to find the pulse. Then all but Abrams, who had the first two-hour shift of the night, turned in under the desert's beautiful star-filled sky. The next day, with any luck, they would reclaim the missing pulse.

Everyone knew the Roman soldiers visited a particular brothel in the city. It was said that Mary Magdalene might have worked there before Christ found her. JJ opted to remain outside watching for trouble while the rest of the team went inside to act as locals checking out the goods. Over the past few days, Abrams had been listening to the locals talk. He knew enough words to get by in this distant time and now he had the dialect down pat. If anyone had to speak for them, it would be Abrams.

White, looking better than most of the workingwomen, made quite an entrance. She immediately attracted the attention of patrons, including a familiar Roman guard.

"My bet is this prick traded the necklace for a piece of ass," she thought to herself, "he's not wearing it." She realized at that point she needed to start looking more at the women than the paying customers.

After rejecting many advances, and the jilted guards become drunker and more agitated, she decided she needed to act or lose her credibility as a prostitute. Abrams read her mind and gave his superior officer a look and a nod. Within seconds Wilson approached White and held out a gold coin. Those two only needed to make eye contact. Any words would let everyone in the brothel know there are strangers among them. White took his hand led him through a curtain, as if she was just another of the girls leaving to take care of her paying customer.

"There it is," Abrams almost shouted out loud.

Sitting across the room at a table with two other women and two Roman guards was a stunning prostitute. She had long flowing brown hair. Her skimpy clothing provided full view of a remarkable piece of jewelry.

Sharif saw the look of astonishment on Abrams' face and then the pulse device as well. They nodded at each other, and then approached the table but stood back far enough to make eye contact with the beauty in hopes of luring her away.

Sharif held up a bottle of wine while a smiling Abrams displayed a gold coin in each hand. She acknowledged them with a glance, but focused on the powerful men sitting in front of her. Never one to quit, Abrams reached into his moneybag and, smiling even wider, held up two more coins. That sealed the deal. The woman wearing their precious pulse necklace whispered something to each of the women she was sitting with and then stood up to attend to the new faces in her establishment.

The Romans glanced up in disappointment, but that quickly faded with the help of the attentions from the other women. After all, the brothel owner was the most attractive woman there, but she also was the most expensive—and a soldier's salary didn't go very far.

She said something, and Abrams responded for both of them. He spoke in a very low voice, explaining that their voices had been hurt years earlier in a fight. He explained that they wanted to spend the night with her and told her that she was the most beautiful thing they had ever seen. She moved as if to sit down with them at another table, but they stayed where they were, looking toward the curtain Wilson and White had disappeared behind.

As soon as they were through the curtain, Sharif grabbed the woman from behind, covering her mouth, and lifting her off her feet. Quickly, they followed White into the room with Wilson. Sharif administered his sleeper hold as the team laid the woman on the bed.

"I can't fucking believe our luck," Abrams whispered.

Wilson removed the pulse device from around her neck and placed it on White as she looked back into the hallway. The coast was clear and there was a way out at the end of the hallway.

Minutes later, Wilson was in front of the brothel

signaling JJ to head to the rendezvous. JJ gave him an "okay" signal without thinking, but almost immediately realized it might look suspicious if any of the Roman guards standing around drinking outside had seen him. JJ looked around to see who might have been watching and, just then, Wilson nodded and returned the thumb-to-first finger circle.

Oh, no! JJ thought when a guard called out to Wilson.

Wilson didn't answer—couldn't answer—but opened both of his hands to show he wasn't a threat, but the guards were looking at him more closely now. The area was crowded with shoppers and merchants so Wilson did what any outnumbered red-blooded American would do, he gave them the finger, turned, and blended into the crowd.

JJ left his perch and walked as quickly as he could, to avoid drawing attention to himself. Luckily the guards had been drinking and were in no condition to run after a lunatic making strange signs at them. But they had seen Wilson's face and would remember it.

Thirty minutes later, JJ arrived at their makeshift HQ outside the city. Everyone was sitting there, smiling. "Okay, did all of you get laid tonight or what?" he asked with a laugh.

White stood up holding a pulse device in each hand.

"No way. There's no way you got it!"

She grinned. "Abrams and Sharif worked their magic tonight. They are the heroes on this one, JJ."

The team briefed him on everything that had happened, each taking a turn to share their perspective, sense of accomplishment, and relief.

"Oh, and Wilson, sir, you still owe me that coin," White said.

It was a huge step forward in trying to get home, but they couldn't lose sight of where they were and how dangerous their situation still was. "Those gold coins came in handy tonight but we're almost out of them, JJ," Wilson stated.

"Yep, it's time to move on out of here for another few weeks. We'll need to stay clear of the Romans who saw our faces. Let's get to the coast and see if there's any money in fishing."

The team settled down for the night. The two loaves of bread and the bottle of wine they had bought earlier in the day was dinner. In the early morning they'd head west again toward the Mediterranean. The star-filled sky provided the distraction and comfort that allowed them to clear their minds and rest. There were so many stars that they formed a heavenly blanket as far as the eye could see. Wilson wanted to sleep, but he couldn't.

"JJ, I still can't figure out what the hell happened back at Andrews."

Lying a few feet away, JJ answered with his eyes closed. He preferred to picture Michelle's face before he fell asleep. "Meaning?"

Wilson thought for a moment. "The only person besides the Doc who knew we were up to something was Anne. I don't think Moretti would have told anyone. I don't think she would have called Petty or anyone for that matter. You asked Anne to look after Michelle for a while and left. She might have called someone and mentioned you were on a mission, just as part of a normal conversation."

JJ had considered every possibility over and over again. They'd talked about it a dozen times before. "My first guess has always been that Scott was involved, but his broke ass was still laid up in the hospital. Brooks wouldn't have gotten out of bed that late. Someone had to see us moving and called someone else to report the activity."

They lay there quietly, thinking.

"Scott was for sure a mole for Brooks, but who the hell was the mole we missed?" Wilson whispered, sleep starting to get the best of him.

JJ sat up as if he'd been fired out of a cannon. "Tommy! You're right, it had to be Anne."

Wilson stood up quickly. He was wide-awake and trying to remember what he must have missed. "JJ, I'm an idiot. I think you're right. She's the only person who could have seen us and would have known something was going on."

JJ's anger was growing stronger now. He counted betrayal as the worst thing a person could do. "She could have called anyone. She knew we were grounded, that our program was shut down, even though she had no idea what it was."

Wilson's anger flared, too. He stood up, which got the attention of the rest of the team.

"What's up, boss?" White asked.

"I think we just figured out what happened. We had our own Judas back at Andrews, and it wasn't Scott. It was Michelle's friend Anne. It had to be." JJ worked his way through the scenario.

"Why? That makes no sense."

Wilson turned to face the group. Everyone was awake now and listening. None of them had been able to figure out who tripped things up.

"Anne must have been seeing Scott. Now it all makes

sense," Wilson suggested, shaking his head in disbelief. "That first night at the bar, when he put his foot in it, talking about Michelle and Anne being hot. After you took Michelle home, I bought Anne a drink and offered to give her a ride later. But when I came back from the john that prick Scott was with her at the bar and she was laughing her ass off. It was clear from the look she gave me that she was interested in him, so I went home on my own."

White was wide-awake and on her feet now. "No way you let an Army prick steal her from you!" Her attempt at lightening up the situation failed.

JJ had always figured Brooks or Scott may have had them under surveillance on base. But maybe they were being watched at home, too. Anne was supposed to be Michelle's best friend, and a friend to all of them. If she had a relationship with Scott, maybe she was reporting their movements to him. Had she effectively sentenced them to a life two thousand years before any of them ever met?

JJ was furious with himself. All of his adult life he had been focused on fighting for his country. He'd put the Marines and the United States before all else. But his love for his dying wife had distracted him, and it had cost him, and others, dearly. He was a trained professional and mistakes weren't acceptable.

Sharif spoke up now. "She might not have known the consequences of telling Scott we were up to something that night. If she's in love with the guy…well, we all make mistakes when we're in love or, for some of you, in heat."

This made at least some sense to JJ. Anne had always been a good friend, but D.C. could be a lonely town. If she had found a friend or booty call buddy in Scott, if she had trusted him, she might not have understood it was dangerous to tell him what the team was up to.

"Okay, so she might have called or texted Scott in the hospital. He'd probably call Brooks. Tip him off that something was up. I wouldn't put it past him to send a bunch of his dumb asses to the hangar, to shut us down.

Wilson looked at JJ. "We left Michelle under her care."

"Yes, we did." But there was nothing he could do about that now. Anyway, Anne might have let news of their mission slip, but he was certain that she'd never do anything to intentionally hurt Michelle."

The team settled back on their improvised beds and gazed up at the night sky above. "Well, that was easy. Guess that's why you guys get the big bucks," Sharif whispered. "It only took you this long to figure out what happened…if that *is* what happened."

White laughed and gave her opinion before anyone had the chance to respond to the joke about military pay. "We've all worked through the fog of war. Someday, we'll have to have a sit down with Miss Anne and see what she has to say. But, for now, she's only half on my shit list."

They were left to consider the only other question that mattered—were they stranded here forever?

"I still can't believe you lost to a redheaded Army stiff," JJ chuckled. No response came from Wilson as the rest laughed and then rolled over for the night. "Maybe that's why the buffalo charged his ass," JJ suggested. "His red hair!"

"Nope. They're color blind just like the bulls that charge the matador's waving cape. It's the wave not the color."

Abrams had been quiet throughout the conversation,

but offered one last thought before falling asleep. "Animals can sense things. I think that buffalo got scared, but he also knew who needed to get nailed."

JJ lay quietly for a moment. It was late, he was tired, and he knew his team was, too. But there was something he had to say. "You all know what we did in Gethsemane was a once-in-a-lifetime opportunity. Nobody has ever dropped back in time thousands of years. Probably, no one ever will again. People pray to God for all sorts of things—help me with my grades, win the lottery, and please make my ingrown toenail stop hurting. Freakin' whiners. We know better. We've all held brave Marines as they took their last breath. They prayed to God at that moment, or we did for them—but nobody should ask him for help with some of the crap that they do."

"Yeah, it's like Lady Gaga's telephone song. Stop calling me!" White added with a laugh. "Please proceed with the sermon, Reverend Jackson."

JJ smiled and went on. "Our maker left us here to fend for ourselves. People can't constantly ask him for help. So, when you do, there should be a pretty serious reason.

I'm not going to ask Christ for help ever again. Not even to get us home. I can't. We're Marines. We'll continue to improvise, adapt, overcome. Heck, we might even make Benny here an honorary Marine for getting that pulse back for us. We're here to survive and carry on."

JJ paused to make sure they were all listening. "We'll do what we signed up for. There's plenty of evil here, just like back home. I told General Stewart and Michelle, and now I'm telling all of you again—I was put on this earth to hunt down and kill bad guys. If we can't get home and do it there, that's what I intend to do here. I might be in trouble if I'm ever lucky enough to face Christ again, but I'll be able to sleep at night. Call it justice, vengeance, or preventive maintenance; someone has to do it. Our world, the one we came from, isn't so different from this time and place. When it comes to dealing with murderous bastards we have to be proactive instead of reactive. It's kill or be killed."

Wilson was shaking his head. "Damn, JJ, I told this crew when we first assembled that you were a man of few words. You need to wind it down and let us get some sleep."

"You also need to let JR rest in peace, boss," Sharif said, his voice soft. "We can't stand seeing you toss and turn in your sleep every night. There's nothing anyone can do about Berlin. From everything we've seen on this damn trip, there must be a heaven. JR's up there right now at some really cool beach bar. He's got a beer in one hand and a babe in the other. He's smiling down on us."

"Yeah, with one helluva headache!" Wilson cracked. The team went silent. "What? Too soon?" He looked concerned. They all just stared at him but then began to chuckle.

"Even JR's laughing at that one!" JJ said.

Turning serious, Wilson looked across at JJ in the dark. "So, what do you think my sister is doing right now back home?"

It had felt good to laugh and think of their friend in heaven, but this new question brought JJ right back to earth. "I hope she's keeping busy with those kids she cares for. And shooting the shit out of DC. I love her photography. I just hope by saving her, but possibly losing us both, we didn't make her life worse."

Wilson took a stick and poked at the fire before

replying. JJ saw the shine of the tears in Tommy's eyes. "She'll be fine. My bet is she moved home to hang out with Mom until our butts show up on that doorstep someday." JJ smiled. "Yeah, and that means you have to come home with us. They'd both kick my ass right back here to get you if I let you stay behind!"

JJ shook his head and surveyed the horizon. "Okay, not to be a party pooper, but you ladies need to get your beauty sleep. Oh, and one last thing. Abrams, stay away from that girl in the village. I saw you looking at each other. We can't interact with anyone. It can get us into real trouble faster than White can down a shot."

"So how long do we do this, JJ?" Abrams asked with a sigh of frustration. "She's a nice girl. If we're going to be here forever I might need to just walk off and start my own life here."

JJ stared at him, unsure what to say but not liking the sound of this. Time to end this conversation. "We'll talk in the morning, Benny. It's your turn for night watch."

Wilson cleared his throat. "No, wait. Nobody's breaking up the band. Once we're home and get some R & R, I say we write out a bucket list and have at it. We can go anywhere. If someone doesn't pay the electric bill and we get stuck up on the moon, so be it."

White laughed and reminded both Wilson and Jackson that if Michelle heard any talk of either of them leaving home again, let alone the planet, their heads would be stuffed and mounted on her living room wall.

"Besides," JJ reminded them. "General Stewart has ordered us to stand down. We may never have a chance to use the pulses again, if we're even lucky enough to get home."

A few hours before sunrise, Abrams was alone on watch but barely awake. The sound of Roman soldiers fast approaching startled him and the team from their sleep. Before anyone was able to get a handle on how many were attacking, or how close they might be, a spear flew through the air.

I'm hit. I'm hit, Abrams attempted to shout, but he couldn't speak. He had been sitting against a large rock but was now knocked flat with the force of the spear. The other Marines around him were engaged in hand-to-hand combat with at least four Roman soldiers. Their modern-day martial arts training enabled them to disarm the Romans of their swords, and now it was a bare-fisted fight to the death that ended quickly.

I'm hit. Someone help me. I don't want to die. I'm not ready to die, Abrams thought, still unable to speak. He was losing a lot of blood. His breathing very labored. He knew he'd soon lose consciousness...and his life. In the dim light of the moon, he saw the six-foot length of spear sticking out from his chest. The end of the shaft pointed straight up to the night sky. He stared at the myriad of stars. Thousands of them. Millions. Slowly, the fear left him and everything became quiet.

"Abrams, Abrams," Wilson shouted, "Stay with us, man, stay with us!"

JJ and White hovered over their fallen comrade, trying to figure out what sort of medical treatment they could give him. But he had a two-inch thick spear running completely through him and he was the one with the medical experience. Sharif gathered the swords of the invaders they'd defeated, cutting each throat to insure the threat was neutralized forever.

Their Navy Corpsman was fading. But he looked up at his friend and leader, and JJ moved closer, bent down on one knee and leaned in as close as he could without touching the spear.

"JJ," Abrams whispered, "thanks for bringing me along." And then he was gone.

The four Marines kneeled around him, heads bowed.

JJ stood up abruptly, a tear running down his face. He shook his head, muttering to himself, the guilt overwhelming. He thought back to Berlin and the life lost there. Now Jones and Abrams were gone, too. The first KIA happened because he had lost focus for a brief second. Now there had been two more KIAs because, caring only for his own agenda, he had taken the team on an unauthorized and, some might say, selfish mission.

Wilson stood up beside him and laid his arm around JJ's shoulder. He directed White to remove Abrams' pulse and watched as she put it over her head, adding to hers and Jones'. Now, more than ever, they needed to get out of there.

They removed some of the soldiers' clothing and used them to wrap the swords so they could carry them without being stopped by other guards. The sun would soon rise, and they had to be far from here long before the bodies were found.

"We can't just leave him here like this," Sharif said. "We have to at least lay him to rest so he's at peace. We've been through so much together."

With a nod from JJ, Wilson pulled the spear from

Abrams' body and threw it into the darkness. They moved all the bodies behind the brush they'd used for cover.

"We've got five minutes to bury him and then we're out," JJ said. "Let's use some of those swords to try to dig a shallow grave. Sharif, you watch our backs." They covered Abrams' face with part of a Roman soldier's uniform and then pushed the sandy dirt over him. They stood over their friend one last time then, in an instant, they were gone. They'd head west to the anonymity of one of the fishing villages. "If we can stay out of trouble there for three weeks, we'll return to Gethsemane on the thirtieth day and hope the pulses will work by then."

15

Three years had passed since the military black ops team disappeared. Michelle had moved home to Montana to care for her aging mother until the end. Since that time, Michelle sat on the front porch each morning, watching the sun rise. She thought of her brother and her husband, still wondering what had happened to them, hoping that, someday, they'd return to her. Bunker, the German shepherd pup, was now nearly a hundred pounds of pure energy. A devoted watchdog and protector, the dog let no one get close to Michelle if she sensed a threat. Michelle spent her days tending to the ranch animals and repairing equipment as needed. She was thankful for the hard work. It distracted her from dwelling on her losses.

Late one afternoon in September, the leaves on the trees already vibrant shades of orange, yellow, red and brown, Michelle and Bunker were making sure the horses were stabled safely for the night. Winter was coming, but the grizzlies, wolf packs, and other predators known to roam the region were hungry and not likely to forgo any animal, large or small, that was left out for the night.

"Bunker, one of these days that damn bear is going to come back and that will be its last time," Michelle told the dog. "Dad's .30-06 put a lot of food on the table when Tommy and I were growing up. If Yogi shows up, I'll drop that son of a bitch and turn it into a rug."

Before JJ went missing, she'd likely have given the creature a few more chances before she brought out the gun. But his absence had changed her, made her harder. Every day she recalled the night she last saw her husband. She could hardly remember what he looked like through the fog of morphine. But she remembered his last kiss. She *fought* to remember it, her last memory of him.

Sure, she was thankful for beating cancer, for the miracle that saved her, but she was angry that she lost her men and the rest of the team at the same time. Abrams, Sharif, Jones, and White were good friends during their time back at Andrews. She missed her friend Anne back in Maryland. She missed them all. She was alone now and resigned to living out the rest of her life in this remote area. Bunker was always at her side, but in her moments of despair she realized that, someday, this love too would come to an end. The only peace she found came from reading from the Bible her father had given her—the same one JJ had read from when she was very ill. She thanked God every night for her life and for those she had lost.

Living here could be lonely, but she was never really afraid. She kept the .45 automatic her brother had given her on the nightstand. If intruders ever set foot in her house, she would stop them dead in their tracks.

That particular morning, just as she finished her third cup of coffee, she heard Bunker's warning barks. She looked up to see the dog's attention fixed on the road leading to her property from the highway.

"What is it, girl?" Michelle asked, listening, watching the road. At last, a government vehicle, one of the familiar Chevy Suburbans, came into view. *Who might be coming, unannounced, way out here?* The recently promoted Major Scott again, acting as if he cared about the missing team? Or someone else with news, any news at all, about the team? As the vehicle came to a stop in front of the barn, a familiar and welcome face emerged—General Stewart.

"I thought you had retired, General?" Michelle asked with curiosity.

He laughed and gave her a big hug. Bunker 's tail was wagging energetically; the dog clearly recognized the man she'd so often seen while with JJ.

"Guess you don't get the news up here too quickly, Michelle. You're not going to believe this, but I'm running for President and, with that, all sorts of entitlements and protections seem to have come along. This ride is one of them. We're just finishing the primaries and things are looking good for the nomination, but I won't count on that until I deliver my acceptance speech."

Michelle stood back and stared at her visitor. "You're kidding me, right?" Stewart's solemn expression answered her questions. "Well, that's amazing news. I'm always happy to see you and catch up on what's going on in the world. What brings you here, General? You knocking on doors, looking for votes? How's Elizabeth feel about you becoming the leader of the free world?"

They laughed and, before long, they were inside the main house drinking coffee and catching up. The General's security team waited outside, keeping guard, but enjoying the fresh coffee and cookies she laid out for them.

"Don't give any of these to the dog," she warned. "She's big enough."

The two talked for a half hour, catching up about the ranch, the animals, the weather, and the political scene she didn't normally follow. The satellite television worked at the ranch, she explained, but she just never turned it on. Stewart stood up to study photographs Michelle had mounted on the wall near the massive fireplace. They were shots she'd take of historic and not-so-historic sites back east. The one that impacted him the most was of JJ and his team, standing in front of the Iwo Jima Memorial in Washington, DC. He smiled, but only to hide his pain.

"Every time I see you it makes me happy, General. But then I have such mixed emotions because I wonder if you have news about the team. Why have you come today? Are you finally going to tell me where they were at the end?"

Stewart put his hand on hers and looked into her searching eyes. "Michelle, I'm running for President. This incompetent everyone voted for has made such a mess of our government that I simply had to step up. I consider it my duty to serve and, for anything to get better, it's going to take someone who isn't afraid of a fight. It's also going to take someone who is intolerant of excuses and political correctness to deal with our national and global issues."

Michelle frowned, listening but wondering where this was headed. Was he talking about his run for the presidency to avoid answering her question?

Stewart continued. "I've brought some documents with me that I need you to read and sign before I say anything else about JJ and the team. They are non-disclosure documents. I'm going to give you the opportunity to learn as much about the team and what happened to them as anyone knows, but before doing so, you have to agree to complete secrecy."

She stood up, taking her hand abruptly from his. "You've known what happened to them all this time and you haven't told me?" Bunker immediately appeared at the screen door on hearing her raised voice.

"No, Michelle, we don't know what happened to them. But I do know where they went. Please, take a minute to gather your emotions, sign the documents and then I will tell you what I do know."

She signed them without reading a word.

"You could have just signed this ranch over to me," Stewart joked. But Michelle wasn't laughing.

She sat back down, pulled her chair closer to his and insisted on information. Stewart laid it out for her as best he could.

"The team was sent into the Middle East on a black ops mission to save a life."

"That's it? No. You have to give me more."

"They were dropped into Jerusalem, actually into the Garden of Gethsemane. If you know that area, you know that, to Christians, it's one of the holiest places on earth. It is still in the center of some of the most fought over real estate on the planet. The team was able to save the life they volunteered to help. That person was very close to death. While they succeeded, and we have confirmation of that, we lost the ability to track them and we haven't heard from them since."

Michelle let the information sink in. She looked to the door and told Bunker everything was okay. "So where are they now? What have you been doing for the last three years? Were they taken hostage? You must know more. Marines don't just vanish, to be forgotten."

Stewart got up from the table, refilled his coffee cup, and looked out the kitchen window at the beautiful landscape. The white aspens made this part of the country unique. He knew much more, but had to hold back.

"We went looking for them, but they didn't leave a trail. No group asked for ransom and no group expressed knowledge of the team." He paused long enough to consider his words carefully. "Michelle, if they were dead, someone would have paraded their bodies on the Internet or in front of the media over there, but there has been no chatter. I personally went to Jerusalem three times—right after they disappeared and then two more times—trying to make some sense of it. We've had help from the CIA, the NSA, as well as Israel's Mossad. Nothing."

Michelle gathered her thoughts. "So basically, you came all the way up here to tell me the team went to Israel on a covert op, saved someone's life, and then disappeared. What am I supposed to think? That they jumped on a boat and went on a tour of the Mediterranean? *Who* did they help? I want to know whose life was so precious that it was worth six of the best you ever had under your command."

Stewart shook his head. "I'm as disappointed as you are that we continue to come up empty. Protocol is that, under the Joint Chiefs, MARSOC and the U.S. Marines will continue to search for them as best they can. The CIA and the State Department will keep their ears open. The trail is cold though, Michelle. It was cold the moment they disappeared."

Michelle was growing impatient. "At least tell me who they saved," she demanded.

"I wish I could, but it's classified. I can personally assure you, I can *promise* you, that every member of the team volunteered for the mission and that the life they saved was a very important one. They all saw the value in the effort, and I commend them for it."

One of the General's Secret Service detail knocked on the screen door. "Don't wish to interrupt, General, but your schedule is tight and weather is moving in. We need to get back to the airport and beat the storm."

Stewart stood up as Michelle acknowledged it was time. "So, what do I do now, old friend?" she asked.

Stewart looked into her eyes. "If it were me, I'd go to Gethsemane. It's a very holy place. Christ gave sermons there and that's also where he was betrayed and taken by the Roman guards. You might not find anything there about your boys, but you might find peace."

She thanked him for the visit. They shared a long embrace that she resisted letting go. She wished him luck. "Don't kiss too many babies out there on the campaign trail, General," she said as she walked him to the Suburban. "Thank you for coming and sharing this information. I need a little time to process it, but at least it has given me a place to start looking for them. While I'm thinking about it, is it protocol for Major Scott to come by and check up on me every few months?"

Stewart laughed. "I think he likes you, Michelle. I can't say it is SOP but don't forget, he's an Army guy, and they do things a lot different from us Marines. Since I retired I haven't been able to communicate with anyone at the Pentagon. The President signed an executive order forbidding anyone to communicate with me. He cited National Security for Christ's sake. Next time I'm in DC, I'll try to have someone ask around and make sure everything's kosher with him. I can ask that they keep him away, if that's what you want."

Michelle laughed. "No, keep him coming. JJ and Tommy thought he was an Army asshole. If there's any way they can possibly know he is sniffing around up here, it will fire them up to march back here to me. We'll use him as bait."

Stewart gave her another long hug. As they backed away from each other, they said simultaneously, "Good Luck."

Michelle watched her visitor drive away. She had chores but now she also had some research to do. Looking down at Bunker she said, "So, you want to stay here or are you up for a flight to Israel?"

Within a week Michelle had made her travel reservations, obtained an expedited renewal on her expired passport, and reacquainted her cousin Wade with the workload at the Wilson Ranch. "Whatever you do, don't leave Bunker out after dark. If you have to go out, take Dad's rifle with you. I only expect to be gone a week, but who knows, anything can happen. I'm not sure how I will feel once I am there."

After a short hop to Chicago and then a long overnight flight to Tel Aviv, she would soon stand where her husband and her brother were last known to have been, the Garden of Gethsemane in Jerusalem.

Stewart was headed east, on a private jet, to Reagan International Airport in Washington D.C. He felt good that he had visited the wife of an MIA, a very special MIA. JJ meant a lot to him and he counted it as his responsibility to be sure Michelle knew as much about JJ's disappearance as possible and that she had everything she needed to carry on with her life.

Late that evening, at his home in Alexandria, Stewart was back to the business of politics and running for President. "I appreciate your coming to see me here, General Brooks," he said when the other man entered his kitchen through the doorway to the garage. "Thanks for agreeing to come so late and through the back way. With all the staffers, security, and the media, it's hard to do anything these days without someone watching."

Brooks smiled and stepped into the house. "It's been too long. I just wish we didn't have to be so secretive. You know if we get caught we'll both be dragged off to Leavenworth. Bad enough we kept the BOTM program from the president, and now this."

Stewart escorted his guest to his home office and closed the door behind them. Other than the security detail outside the property, they were alone.

The two exchanged pleasantries and talked shop for thirty minutes before Brooks' voice took on a more solemn tone. "Stew, I wanted to tell you how happy I am for you that Mrs. Stewart has come home. I saw her on the news before coming over. She looked like she was actually enjoying being out on the campaign trail. You two have been through enough. Hopefully, before long, we can address her as First Lady in the White House."

Stewart nodded in response, surprised at what seemed genuine sentiment from his former adversary.

"So, what really brings me here today, Stew?" Brooks asked.

"I'd like to get an update on BOTM, General. Once I left the Pentagon and the President issued his little decree, I lost all access to military personnel and intelligence. But considering that we set up that program and how it terminated, I was hoping, as a friend and former colleague in arms, you would let me know what you know."

Brooks thought for a moment. The working relationship they had was a good one, despite their occasional philosophical differences and "who's better—Army Ranger versus Marine Raider—rivalry." A rivalry between the two services that ran from the grunts at boot camp all the way up to the Pentagon's highest authority.

"Are we operating under the same confidentiality that we did back at the shop?" Brooks asked.

"Of course. We both know that setting up BOTM and burying its existence would have gotten us canned back then and would still cause us problems today. What we discuss between us will remain here."

Brooks looked around Stewart's study, as if admiring the room and its many military paintings, photos, and artifacts. He noticed the large painting of the Enola Gay and raised his glass to it.

Stewart said, "That was the day America told the world we wouldn't put up with anyone's shit ever again. I looked at that every time I need to make a tough call. Hopefully it'll be hanging in the Oval Office someday and can help me there."

Brooks nodded and got back to the top-secret briefing Stewart's requesting. "It's going to cost you another Scotch," he said with a laugh then leaned into the top-secret discussion. "We've been able to get the program back into action."

Stewart's heart gave a lurch. Maybe there was hope yet of getting JJ back. "Tell me."

"Well, you will remember that the night Doctor Moretti died they did an autopsy on her and discovered not one, but two, pacemaker-like devices implanted in her chest—one on each side. The first was a standard issue defibrillator type, but the other was something nobody at Bethesda had seen before. Luckily, Colonel Petty had been keeping an eye on things and was able to get hold of that device, and sent it back to the research team at Nellis."

"Wonderful. But it's now been a long time since then."

"Yes. It took two years to identify the parts they could and another eight to ten months to match the other pieces with specimens they found buried in Moretti's research rubble. Two of the scientists working for us on top secret programs were able to figure out the dating and location elements and, while they still don't fully understand some of the elements in the extra pacemaker and the device we found in her pants pocket, they were able to make it work. They were also able to fix the near-past issue."

Stewart could barely contain his excitement, but took a moment to consider what he had just heard. "So, have you been able to send T2 back to look for the team?"

Brooks took a sip of his drink and continued. "Yes and no. First, they reproduced the domestic testing Moretti had done with animals. They then sent a human team, T2, between hangers at the base. That all worked fine. Once we had confidence they could go back to wherever we wanted to send them, we set up a possible rendezvous. The protocol on T1's side was to try every day, for five days, then at thirty days, and then each year. They were to attempt their return from the same spot where they'd originally landed. It wasn't until two months ago that we had everything on our side tested and ready. Then we encountered a personnel issue with T2. You'll remember that Captain Scott was the sole Army officer on the team."

Stewart gave him a stiff nod. "Yes, to support the program you wanted one of yours on board and you hand selected Scott, just as I did Jackson."

"Yes, but the rest of T2 was staffed with Marines. The friction within that team and between the team leaders escalated after the abortion at Yellowstone. Scott wanted his own team of Rangers. The Marines from T2 expressed concern that payback, rather than rescue, was on Scott's agenda and started all kinds of trouble."

Stewart sat back in his chair, digesting what he had heard so far.

"Stew, you don't need to say another word. The most important thing was, and is, bringing that crew back, so we replaced Scott. Hell, he was so banged up after that Buffalo nearly killed him that I pulled him and stuck him back at a desk outside my office. I thought it best at this point to limit the number of people involved, so we asked Petty to take the lead, and he accepted."

"Good choice," Stewart said, for once agreeing with Brooks.

"By the way, it took Petty a long time to accept that he wasn't able to communicate with you. He's a good man. We sent them back to the exact location and the same time of day that T1 went to, one year to the day after their trip. They spent eight hours there and then returned without a clue."

Stewart felt a sharp stab of disappointment. "Son of a bitch."

"It gets worse, Stew. Of all the places they could have gone, they chose the Garden of Gethsemane back in the time of Christ. That's 33 AD. They went virtually empty handed. Jackson took a bunch of high-tech warriors into an ancient, barbaric world. T2 saw no signs of them, no markings on a tree, nothing. T2 left their mark: 'SF-T2', carved into the tree closest to the landing spot, although they tell me there were dozens of olive trees all around there. The truth is, we don't know where any of them are. We don't know if they are alive, imprisoned by the Romans, nothing. Someone pointed out that, for them to know when to be at the rally point one year later at the correct time, they'd better have a means of accurately counting the days. No modern calendars back then."

Frustrated, Stewart asked, "Did you try sending T2 back to the exact same time that T1 went or perhaps every day for the following five days and then 30 days as we laid out?"

Brooks nodded but looked away before saying, "We did. Nothing."

Stewart observed him for a long moment. Although they'd worked well together at the Pentagon and, as far as he knew, Brooks had been honest and forthcoming when operating in the best interests of the United States—Stewart didn't trust him. He wondered if the General was being totally forthcoming.

He knew that Major Scott was like a son to General Brooks. After Scott came home from Yellowstone, nearly dead, he'd wondered if T1's fate was sealed. Brooks was a man who held a grudge. If he saw an opportunity for revenge, he'd take it. But would he intentionally leave a BOTM team stranded in another millennium? Something told Stewart he just might. But he couldn't let the General know that he was suspicious.

"Well, we did the best we could. We all knew when we agreed to run the program that it had special risks, and these seemed to have come to fruition. Thank you for briefing me, General. I appreciate the intel." He paused to gather his thoughts. "I want to discuss another topic with you, one that still involves BOTM."

Brooks looked at him with interest. "Oh?"

"They're saying I have a 60% shot at winning the nomination, winning the election and becoming President."

Brooks smiled. "It's been a long time since a military man was in the White House. Knowing you as well as I do, I believe you will fix a hell of a lot of things pretty quickly."

Stewart refilled Brooks' Scotch and poured one for himself. "Well, this is where I want your help. I need BOTM to help me win the election." They had agreed, years earlier, that the technology would never be used to advance a career. But the country was now at risk, and extreme measures would be necessary to insure its safety.

The men debated Stewart's request but finally came to a

general agreement as to how the time travel program might be used to assure him the Presidency.

"Okay, Stew, what exactly do you need BOTM to do?"

Stewart smiled and laid out his plans for domestic and international espionage. His biggest rival for the Presidency, Senator Maxwell of Colorado, would be in Washington in two days for meetings. Maxwell was quite the ladies' man and cheated on his wife as often as he changed his shirt. The first mission would be to go back in time and insert the T2 team into the hotel room Maxwell would be using, before the Senator arrived. They would plant high-tech audio and video equipment and then return the next day to remove it. The bugs would transmit live. Stewart would use the footage to push his opposition into leaving the race. Security would check and then seal the room sixty minutes before the Senator's arrival, so timing and stealth were essential.

"Consider it done, Stew. What's next?"

From there he outlined the next ten missions targeting various individuals, foreign and domestic, ranging from the Russian President's personal office in the Kremlin to the big banks and brokerage firms on Wall Street. Not only would he be gathering intelligence to win the election, he also wanted to put the country's external and internal adversaries on their heels using whatever intel he was able to gather.

They already had the ability to hack foreign governments, and the professional and personal email accounts of the movers and shakers from around the world. The ability to covertly place a team in the offices and homes of these same people could really shake things up. Not only based on what they learned but from the ripple effects of their stealth. Gaining information from Russian and other leaders would at least make them paranoid about trusting people in their inner circle. Subvert, disrupt, corrupt—whatever it took to not only win the Presidency, but to put America back on top and in full control over all enemies, foreign and domestic.

"Any issues so far, General? I mean, Secretary Brooks?" Stewart asked.

Brooks smiled and shook his head. He now saw what was in it for him, the leadership of the Department of Defense. Stewart knew Brooks would have gotten around to asking, but he probably was pleased he didn't need to.

"General Stewart, your Marines, and the rest of the military, know you have America's best interests at the forefront. The civilians who don't get you now will understand you when they see you in action. If you need to be in the Oval to make things right, then the assets under my command will do whatever is needed to put you there."

Stewart smiled. "Very well." Brooks would direct the T2 BOTM team to target candidate Maxwell immediately and fully develop the additional missions from there.

It was just before midnight when he escorted the Chairman of the Joint Chiefs to his Suburban, parked in the garage, Brooks shook his hand and looked him in the eye. "Mr. President."

Stewart placed his left hand on Brooks' shoulder. "Mr. Secretary." The deal was made, assuring two Generals of their rise to the top.

The Pentagon

"This seems very Watergate-ish," newly promoted T2

commander Lieutenant Mike Buchanan protested as General Brooks sat back in his chair.

The new commander had been a part of the BOTM program since the very start, participating in the first testing of the program with Petty and Doctor Moretti at the top-secret facility in the southwest. He was there when Corporal Richards' body was brought back to Andrews from 1945 Berlin. He watched quietly as his second in command, Sergeant Jones was chosen over team leader Scott and transferred to T1. When Scott was critically injured in a freak accident with a Buffalo at Yellowstone, he helped carry him to the trauma unit. He followed orders, kept his mouth shut, and bided his time, believing his chance to get into the game would come. And now he was surprised to hear they wanted him to help undermine an election.

"You have a problem working to put an extraordinary military man in command at the White House, Sergeant?" Major Scott asked. Still not operating at 100%, Scott did the best he could at the Pentagon to assist General Brooks. Buchanan knew he was in a precarious position. There he was, in the massive Pentagon office of the Chairman of the Joint Chiefs, the most powerful military man in the country, and he was being asked to perform a duty that he wasn't sure was even legal.

The General's predecessor had resigned the position to protest the weakness, as he called it, of the President of the United States, their military Commander in Chief. Buchanan admired General Stewart and was proud to see him stand up to the limp politician who had allowed the armed forces to become undermanned and ill equipped, tarnishing the country's reputation as a force to be reckoned with. Buchanan wanted to serve; he wanted to advance up the ranks. He just didn't want to wind up in a federal prison or get shot by the Secret Service.

"General Brooks, Major Scott, may I speak frankly?" With their nods he proceeded. "I have fought around the world defending this country and protecting our interests. As a Marine Raider, as a special operative and black ops participant, I've engaged in actions on foreign soil that could have gotten me killed or, worse yet, stuck in a third-world, rat-hole prison for the rest of my life. Yes, I do want a Marine in the White House. Maxwell's the only person who can challenge the general in the primaries. And that dipshit running on the other side won't have a chance at re-election. I just don't want to get arrested for carrying out your orders."

"Okay, son, I get that." Brooks left his chair and came around the desk to lean against it in front of Buchanan. "All we're suggesting is that you enter the hotel room of a two-faced bastard who cheats on his wife, who abuses the women he seduces, and help expose him for the POS he is."

Buchanan thought for a minute. Looking at Scott, he smiled and responded, "Are we talking about hiding cigars or rough stuff, General?"

Brooks looked baffled, but realized this meant Buchanan was in and would do whatever he could.

"I must have your word, though," Buchanan said, "that in the event something goes wrong and we get caught, you will get us out of it—and I don't mean by way of a body bag or a pine box, sir."

Scott laughed and then gave Buchanan what he needed to hear. "We will have your back and we will never leave you behind."

Buchanan thought it funny that an officer perceived as impotent was making any promises, but he let it pass. After exchanging salutes, he was on his way out of the Pentagon and back to Andrews.

A week later, the six-member T2 team followed the usual BOTM procedure—mat-up, and go back in time just twenty-four hours. They landed in one of the executive suites at the Willard Hotel in downtown Washington, D.C. Their guest of honor was due to arrive within fifteen minutes. His suitcase had been placed on an antique-looking luggage rack against the wall and opened. As standard operating procedure in the protection of a party's top Presidential candidates, the U.S. Secret Service had swept the suite once already for intruders, explosives, weapons, and listening devices. They'd also checked the environment for toxins and radiation. Once the all-clear was given, two agents would stand guard just ten feet away outside the door in the hallway. One unexpected sound would bring them charging in, guns drawn.

While one Marine remained in place, standing on the travel mat, the other five moved quickly to install audio and video transmitting devices in the living room area, bedroom, and bathroom.

Suddenly, someone was speaking outside the door. The signal to abort was given. *No time, there's no time,* Buchanan thought. The mat was too far from most of them to reach. Buchanan and three others slid under the expansive king-size bed, while the fifth headed for a closet. The sixth man grabbed the mat and followed him in. Special operatives were the quickest, stealthiest, fittest, most highly trained military machines on the planet, but in this case, they needed to move with the grace of a Cirque du Soleil performer and the speed of a bullet.

"Come in, my dear," the familiar voice said. From his cramped vantage point under the bed, closest to the door, Buchanan could see the dress shoes of two men entering the room. A pair of red stilettos followed. The woman was clearly the entertainment for the evening.

"Just one second, Senator, and I will be out of your way," the agent said as he walked past the bed and toward the bathroom.

"No need, Agent, I got this. You may leave now."

"We're right outside if you need us. Good night, Senator. Good night, ma'am."

Buchanan knew the Marines in the closet could also hear what was going on. Luckily, the recording devices had all been staged and were operating. He just hoped neither of the people in the room had a reason to look under the bed or hang a coat in the closet.

Miles away, at the BOTM hanger at Andrews, things were not so quiet. "Are you kidding me, Major?" General Brooks yelled into the phone.

"No, General, all the bugs were placed and operating perfectly. But the senator showed up early and the team had no choice but to hide. If they had engaged the Secret Service, there would have been a shootout."

Brooks was furious. Why had he let Stewart talk him into this? Yes, he wanted to be Secretary of Defense, but this had shades of Watergate, jail sentences, and Nixon's resignation all over it. Even worse, exposure of the BOTM program could set politics in Washington and around the world on fire. Some might see this as a coup of sorts, the military participating in the presidential political process.

"Let me know when it's over and they are out of there safe, Major," Brooks ordered. After the call, he wondered for a brief moment which country he'd head to if things went astray.

Back in the hotel room, the candidate's evening proceeded as planned. He and his female guest got to know each other better after sharing countless glasses of Scotch. The only close call came when he dropped a blue pill at the side of the bed and it bounced under the bed skirt.

Shit! Buchanan silently screamed as those watching the video feed yelled the same thing.

Luckily, the Scotch had slowed the senator's senses, and his female guest was using the bathroom to get ready for whatever he had planned. Buchanan quickly moved the pill out from beneath the skirt, to where it could be seen and recovered. Those beside him under the massive bed lay there, eyes alert, bodies tensed. The looks they gave him mirrored his own thoughts: *That was too damn close.*

Minutes later, the woman joined the senator on the bed and, before long, as uncomfortable as it was for those under it, they learned the politician's appetite was unquestionably sadomasochistic. He'd left the television on, turned up loud, so their conversation and any other sounds were drowned out, in case anyone in the hallway might be listening. He clearly had little respect for the woman in bed with him. It wasn't long before her feet hit the floor.

She dressed quickly, snapping at him as she pulled on

each piece of clothing. "That's no way to treat a woman, you creep. You think choking a woman is exciting? Sexy? Don't ever call me again! You can stick my vote in *your* ass!"

The senator just laughed.

Buchanan couldn't believe it, and suddenly felt more than justified in doing what they were about to do to the man's career.

The door to the suite opened, and then slammed closed.

A second later it opened again. "Everything okay in there, Senator?"

The response was another laugh. "Yes, I'm fine. I'm just going to take a shower. See you men in the morning." The door clicked shut again.

Buchanan looked at the other three men, still motionless under the bed with him. This would be their chance to exit. Maybe their only chance until the man fell asleep. More than anything, he wanted out of that room.

He watched the candidate slowly wander to the bathroom and start the shower. The door was open, steam starting to pour out. He figured they could grab the two from the closet, assemble on the mat, count to three, and be out of there in as few as fifteen seconds.

One problem, Buchanan was a Marine. And, like most Marines, he couldn't tolerate anyone who hurt women or children. He was last out from under the bed. "Everyone on the mat and ready to go. I'll be right back!"

He grabbed the video and audio bugs that they had placed around the suite's living room and bedroom. The feed to Andrews went out as he clicked off each unit and headed past his team for the bathroom.

Moments later, just past midnight, the team returned

safely to Andrews. Scott took Buchanan aside and said only one thing, "Steam. We lost everything in the bathroom after the shower steam killed the video. Glad you men got out of there all right. It was too close. I'm sure the bedroom video will hurt his chances once we leak it to the media. I don't think his wife will be too happy with him either. Well done."

Buchanan smiled and saluted. Before turning to leave, he said, "Score one for the good guys, Major."

At 7:00 a.m. the next morning, the Senator's aide insisted the agents check on him. They found him slumped over in the tub, shower water still running. Dead. It appeared he must have slipped on the soap and broken his neck as he fell to the tub floor.

Days later, after publicly expressing his surprise and sadness at the loss of his opponent, Stewart had his assistant place a call to Colonel Petty, requesting a confidential, off-the-books breakfast meeting at the residence at 07:00 in the morning. With that scheduled, Stewart sat back for a short time, reviewing polling reports and the busy travel schedule his campaign had laid out for him with only three more primaries left before the party conventions and the fall campaign. With Maxwell gone, Stewart was all but assured of the primaries and the nomination.

The next morning, Stewart was waiting for Petty in his den, coffee and hot food already set up. Petty had served with Stewart years before. Falling back on the great, candid relationship they'd had at the Pentagon, they acted as if it had been days, not years, since they last spoke.

After the typical pleasantries, they sat down to pass the

cream and sugar back and forth, and remove the silver chafing dish covers. Stewart told him about his latest visit with Michelle Jackson and expressed his shock at the tragic death of his opponent.

Petty sighed. "It surprises me that sort of thing can happen, in this day and age. A simple accident ends a man's life and, likely, alters history. General, you had my vote the day you announced you were running, and you do today. I know you are a very busy man, so tell me how I can be of service."

Stewart always had appreciated the Colonel's cut-to-the-chase manner and got down to business. "Colonel Petty, I appreciate everything you have done for me, for the Corps, and for your country over the years. I'm hoping you can bring me up to speed on a few things. I would also like to discuss your role in the Stewart Administration, if that comes to be."

Petty's gaze sharpened with interest, as if this was something he hadn't expected. "Whatever you need, General. You and I go back a long way. It would be an honor to continue to serve you in your role as our Commander in Chief."

Stewart smiled and sat forward. "Tell me a bit more about the T1 rescue attempts. I can't believe you didn't find a single trace of those Marines."

Petty looked stunned. "General, I'm sorry to say—despite my urging—we never actually looked."

16

It had been two months since Michelle arrived in Israel. She wanted to walk where her husband and her brother walked before they disappeared. She hoped that by following in their footsteps she might connect with them—if only spiritually. Feeling closer to them was all the more important to her as she began to realize that she might never see them again.

The moment her plane landed she'd felt drawn to this area. Incredibly, she also felt safe here. She'd learned where she should and shouldn't go. It might be a holy place, but it was also the site of fighting dating back thousands of years.

There were the Christian, Jewish, Armenian and Arab sections. Flags, markings, and signs in the markets changed abruptly. The expressions on people's faces sometimes warned her away. She paid close attention to her surroundings. She was aware that there likely were terrorists mixed in among the less dangerous pickpockets that tourists were warned to be wary of. Whenever she felt someone getting too close to her, or suspected she was being followed, she stepped into a shop or headed for a family or tour group where she felt safer.

Her brother had taught her years ago how to protect herself by reading the intentions of those around her, knowing the difference between the hungry who might be forced to steal just to get food…and those who sought to harm her out of pure evil. Tommy also instructed her in self-defense when he returned from boot camp so many years ago. She knew she'd be okay here, as long as she remained vigilant. She intended to remain in Israel until some news, any news, came to her.

The geography was startlingly different from both rural Montana and suburban D.C. Most structures were the color of desert sand and only versions of palm trees thrived.

She familiarized herself with the sights and sounds of Jerusalem, taking guided tours and then returning to those places on her own to let them soak in. It wasn't long before tourists were asking her questions.

"Where's the loo?"

"Where was Christ crucified?"

"How far is Tel Aviv?"

She had the look of someone who was there to help. Before long, she realized she might just have discovered a way to support herself, which would enable her to stay longer.

After finding a very small apartment to rent she decided to become a paid tour guide. That would take care of her expenses and, at the same time, keep her close to the last known places where her men had been. Occasionally she landed a side job, a well-paying one, guiding a lone traveler or a couple who wanted a private tour of the major sites or the more remote areas outside the Old City walls.

Gradually, she found peace in this foreign land. More importantly, she began to feel the connection she had sought. "They were here, I can feel them," she told her cousin Wade over the phone, when she called to check on Bunker and the ranch back in Montana.

"How long do you plan on being there, Michelle?" he asked. "I can't watch the place forever, and you can't stay there forever."

"Time will tell," she said. "I'm making enough money to cover my expenses. If I have to sell the ranch and have Bunker shipped over, I will. But if you can hold on for another month or so… I really appreciate your being there, Wade. But just tell me if it becomes too much for you."

"I will," Wade said. "But sooner or later, you're going to have to accept that the boys are gone."

"Maybe." She closed her eyes against the thought. "But not yet."

The hardest part was trying to sleep. She couldn't. She still kept her Bible close by but, for some reason, she didn't feel the need to read from it as often.

"You stay there as long as you need to," Wade said. "If that's what you feel you have to do. But I have to say, I worry about you. A pretty American woman wandering around that part of the world—it's just not smart, or safe. Tommy would be pissed if he knew you were there alone."

She couldn't help chuckling at that. "I'm sure he would be."

Thirty-seven miles to the west of the streets she walked

was the Mediterranean Sea. If only Michelle had known how close, yet how far, JJ and Tommy were.

The four remaining T1 operators, Jim Jackson, Tommy Wilson, Christy White, and Omar Sharif, made it to the Mediterranean after their escape from Jerusalem two weeks earlier. They were able to blend in among the fishermen in scattered villages and find work. At first they worked for food and shelter. Eventually they were able to earn coins for whatever other necessities they needed.

Their willingness to take on hard labor won the stranded Marines a safe place in the community, at least temporarily. Their missions had prepared them to survive high altitudes and cold in the tallest mountain ranges, to fight in rain forests, deserts, and monsoon conditions. But stepping back 2,000 years for an extended stay in a world where they couldn't talk to anyone but themselves was something they hadn't prepared for. Luckily, the people here were kind and welcomed the strangers, seemingly unconcerned with their inability to communicate with them.

The team hadn't seen a Roman soldier since the early morning encounter that took the life of their friend Abrams. He and Jones were the first two Marines they'd ever left behind. Failing to bring them home was something none of them would ever forget.

"JJ, I've been thinking," Sharif said. He had stopped his work, mending the fishing net spread over his lap, and was looking at his team leader. "If T2, or anyone at Andrews, came back to get us, wouldn't it be possible to go back in time before Jones and Abrams died. Couldn't we save them and bring them with us back to modern-day Maryland?"

JJ studied his sergeant's earnest expression. "I've considered that a thousand times, but I get totally conflicted over the possibilities. We could have done that for Richard, but then we would have changed history."

"Yes, but in killing those Romans back there we changed history. Same for the cook and the krauts we killed in Berlin."

"True. But the Russians would have killed anyone they found in their sweep across Berlin, and they would have violated that poor cook before putting a bullet in her head. I know. I've thought a lot about that. The entire question compounds itself over and over and over. That's why all of this was supposed to be an observational program until the guys above our pay grades could figure out how best to use it. Maybe we haven't been rescued because they killed the program before it got out of hand."

Wilson and White joined in the conversation. They had just completed their work for the day and were hoping for dinner and another beautiful sunset. Instead they got into a debate about history and their roles as time travelers.

Wilson gestured for the team to be vigilant. "If and when we get home," he said, "I'd like to take a trip to listen in on the Joint Chiefs to see what other things they had in mind for us. With the exception of General Stewart, we might have been nothing more than expendable guinea pigs."

Jackson was frustrated at the thought. "We're not like the chimpanzees NASA used before they finally put a Marine into space. Stewart wouldn't have allowed us to be used that way. We'll find out what happened, someday."

An hour later, with their work complete, they were

seated around a fire, eating fish, and enjoying the bread and wine made by the locals.

"So, everyone's agreed. If we ever get out of here, we're going to toss these damned necklaces in the Potomac and hope nobody else ever has the chance to screw with the past. What's done is done, so let's worry about the present and the future," JJ summarized.

"Can I get an Amen?" White joked.

"Don't forget, there's another set of pulse devices back at Andrews. Who the hell knows what they're being used for at this point. They sure aren't chasing after us," Sharif reminded them.

"Let's keep counting down the days. We move again in three. If nothing happens in the Garden, then I guess we make more money fishing and then set sail to Mykonos. Hell, we'll all go!" JJ said with a smile. "Who's up for a boat ride?"

"Roger that," White and Wilson said at the same time.

Their day ended soon afterward. It had been a very long time since they felt the need to stand watch at night. The threats seemed long gone, and fishing started at sun up.

Washington D.C. – Modern Day

The Inauguration weather was perfect. The newly elected President gave a speech that echoed everything he'd said during the primaries and the general election. Putting the country back to work, instilling a sense of pride, and demonstrating strength against all enemies, foreign and domestic, gave the country what it wanted, needed, to hear.

Having chosen the brightest and most popular woman

in congress, Senator Williams from California, as his running mate, assured him of the support he would need up on The Hill to get the agenda they shared enacted. The United States would soon be back in business with the same sense of hope, unity, and love of country that was felt after the terrorist attacks of 2001. It was a long night of inaugural balls for Stewart, and he made his last stop the Marine Corps Barracks for a special midnight parade.

Excusing himself briefly from the festivities, he met privately with his trusted friend and advisor, Colonel Petty.

"Congratulations Mr. President," Petty said proudly as the two stood, shoulder to shoulder, in the men's room.

"Thank you, Colonel," Stewart responded. "I'd be happy to hear any news from your end."

"Nothing yet, Mr. President, but we are on it. The technology allows us to come and go quickly, like opening one door after another. We started the minute you uttered the words, 'So help me God,' at the swearing-in. We won't stop until we catch who we're looking for. I'll be back in there checking on things shortly and see you in your new office in a few hours. Hopefully we'll have something to report."

Jerusalem – 36 A.D.

"How long do you want to stay here, sir?" one of the rescue team members asked.

"You know the protocol. We stick for ten minutes and then go back and re-launch for another time slot," Buchanan replied. The six members of the T2 rescue team were laying low, under the cover of darkness and behind the familiar olive trees that painted the hillside at Gethsemane.

The six U.S. Marines of T2 had returned to this same spot at least a dozen times, in search of the missing T1 team. While they were dressed in the same style robes and leather sandals, these six had come heavily armed and ready secure the safety of their fellow Marines and bring them home to modern times. Glock 19 automatics with laser sites and four 17-shot ammo clips were strapped on their thighs. Stun grenades, knives, zip ties, one set of night vision optics, and a small medical kit rounded out their equipment.

"This still freaks me out," one Marine whispered. "They say Jesus Christ used to walk these hills giving speeches and Major Jackson came back here to ask Him for help with his sick wife." A minute passed as they continued to scan the horizon watching for movement, listening for any sounds.

"Sermons," another Marine corrected him. "Jesus gave sermons, not speeches. I used to get dragged to church every Sunday by my mom. I'd listened to the priest talk about burning in hell, miracles, giving money to the poor, don't curse, respect your elders, and on and on. Blah, blah, blah. Then I heard stories about priests screwing with kids. I stopped going."

A few of the Marines chuckled but kept their eyes trained on their surroundings.

"Kneeling here in this holy place, I remember one sermon that still sticks with me. Let the man without sin cast the first stone," one said

"You ladies need to keep it quiet," the second in command admonished them.

"Quiet the fuck down!" Buchanan whispered sternly. "I hear someone coming."

Up the hillside, along the path worn by sheep, goats,

shepherds, and the faithful, four figures slowly walked their way. "Someone finally shows up and there's no moon!" the SIC whispered to her team leader. Looking to her left, she asked the Marine wearing the night goggles, "What's coming?"

"Looks like four villagers," he whispered.

"Great, another set of followers looking for their savior." Suddenly, the four on the path stopped dead in their tracks as if they'd already spotted T2 among the olive trees.

"Shalom," JJ called out to the figures he could barely make out in the darkness. There was no response. He slowly turned to Sharif, White, and Wilson at the rear. "Get ready to move. I'm not sure who or what we just walked up on."

"Shalom," he called out again. "On the count of ten, we are going to turn and walk in four separate directions. We'll rendezvous back at our spot as always." He began the slow count. Halfway through, he heard a word whispered by one of the strangers. A word he'd never thought he'd hear again: "Quantico."

The four dropped to a knee. This couldn't be happening. White was beside herself. "Marco!" she called out.

"Shalom and Marco are the best you lost bastards can come up with?" Buchanan said, stepping out from behind his cover. "Get over here, under these trees."

As quietly as they possibly could, the four survivors of T1 and the six rescuers of T2 fist bumped and patted each other on the back as they quickly kneeled to form a ring and watch for anyone who may have followed them.

"Buchanan, you son of a bitch!" Wilson whispered. "Been a long time since Andrews."

"Where are Abrams and Jones?" one of the Marines

asked, "they coming up from behind?" JJ motioned for everyone to fall back into shadows now that the area seemed secure.

Wilson delivered the news. "They didn't make it. Abrams took a goddamned six-foot-long spear in the chest and Jones went looking for a group of Roman soldiers after he watched them torture Christ. He gave it his best, but he lost the fight. Both of them are buried out there somewhere."

Reliving those moments in his memory, JJ said, "I don't think there's any chance of retrieving them."

There was a moment of silence while the news sank in. Buchanan spoke at last. "Well, then, time we get moving."

"Home?" Sharif asked. "Can you get us back there?"

"Looks like all we need to do is grab a few goats or whatever else is wandering around out here to take Jones' and Abrams' spots,' Buchanan said. "Complete the chain and you guys are out of here. Oh yeah, and you'll have to swap pulses with me to refresh the technology. Once T1 is out of here we'll have to wait a few minutes. Then we can circle up and be right behind you."

Wilson looked at JJ, who couldn't hold back any longer. "My wife. I need to know—"

"Michelle is fine," Buchanan said with a smile. "I went with the general to visit her at the ranch. She's healthy and that damn dog of yours weighs ninety pounds now. Colonel Petty will brief your team back in DC on all your family intel. He'll also tell you why it took us so long to find you, and what's been going on back home, so let's execute and get the hell out of here."

White looked at Wilson and said, "Petty's still on board but they keep saying D.C. Why not Andrews?"

Buchanan overheard. "Petty is in charge of BOTM now. Dr. Moretti passed away the night the technology failed."

JJ's exuberance at being found soured at the news. They'd all cared so much for her. She was a loveable old woman, a grandmother to them all. She'd chosen to work in science and had done incredible things for her country, and for them personally. JJ wanted to know more, but it would have to wait until they got home.

"We're headed to D.C.," Buchanan explained, "because The White House sent us to get you. President Stewart will always be a Marine. He told us not come back without you."

JJ couldn't stop himself from grinning now. The relief he felt was overwhelming. He could tell the others were as happy as he was. Within twenty minutes, they managed to capture two goats that had wandered from their herd. JJ laid the last of his coins at the spot where they'd seen a shepherd return nightly to sleep. They formed two rings.

"Ready?" Buchanan asked.

"JJ," Wilson laughed, "there's no way you're taking these guys home to Michelle!"

"I suspect we can find a few Navy boys over at Annapolis who would love to have backup mascots. Now, let's just go home!"

The White House

General Brooks had supported Stewart's candidacy covertly through the use of the BOTM program. He had then pushed to use the program to spy on the general's other adversaries, but the candidate resisted. Stewart knew that his election victory was secured with the conveniently timed death of his only real opponent. He directed Brooks to park the BOTM program until after the inauguration. It would continue to be an invaluable asset in the war against crime and terrorism he, as President, intended to wage.

Stewart took the precaution of taking control of the six remaining pulse devices. Without Brook's knowledge, he had Colonel Petty hand deliver them to him at his home for safekeeping.

The cause of Maxwell's death, considering who was present in his suite that night, concerned Stewart. He wanted to lock the program down until further notice. He also wanted to eliminate any chance of Brooks using the pulses for personal benefit or against the President-elect. The man was not to be trusted.

Stewart directed Petty to contact the military leaders of America's allies to let them know that this new President would be swift in keeping his campaign promises to work with friendly governments to annihilate those who sought to attack freedom and democracy. On the morning of January 21, General Brooks is one of President Stewart's first appointments in the Oval Office.

"Good Morning, Mr. President." Brooks saluted his new Commander in Chief.

Stewart turned from the window that overlooked the South Lawn of the White House. "General." He returned the salute. "Take a seat with Colonel Petty. I'll be with you both in just a minute."

Brooks looked surprised to see the Colonel there. With everything on Stewart's plate, he couldn't imagine why Petty would be there ahead of him on the morning after the swearing in. Brooks sat on a sofa with Petty across from him on a matching one.

Stewart walked around to the front of his massive desk and sat against it. He gave them time to slowly soak in their surroundings, and then, set his eyes firmly on the General.

"General Brooks, I am sure you are here today, expecting to accept the position of Secretary of Defense."

Brooks frowned. "I am—after all, that was our agreement, wasn't it?"

"It was. But I'd like the Colonel to give us a quick review of the BOTM program before we get down to the real business at hand."

Brooks nodded. He'd follow his new Commander in Chief's lead, for now.

Petty dove right in. "Thank you, Mr. President. As you directed, I prepared a brief summary and will run through it quickly for you."

Brooks sat complacently, at first. Soon, his hands were

making restless motions in his lap as if he wasn't really paying attention to what was being said. Stewart sensed the other man's growing impatience with Petty's report. They all knew the program; they all knew how it was tested, how it faltered with the sudden death of Dr. Moretti and the disappearance of the T1 team, and how Petty got it going again. And they all knew that Stewart had asked for Brooks' help in breaking laws to help him win the election.

Petty went on describing the course of events after T1 went missing and General Stewart was banned from the Pentagon. In a directive from General Brooks, he got his orders: "Get BOTM operational." There was no mention of a rescue, of finding and bringing back T1. "Get the best scientists on it and get it working again." Brooks told Petty that, all along, he'd wanted to pursue his own agenda. "General Brooks stated that there would be a place for me, alongside him, as he continued his pursuit of power. He said that he wanted his agenda enacted before the sitting President, or anyone else, found out about it. He reminded me that Stewart was gone, that intel was not to be shared, and that was an order."

"So," the President interrupted, "it seems that this was your priority, General. Five Marines and a Navy Corpsman were MIA, but they weren't high on your agenda. In fact, they didn't even appear on your agenda."

"I'm not sure where this is going, Mr. President," Brooks interrupted.

"It will become clear. Proceed, Colonel."

Petty related how he intended to do whatever he had to—go off the books on a rescue mission of his own, if needed. The rest of the T2 team were also Marines and they were chomping at the bit to go. It took time, but eventually, with the 24/7 focus of the late Dr. Moretti's colleagues at Nellis, they were able to figure things out.

"Moretti had indeed hidden the centerpiece of the time travel equipment in her chest, in the casing of a modern-day pacemaker," Petty explained. "The functional one on her left side had been there for years. The new one, not connected to her heart, was implanted on her right side by a medical team working at Nellis under the guise of R&D. The doctor's antiquated cell phone, the one that wouldn't take pictures, was actually the computer for the program."

The impatient expression on Brooks' face had turned into one of astonishment. "But this is outrageous! You ignored my direct orders to—"

"Quiet, General," the President said in a tone that carried weight. "You need to hear this. Go on, Colonel."

Petty looked more than a little uneasy under Brooks' glare but continued his story. "Everything that was needed to activate the pulses, set the time, date, and travel coordinates, and act as a homing beacon to bring a team home, was in that phone. A brilliant team working on top-secret programs for the government was able to connect all of the dots and get the program going. They called it 'The Moretti' in honor of their fallen friend. They were honored to help. I asked them to run the same tests we'd used to make sure everything was in order. First, they moved animals around, then the T2 team. In little time, they were ready to go. Then, all we needed was the destination. Moretti must have deleted the last mission from the phone when Scott and the others charged into the prep room that night."

"This is ridiculous, Stew…Mr. President," Brooks protested, his face flushed a bright red.

Stewart raised his voice, "General, you need to sit there and listen. When he's done you'll have your chance to defend yourself!"

Petty continued, "We asked ourselves: Where did they go? Why weren't they able to return as they always had?"

Stewart took over from there. "It was actually pretty simple to figure out at that point. Michelle Jackson was on her deathbed. We had given these Marines the ability to travel back in time and return. The ancient wardrobe they used to visit the Coliseum was gone. We knew they didn't go back to Italy. The Major and his team, which included Michelle's brother, decided to go after a miracle worker. There was only one person I could think of, the same one Jackson must have thought of, who could perform such a miracle." He took a deep breath, feeling anew the amazement of what he was about to say. "Yes, it does sound outrageous. To anyone reading our report, it will seem impossible. But it happened."

Brooks snarled, "You can't mean Jesus Christ. The idiots thought they could actually—"

"They didn't just think they could do it. They did it. And we, that is the team Petty put together, figured out where and when JJ's team would have attempted to meet up with the man. After all, Moretti's last words were "they went to the garden." We may never know if the miracle that cured JJ's wife was a result of their trip back in time. All I can say is that this woman, who was at death's door, is now healthy."

Petty looked at Brooks and cleared his throat before attempting to speak again. Stewart could tell by the glazed look of the man's eyes that he was deeply moved by the tale he was telling. Petty said, "It took an incredible number of attempts, but T2 kept going back to the Garden of Gethsemane on various days, starting a few days before Christ was taken prisoner there in 33 AD. Then they followed the recovery protocol. On their third mission, they came across an olive tree that had a small "SF" carved into its trunk, and we knew they'd found the right place. *Semper fi.* Leave it to a Marine to leave a calling card only another Marine would understand. Many missions later, there they all were. Ten relieved Marines and two scared goats, standing on the hillside where Christ once walked."

While Petty continued the briefing to an increasingly uncomfortable looking General Brooks, President Stewart thought back to earlier that day as he stood and watched Buchanan lay out the travel mat a thousand feet below, in a White House security bunker. He and Petty had watched in awe as Buchanan and T2 literally disappeared into thin air. They'd waited anxiously as the minutes ticked by, unable to communicate with them, or know what they had or hadn't found.

When the four members of T1 followed by T2 flashed back into the bunker, the President felt a surge of joy and relief. "Thank you," he'd whispered. "Thank you, God." His Marines were finally home.

He immediately embraced JJ, the young man who had been like a second son to him. Only after he'd released JJ and wiped the tears from his eyes did he take in the two goats…and realize that two of T1 hadn't made it home. He told himself that there would be time, later, for him to find out why and to mourn their loss.

JJ and Wilson wanted to head straight for Michelle, but Petty told them she had moved away.

"Michelle's doing great. She's fully recovered," Stewart reassured the two men. "The doctors all said it was a miracle. I suppose you know that better than anyone."

"We'll connect you once she answers her phone," Petty said. "We started trying the moment you arrived. Once we get you checked out and deal with something a few flights up, we'll have you on a plane headed her way."

Jackson and Wilson bear hugged each other, tears of joy running down their faces.

Sharif, still looking stunned to be back home, muttered, "Thank God."

White patted Sharif on the back then pulled Wilson to her and wrapped her arms around him.

As they all stood back, smiling and laughing, Wilson looked at JJ. "She must have gone back to Montana to be with Mom."

Petty was already shaking his head. He and Stewart knew that her mother had died recently, but decided to leave that news for later. For now, they'd agreed to give them only good news.

"Israel," Petty said. "She's in Jerusalem looking for the two of you. General Stewart told her that you had gone to Israel on a mission to save someone, and she wanted to go there, too. She thought she might feel closer to you there. I'll tell you more about that later. Suffice it to say, she was doing fine last we heard from her."

Stewart had shaken the hand of every man and woman on the two teams. He told them how proud he was of each and every one of them. On JJ's order they snapped to attention and saluted their new president. He returned the salute and then suggested they get cleaned up so he could include T1 in something special upstairs in the oval office. "Oh, and T2. You will like what I have in store for you six. Just give me a few weeks to figure out where the hell everything is in this place and then we'll have a meeting to discuss what's next."

After the medical team gave them all the AOK, everyone inhaled pizzas and sodas while Petty brought the team up to speed on what was going on in the world—and all that had transpired with Brooks and Scott while they were gone. CNN was on the televisions in the bunker. The four time travelers had been laser focused on the replay of the Stewart Inauguration, from just twenty-four hours earlier.

Petty explained how they were betrayed and abandoned, but somehow JJ and Wilson couldn't stop smiling at each other and their team. They were home! For the moment, nothing could spoil this feeling of returning to their lives.

17

In the Oval Office, Stewart looked up out of his thoughts of the reunion celebrations when he sensed Petty had finished talking. He focused pointedly on General Brooks then walked over to his desk and pushed the intercom button. "Will you show our guests in, please."

The door from the President's study opened and, escorted by three Marine guards, in walked Jackson, Wilson, Sharif, and White.

Brooks gasped. The expression on his face said it all: *They're supposed to be dead!*

Stewart smiled at the four. Their faces had aged and their plight had worn on them emotionally, but they were home safe, which was all that mattered.

After AGAIN exchanging salutes and handshakes with their new President, it was time to get down to the business at hand. Petty added one last piece to the puzzle. "You might recall Doctor Moretti's last words. I said it sounded like she said 'shot' or 'hot.' Well, it didn't take long to figure out what she meant. We now know who *shut* down the operation and sent T1 adrift."

The door opened one more time, and Major Scott was then brought into the Oval Office by the five Marines from T2. He seemed stunned by being in the most famous room in the White House. But on realizing that among those present were four members of the lost T1, his eyes widened.

Scott only missed a beat before putting on a display of excitement. But his forced smile faltered at the look on Brooks' face. Stewart's investigators had learned that Scott, with the help of and two of his buddies, had snuck up on Moretti and scared the old woman, causing her heart attack.

Stewart could no longer contain his contempt for the two guilty parties. "All bets are off, General Brooks. All deals are dissolved," Stewart growled. "You son of a bitch, you lied to me. Lied while sitting in my den with a glass of eighteen-year-old scotch in your hand, while these four were left stranded in the desert! Two of their team died over there! We don't abandon our own, General. We don't leave people behind!" Stewart took a step toward Brooks. "And then you lied to me about going back to find them. You intentionally left them there and made it impossible, or so you thought, for anyone to go looking for them."

"Stew," Brooks began, throwing a glare in Petty's direction. "We need to talk about this. There's been some sort of misunderstanding."

Before he could say another word, Petty gestured to the Marines, who stepped forward with handcuffs and gags in hand.

Wilson whispered to JJ, "Bet it's not the first time someone's used them in here." Wilson and Sharif found it amusing, but JJ was too intent on how this was going to end.

Stewart looked at Scott, "You are just as guilty as he is.

Treasonous sons of bitches. I'm done with the both of you. If you wish, you may walk out of here, under guard, with your mouths shut—and take your punishment like men. If not, I'll have you bound and gagged. Your choice."

Brooks and Scott's eyes opened wide. The mention of treason meant only one thing—if found guilty they might be put to death for their actions. But who was to say there would even be a trial? Stewart was now the supreme commander of the military, the intelligence agencies, and the President. He could do just about anything he wanted, officially or covertly.

"Once I learned the truth of what you'd done, I began to consider fair punishment for your actions. Since you have so much experience with time travel, we could send you somewhere special, somewhere with historical significance, like those our team went on. Maybe we'd send you to Hiroshima so you could witness Little Boy go off above you, to the top of the World Trade Center just before the first plane hit. Or to another, very distant planet. I hear Mars is nice this time of year."

"Mr. President," JJ said, "this sounds like vengeance. Someone very special once told me that wasn't our job. It was his alone."

Stewart looked directly into JJ's eyes. This was something they needed to talk about. And they would, at a later date. He paused briefly then softened his tone. "This isn't vengeance, son. This is justice. Don't confuse the two."

Turning to the captives, he stated, "They're headed to Guantanamo. They'll look good in those orange jump suits. The Marines looking after them will be sure they have the same comforts of home your team had while you were stranded. I am going to leave them there for the same amount of time they left you adrift."

"But their families," JJ began, "how will you explain to them—"

"Turns out they don't have any. Believe me, they won't be missed. And no one will look for them, which seems ironically fitting, I think you'll agree. As far as anyone's concerned they will be working on special, top-secret assignments overseas. Once they return to society, they will be dishonorably discharged for violating their duty. And, thanks to their clearance levels and the secrecy oath, they won't be able to tell anyone a damn thing."

JJ gave his mentor a nod of agreement. Neither Brooks nor Scott said a thing.

"Good," said Stewart. "Now, I think there's somewhere else you'd all like to be and I've got to get to work. Apparently, I've got a country to run. I'll have the four of you all back here at a later date to discuss what I have in mind for you, if you are interested in continuing to serve your country. Colonel Petty here is going to be nominated to be my Secretary of Defense today. I'm sure that, between the two of us, we can find something fun for you four to do.

"Thank you, Mr. President," JJ said, snapping him a salute.

"Meanwhile, we have fast jets waiting over at Andrews. One's headed for Cuba, and the other will take you, JJ and Wilson, to Israel."

Petty turned to White and Sharif. "Where do you two want to go? Are you sure there's nobody you want us to get on the phone for you?"

"No sir, I want to go to Jerusalem with the Major," White said. "If that's okay with you, JJ?"

"Not without me, boss," Sharif added with a smile. "I wouldn't miss this reunion for the world. I haven't talked to my parents since before I joined the Marines. We didn't part on the best of terms. I guess it's time for me to make peace with them, but that can wait a little while longer. I want to see this miracle for myself."

Petty wrote something in the folder he was holding. "Fine, the four of you can leave as soon as you're ready. I'll notify the pilot." He smiled. "Unless you want to use your pulse devices to get there quicker?"

Without hesitation, all four of them shook their heads no. Stewart suspected they could use the time in the air to decompress and begin the process of fitting back into the modern world.

"Can you imagine her walking around the Garden?" Wilson asked.

JJ grinned. "Not without me. The sooner we get there, the better."

The Marine Guard led Brooks and Scott from the Oval Office and into the President's private study. The Secret Service detail, under the leadership of veteran agent Jason Hill, and fully supportive of this new President, intended to accommodate his Marines. They'd stand back and let Stewart take out his trash before he got down to business. There was a new sheriff in town, an impressive Marine President, and Hill would acquiesce until much bigger lines were crossed.

A small elevator took them four levels below to a

pedestrian tunnel that led to the garage under the Old Executive Office Building. From there it would be a short ride to Andrews.

JJ remained with his team, President Stewart, and Petty in the Oval Office. Wilson and White were standing in front of the fireplace, admiring the portrait of George Washington that hung over it. "Pretty good job, don't ya think?" White said. Wilson just smiled and winked at JJ.

Petty seemed totally absorbed in Sharif's description of their time in Israel. He patted Sharif on the shoulder. "I can only imagine what it must have been like. After you've all had a chance to reintegrate and fully decompress from all that has happened to, I'll want to hear every word of your adventures."

JJ moved over to stand beside the President at his desk.

"Someday," Stewart said, "you could be the man behind this desk, if you wanted it, JJ. You've been on a fast track for some time. I know your parents would be proud of you. Just like I am, young man. Mrs. Stewart will be overjoyed to see you. Don't know if anyone has told you yet, but she moved back home after I retired and hung up the uniform. She's upstairs trying to figure out where everything goes."

"She'll make an amazing First Lady, sir," JJ said, "she's an extraordinary woman."

"Indeed." Stewart thought for a moment. "Neither one of us will ever get over our loss, but you are like a second son to the both of us and…" Tears welled up in his eyes. "I'm just thrilled to see you back in one piece."

JJ drew a deep breath and felt a long-delayed warmth spread through him. To be home after being so long away—he savored this feeling. "You can't be any more thrilled than

I am. And thank you, sir. But now, all I want is to get on that bird, have a few celebratory beers on the way, and find Michelle."

"Understood."

JJ shuffled his feet, considering his next words. "Mr. President, you'll be in here for eight years, so we have plenty of time to figure out what I want to do." He hesitated. "But as to Brooks and Scott—are you sure you've finished dealing with them? Army Generals don't just disappear."

Stewart coughed on a laugh. "JJ, don't you worry about a damn thing. Petty's on top of that. If the press comes snooping around, all they'll discover is the information we've planted about their secret assignments at an unknown destination—and then a dead end. By now, they'll have signed their retirement papers which will be filed on their release from Guantanamo."

A few minutes later, the Marine Guards returned to escort the team to the Suburbans waiting down below. Everyone snapped to attention, saluting their new President.

In the now quiet Oval Office, Stewart looked to Petty. Time to get to work. The first order of business would be to place calls of condolence to the Abrams and Jones' families.

The flight to Israel would take just under eleven hours. The team boarded the small Bombardier luxury jet maintained by the Department of State and flew in comfort. The plane would set down in the diplomatic landing zone at Tel Aviv's Ben Gurion airport.

"Man, this sure beats a C-130," JJ said to his team with a cold beer in hand.

"Yeah, well, Magic Carpet rides are faster but I'll settle for this tin can tonight," White joked.

On the plane none of them felt able to sleep or eat. Too much meat lover's pizza and soda after so many years of simpler foods—bread, fish, cheese, water, and wine. However, they were soon on their way to cleaning out the galley of every can of beer and bottle of water on board. The anticipation of being back in the modern world and, especially for JJ and Wilson, finding their girl, had them fully charged.

"God, I can't believe she was out there taking care of the ranch all by herself," Wilson remarked. "That's a hell of a lot of work for one person."

JJ laughed, "Well, we are talking about your sister. There's not much she can't do."

Sharif leaned in, "I know they gave us a ton of info this morning but did Petty really say Bunker chased a grizzly bear away from the ranch?"

White laughed. "You know how protective a female can be, especially if she's pissed off."

"How do you want to play it, JJ," Wilson asked. "Once we find Michelle."

"Let's show up on one of her tours and surprise the living hell out of her," JJ suggested.

"Oh no!" Sharif scolded. "You aren't going to scare her to death, not after what she's been through."

"I like the tour idea, JJ," White said. "It's right out of the movies."

"That's the plan then," JJ decided. "Don't worry, Sharif. She'll love it."

They would call the tour agency Michelle had told Stewart about when he'd last spoken with her over the phone. She had used the agency to orient herself to the city, and then took employment with them.

As soon as they got into the city, they would go to one of the agency's offices and ask to be booked on one of her tours.

The only other passenger on the flight was a State Department analyst, seated at the back of the plane and on his way to Israel to give the Ambassador a security update.

"Dude, you're CIA, aren't you?" White joked with him as she left the bathroom. She only got a wink in response. "Do all the cloak and dagger bullshit and see the world, right? Damn, wish I could get me some of that."

The analyst smiled politely. "Giblin, State Department. Nice to meet you."

"Do I know you?" she asked but he plugged in his earbuds and continued reading the paperwork on the minidesk in front of him. She returned to her seat up front with the rest of the team.

"That's it. Riding around in private jets all over the world. I'm joining the CIA, if Stewart offers me a spot. What about the rest of you? What kind of job do you want?"

Sharif went first. "I got a kick out of the BOTM program. If they give it the green light to go after terrorists, I'm in. No questions asked."

Wilson smiled. "I might just ask for a diplomatic job. I could see myself sitting in some air-conditioned office in the embassy in Rome. I loved it when we were there in modern-day on leave and loved it way back when." Wilson considered what he'd just said.

The others looked at him and laughed. No way would this warrior sit behind a desk for long.

"What about you, JJ? You think Michelle's going to let you leave the ranch once she gets you back there?"

JJ had been listening, but he didn't know how to answer. The weight of everything that had happened since the program started was finally hitting him. What they'd seen, who they'd met. "I think I'll ask if they'll send me and Michelle back to Hawaii, maybe around 1500. Nothing but coconuts, palm trees, and beaches."

White laughed. "And pirates."

"Didn't I mention that I'm taking special gear with me? Nothing like a Gatlin gun and a case of grenades to chill out a boat load of bad guys."

Everyone laughed and then sat back to gaze out the jet's windows at the stars and be alone in their thoughts.

Before long the sun was rising on the horizon and the landing gear down. After a quick trip through Customs, two U.S. Marines greeted them from the Quick Reaction Force at the embassy in Tel Aviv. They were dressed in plain clothes but heavily armed, holstered handguns and ammo clips under their un-tucked shirts. Their vehicle was equipped with anything and everything needed to protect a VIP or confront a hostile force. They had orders to take their guests anywhere they wanted to go.

As they climbed into the white Suburban bearing diplomatic plates, Sharif laughed and hopped into the very back before anyone had a chance to suggest it.

"I know, I know!" he said. "Damn, I've been in a lot of these but this one is a real war wagon. You guys have added a lot of weapon and comms upgrades in the last few years." The U.S. Embassy was a twenty-minute drive west toward the Mediterranean. Jerusalem, and the U.S. Consulate there, was forty minutes to the east.

"East," JJ and Wilson said at the same time.

"We'll have you there in thirty minutes," the driver assured them.

Stewart and Petty had both tried to reach Michelle by phone, but only connected to her voicemail. JJ tried Michelle's cell and was thrilled to hear her voice again, even if it was just her recorded message. White called the tour office where Michelle worked.

"Michelle Jackson? Yes, she works here," the woman responded. "She was supposed to give a tour today to a couple from Canada. They called earlier looking for her, but I haven't heard back. She's usually on time. I don't know what's holding her up."

White looked frustrated. "Her office seems to have lost track of her," she reported to JJ, then returned to her call. The woman was still talking: "We've tried calling her mobile but there is no answer. Are you sure she's okay?"

The office worker assured her that Michelle should be fine. "She had her bag stolen yesterday in the market. They got her phone, her credit cards, ID—everything—and it will take some time for her to replace it all. If you are in Old City now you should go to the Church of the Holy Sepulcher. If they are following the normal stops she will be there or the Garden. That would be her next stop on the tour. Sometimes if the crowds are too large it adds a lot of time. Do you know the area?" White killed the call, passed along what she'd learned to JJ and Wilson, and told the driver where to go.

The Garden of Gethsemane – Modern Day

"She's going to have to show up here at some point," JJ said. Never the less, he was beginning to worry. "Man, a lot of this place looks the same, but other things are so different. Some of these trees must have stood here dating back to 1000 A.D. Whenever the raiding armies invaded the area they burned everything to the ground but these roots just kept coming back. There's a damn good chance these roots were here the first time we visited."

Wilson looked around at the buildups of houses and mosques on the nearby hills. "I remember standing on this hill; it feels the same. I remember the lantern and candle light from the homes."

White added softly, "Reminds me of Abrams and Jones."

JJ took a step back and observed what remained of his handpicked team. "With everything we've been through, there's one thing I wish I had gotten out of the Doc. I asked her at least ten times what drove her to build the device in the first place, but she always smiled and said 'someday.' I guess that day will never come."

Wilson laughed and patted his brother-in-law on the shoulder. "Guess I got the scoop on ya, JJ. One night, we were sitting around talking about travel and movies, and I asked her the same question. Without blinking she told me her mother had died in childbirth and, although her father had shown her photos of her, she'd always wanted to see her face, to see her in person. That was a bond we shared that I never talked about. She wanted it that way. I pushed her to let us take her on the ride, but she said no. In the end, she wanted to leave things as they were. She felt that her opportunity to take the trip had come too late."

They considered Wilson's story about their lost comrade. There was nothing more to say.

Sharif said wistfully, "I could stay here forever now that I know we'd at least have running water and hot showers."

"Speaking of that, I have to hit the head," JJ said. "That airport coffee was something else. Hang loose and I'll be right back." He walked away toward the entry gate. Surely there would be a public toilet somewhere around there.

Minutes later, Wilson spotted a familiar face among the crowd. The woman was walking up the hillside followed by a young couple. "Holy Shit, there she is!" he yelled to White and Sharif.

They were beside themselves with joy and started running toward her. In that region, when people suddenly began running, it could scare people but Michelle recognized the threesome. She rushed toward them, shouting, "Tommy, Tommy!" but then stopped when she saw that JJ wasn't with his team. The joy fled from her eyes, and her expression mirrored her shock. She dropped to the ground.

White understood instantly. "Michelle, he's okay. He's okay! JJ will be here in a few minutes."

Wilson reached his sister, scooped her up off the ground and hugged her, tears of joy running down his face.

"I can't believe you are here!" Michelle gasped. "I just… can't. Oh, God, I thought I'd never see any of you again."

Michelle and the three T1 team members laughed, cried, and talked over each other while the Canadian couple snapped pictures of their reunion. Then Michelle heard a familiar voice shouting her name.

"Michelle, Michelle!" JJ barreled up the hillside and toward her at a full run. She broke free of the group and ran to him. She tripped over an olive tree root and fell hard to the ground. JJ quickly helped her up, his expression a mixture of happiness and concern. "Are you all right?"

"Fine! Oh my God, I'm more than fine. JJ, you're here! You're here!" she cried.

Wilson reached them and they formed a tight ring.

"We were here all along!" he whispered with a grin.

18

It had been a week since the team reunited with Michelle. Their days were full, from sunrise to well past the beautiful Mediterranean sunsets as they celebrated her good health and their return to the modern world. They also spent time remembering the two who were left behind.

Michelle understood their sorrow, but she would never learn the details of the loss and all that JJ and Tommy had been through. Wilson and Michelle mourned the loss of their mother as Michelle told of her final days. She also shared stories of her life on the ranch with only Bunker to keep her company. Slowly, she began to realize that the person her husband and her brother had set out to save three years ago was, indeed, her. How that could possibly be true, she had no idea. But hadn't the doctors called her recovery a miracle?

"Bottles!" Sharif held his bottle of beer high. "What I would have given for a friggin' bottle of anything and a Whopper with cheese." They laughed.

Wilson finished his beer. "If I never taste bread, wine, or fish again, I'll die happy."

The Marines raised their drinks and toasted that thought.

"Sharif, I'm not sure we're going to know what to do around here without ya," White said sadly. "We've been inseparable for so long. You were starting to grow on me."

Sharif looked around at the four seated with him. "It's time for me to go home. I had to come here to see this healthy young lady and to join the reunion, but it's been a week now. I've gotten used to this modern world again. I'm need to return to my family. The last time we spoke didn't end very well. I want to enjoy some home cooking and catch up on everything that I've missed. I need to go see my mother.

Sharif laughed. "Yeah, they call this acclimation or reintegration, I think. I can't wait to get back to Montana and acclimate myself with some Scotch and the biggest piece of prime rib I can find."

"Bison. I thought you'd want a bison burger, Tommy," JJ responded.

White straightened suddenly. "Excuse me, Captain Wilson, sir, but we're going east to Mykonos and Santorini, before your butt's headed anywhere else. You promised!"

Michelle looked at her brother with surprise, a smile spreading from cheek to cheek.

"She's right, sir, you promised," Sharif said.

"Okay, okay, I did promise. The Embassy car is picking up Sharif in the morning. We can ride over to the airport to check out commercial flights. All we need to do is pick up our new passports at the Embassy, and we can go wherever you want. Remember, Petty said the Marines are buying!"

White's smile rivaled Michelle's. "We can leave these two lovebirds alone and we'll go do our thing."

Michelle and JJ said their goodnights and left the dinner party before anyone could order another round of drinks, forcing them to stay any longer. The rest of the group continued to celebrate clean clothes, ice, electricity, hot water, music, and the sea of stars above. This would be their last night together, possibly forever.

The next day, after a quick buffet breakfast and goodbyes filled with tears, smiles, and hugs—Sharif, Wilson, and White left the hotel in the same vehicle they'd arrived in, accompanied by two plain clothes U.S. Marines.

"Tommy," Michelle said before the car started away, "the only thing I ask is that you're back at the ranch by Christmas. Christy and Omar, you are both welcome, as long as you like lots of snow and thirty below." She grinned at them. "I can tell you right now, if you do show up, you're getting a puppy for a present."

Sharif laughed. "You can count on me showing up—despite that threat."

JJ stepped back and pulled Michelle away from the car so they could leave. He had something special planned for his girl that day. It has been many years since he walked through the Old City, but he remembered it well. He had toured the area many times with his friend and fellow Marine, Ben Abrams, back when they were stationed in Tel Aviv. As he approached the massive Jaffa Gate, one of many that lead to the walled Old City, he looked out over the hillside and thought about his friend. How he had died there so many years ago. The pain of leaving him there, although they'd had no choice, would stay with JJ forever.

Michelle reached for his hand, knowing that look on his face. Perhaps, someday, her husband would tell her more. But, for now, she held his hand tight until he came back to her.

"Let's go," he said at last.

Through the opening in the massive stone walls, they entered a large open space. The market, full of shops and tabletop vendors, was to the left. Stone walks and the moat that had protected the Tower of David were to the right. Merchants called to them to come inside and see their offerings. Gold and silver religious medals and chains, rosary beads, holy water, holy oil, statues, pieces of stone—relics from the Old City—maps, tea, water, and prayer rugs. JJ became annoyed by the incessant calls from the vendors, but stopped to look at one prayer rug in particular.

"It reminds me of a flying carpet that Abrams used to have," he told Michelle with a smile. His focus returned, and he was back to the mission at hand.

Michelle gave him a curious look but didn't ask for an explanation. He sensed she'd want to learn much more but would wait until they were back home.

He had a keen sense of direction and knew the way from taking a quick look at a map in the lobby before they left. She had been here recently, sometimes two to three times each day, taking tourists through the areas filled with street vendors and holy sites. But now he led her as if he were the guide.

"There's one spot I have to go to before we head home. And you need to be right there beside me when I do."

"All right."

The narrow streets were crowded with merchants and tourists. They turned to the left through the Daniel Street market, then left again onto Ha-Notsrim Street. Before long there it was, The Church of the Holy Sepulcher. It was still early in the day, so the crowds were relatively small. JJ stood still, looking at the edifice for at least five minutes before leading Michelle through the massive wooden doors.

"JJ, how long has it been since you were last here?" she asked.

He didn't respond, his thoughts elsewhere. Eventually, they moved on. He found himself standing in front of the Edicule. Inside was the Chapel of the Angel, and beyond that, a very sacred place. The line moved quickly and quietly, passing the many I-beams that supported the walls of what looked like a church within a church. A monk in black robes waved them inside. They ducked their heads and stepped into the innermost part of the structure. There, on the right, was the marble bench that covered the place where Christ's body once lay.

JJ knelt down as Michelle made the sign of the cross and knelt beside him. They prayed until one of the monks asked them to keep moving, making space for others to experience this holy place.

JJ thought about everything he had been through since that night back at Andrews when he realized what he had to do. He had met the Son of God, who had saved his wife, and been laid to rest on this very spot almost 2,000 years ago. He also couldn't forget the lives that were lost under his command.

Michelle tugged at him to get moving. He stood up, tears running down his face. "Thank You, Jesus." He drew a shuddering breath. "Please forgive me, Lord. Please forgive us."

Michelle made the sign of the cross again. "Thank you, Jesus for bringing them back to me," she whispered as they turned to leave.

Once outside the Edicule they stood apart from the

crowd, holding each other, soaking in the aura of the holy place. They were finally together and at peace.

They didn't talk much as they walked away and past the vendors, through the gate, and up the sloping sidewalk toward their hotel.

Stopping abruptly, JJ turned to face Michelle. "What do you think about adopting a baby once we get home?"

She screamed and jumped into his arms. People smiled and walked around them on the busy sidewalk. Michelle didn't need to say anything. It was what she had always wanted. They held hands and smiled at each other until they reached the hotel lobby. There seemed to be more than the usual activity in the hotel bar. People crowded around two televisions. JJ looked up at the nearest screen. BBC News flashed a breaking headline across the screen: "Terrorist Attack on American President's Motorcade."

JJ stared, stunned. He turned to the closest group of people who had been there when he and Michelle arrived. "Was he hurt?"

"I don't think anyone knows yet," a woman said.

JJ and Michelle rushed out to catch a cab to the U.S. Consulate. He insisted on checking the driver's license so he'd know who was at the wheel this time. JJ asked the cabbie to drop them a block away so they could walk up rather than approach in a speeding vehicle.

Security was obviously elevated. The formal dress Marines who customarily stood at the gates were now accompanied by Marines in riot helmets and fatigues, brandishing the latest in hand-held weaponry. JJ saw Wilson and White had already arrived at the facility and were inside the gate. When they saw JJ and Michelle, they were able to get them cleared quickly and escorted inside.

"Any news?" Michelle asked, hopefully.

"Nada," Wilson responded. "I was able to get Colonel Petty on a secure phone, and he said the Secret Service has an intel blackout in effect. Nobody is saying anything right now, whether they're in the know or not. He said he understands how close you and the President are and we have clearance to get on a State Department jet in a few hours to head back to Andrews."

JJ couldn't wrap his mind around the attack—so soon after Stewart's inauguration. He desperately wanted to get back to DC.

Twenty minutes later, word came that CNN's feed had died. The BBC channel broadcasting from London reported, live, that power grids in New York City and Washington, DC may have been attacked. Speculation was that Russian hackers were somehow interfering with broadcasts. Meanwhile, the President's health and whereabouts were unknown. Confusing reports had reached London, but the one thing that was clear was—something was very wrong on the East Coast of the United States. Consulate staffers quickly confirmed the information, although details were nonexistent.

The Ambassador, who had traveled to Jerusalem from Tel Aviv earlier in the day for meetings, had been moved to a bunker within the complex. Before long, Michelle and other non-essentials would be escorted to another room for their own safety. JJ, Wilson, and White were issued holstered.45 caliber side arms, MK 18 assault rifles, additional ammo magazines, and radios with earplugs.

Michelle looked at JJ. "I'm scared. This sounds bad,

really bad." She gripped his hand. "Let me stay here with you!" she begged. "You know I'm a damn good shot!"

"No. They won't allow it, and I want you in a safe place." He gave her a quick hug.

She gave her brother a hasty embrace then followed the guards sent to round up the civilians. "Don't get lost on me again, guys?" she called back at them.

But their attention was already fixed on preparing to defend the consulate. The Quick Response Team leader directed JJ, Wilson, and White to the emergency exit and stairway on the left side of the lobby. They'd guard that post and await orders.

"And so, it continues, the eternal battle of good against evil," JJ murmured.

"Oorah," his fellow Marines chorused. It's all he needed to hear.

"Son of a bitch," White whispered.

JJ looked at her. "What?"

"I saw someone in the group being led down to the safe rooms. I knew I'd seen that bastard before."

Wilson looked at JJ.

"Who?" JJ asked.

"That CIA dude from the jet. He said he was State Department, but I busted on him. I knew I had seen his face before. He was at the bar that night we took Doc Moretti out for her birthday. That prick isn't CIA or State, he's Army, or at least he was."

JJ's mind raced. *There's an Army prick locked in a secure bunker with my wife three levels below us.* He looked at Wilson. "What the fuck!"

19

THE MASSIVE EXPLOSION that erupted from beneath the street threw the President's limousine into a series of rolls. Before Stewart lost consciousness he knew they had just been struck by an IED. Lead Agent Jason Hill and the rest of the agents jumped from their vehicles, guns drawn, and assumed the 360-degree protective posture. They'd drilled so often for just such a moment that every move was instinctive. The second and third massive Cadillac limousines stopped on either side of the crater the explosion left in the street.

Rapid Response agents in military fatigues snapped into action. Rooftop hatches popped open on the black Suburbans in the motorcade. Dillon Aero machine gun turrets rose from within the vehicles. The high-volume, Gatling-style machine guns could be operated from inside the armored vehicles or, in the event the operative was disabled, aimed and fired remotely from the Secret Service emergency center. Any unwanted threat—be it person, vehicle, aircraft or drones—moving toward the President or the security perimeter would be shredded in an instant.

The Beast, the President's heavily armored limousine,

lay on its side. The roof was leaning against the front entrance of a bank. Sirens screamed and people shouted for help. Smoke and fine debris in the air made the area look like a war zone.

President Stewart and his Chief of Staff lay unconscious inside the car. Neither had been wearing a seat belt and both were thrown around the inside the airtight compartment. The driver and the agent who rode shotgun were strapped in. Shaken but conscious, they operated communication and vehicle security measures from their compartment up front.

Agent Hill, assigned to the President's vehicle, had to make quick decisions. Extensive, repetitive training he and the other agents had gone through allowed him to assess the situation and move. "We need to make sure there are no secondary explosives, shooters, or chemical agents in the area," he shouted at the driver. "But, damn it, first priority—we get the President out of this heap and into another limo STAT!"

Time was of the essence. Seeing everyone was in place, including the Gatling gun operators, Hill activated an electronic switch under the Beast. A two-foot square escape hatch flipped open. Another popped open under the floorboard of the driver's compartment, allowing the two agents to emerge and help others with the rescue.

They pulled the President's body from the Beast, placing him in a second armored limo. Before the vehicle's doors had closed, an agent with trauma training began attending to Stewart.

"GW?" the new driver shouted at Hill over his communication piece. George Washington Hospital.

"No. Plan B. This is no lone wolf scenario." Hill forced his tangled thoughts to unknot long enough to communicate next steps to the driver. "GW might be a target. There might even be an IED planted near their ER for all we know." He sucked in a ragged breath. "EOB. And don't stop for anything or anyone!" As the surviving vehicles in the motorcade raced toward the Executive Office Building and away from the scene, the carnage they left behind became obvious.

Almost instantly, cellphone videos were circulating over the Internet. They showed the Presidential limousine flipping over and over, engulfed in a flash of flame, concrete and asphalt flying in all directions.

Eyewitnesses to the attack called local television stations and network news offices. "It was horrible," a tourist from New Jersey said over the phone to a news anchor on live television. "We were waving at the President. We could see him as his car passed us. And then, just as it turned the corner, a huge explosion knocked all of us to the ground." Other callers reported multiple dead and wounded.

The Executive Office Building and Treasury Building served as bookends to the White House complex. The White House had below-ground bunkers and was secure against attack, but those in charge of POTUS's safety had assumed that anyone wishing harm to the President would take aim at 1600 Pennsylvania Avenue.

Taking the President underground through the EOB might make it look as though he was headed to the Oval Office, or a Presidential bunker hundreds of feet below it, which was what Agent Hill counted on. Located deep under the EOB was everything needed to run the country, fight a war, survive for months, and save a critically injured person, including a top military trauma team.

People across the country and around the world watched and listened to those news feeds still functioning on their phones, computers, and televisions—hoping to hear reassuring news about their president. Across the country, many gathered in churches, synagogues, and mosques. Most disconcerting was the fact that the identity of the terrorists who had attacked the President was unknown. Because no one knew what might happen next, gun and ammo sales skyrocketed, and stores sold out of everything.

The media was told only that the President and Vice President had been taken to secure locations. There was no mention of Stewart's condition. Rumors circulated that North Korea, Russia, or China could be planning more attacks. There was an immediate run on banks, food stores, gas stations, and pharmacies—emptying them of anything of value. The Joint Chiefs of Staff assessed all possible threats. The biggest concern was that other terrorist groups, or countries considered enemies of the United States, would realize the country was at a vulnerable moment. If ever there was an opportunity to make a big move, this was it.

JJ, Wilson, and White remained at the U.S. Consulate in Jerusalem to help provide security for the facility and its American staff. The first night at the consulate, JJ realized that Michelle might again be at risk. Wilson and White wanted to head down to the bunker and place themselves between her and the man who had flown from the U.S. with them.

"This has to be more than a coincidence," Tommy Wilson argued.

"Giblin, if that's his name, could be another of Brook's moles," White said. "Maybe this attack has something to do with what President Stewart did to Brooks and Scott.

"Sounds unlikely," JJ said. Then again, if there had been a leak within the Oval Office that morning, either from the Secret Service or the Marine Guard… Something wasn't right and they needed to do something about it. "I think Michelle should be safe for now," he said. "If the stranger means her harm, he isn't going to make his move in a room full of witnesses. That is, unless he intends to harm everyone in there."

As soon as reinforcements arrived at the consulate and took over for the time travelers, all three headed down the steps to the bunker. It had been two hours since they saw the worried expression on Michelle's face. The "actor," as they had quickly come to call him, had been right behind her, his attitude confident, almost as if to communicate that he would look after her.

Through radio communication, JJ gave the Marines standing guard outside the bunker a heads up that only U.S. Marines were coming down and there was no reason for alarm. He briefed them on his concerns and warned them about Giblin being in there, not only with JJ's Michelle, but also with the U.S. Ambassador.

"Listen, I don't know who the son of a bitch is, but there's something not right. We believe he lied about his identity and we are totally unsure about his intentions. We'd like to walk in there as if everything is okay and, once he's contained, we escort him out and away from the Ambassador." The Marine in charge knew Jackson. They had trained together years before. Without hesitation, he gave JJ the thumbs up.

"Go get his ass!" one guard whispered to Wilson.

The door opened into a small meeting room with a large table surrounded by chairs. There was a couch with two easy chairs as bookends and a coffee table in between. The Ambassador and his two assistants were working the phones. JJ nodded to the lone Marine guard standing with them.

Discarded water bottles and wrappers from protein bars were stuffed in the overfilled refuse cans. Three flat-screen monitors displayed feeds from Sky News and the BBC in London with the third acting as a security monitor focused on the front gate of the consulate. There was still no news about the President or the situation in Washington and New York. JJ estimated over twenty men and women had been crowded into the room. They looked to the men and woman who had just entered, as if hoping to get an all-clear.

JJ found Michelle immediately, leaning against a wall at the far end of the conference table. Her concern quickly changed to relief on seeing him. Wilson and White moved through the crowd, looked for their target but, so far, hadn't seen him. The Ambassador ended his call and looked up at JJ.

"Nothing yet, Mr. Ambassador. No news, but everything is quiet up on the street."

Seconds later, the door to the restroom opened and out walked their actor.

"Hands up!" JJ shouted. He pointed his assault rifle directly at the man's chest.

Wilson and White also had the man in their sights and approached him slowly from opposite sides of the room. Everyone was startled and seemed confused as to what was happening.

"It's okay, Major Jackson. I'm here on Colonel Petty's orders. I can tell you more once we can talk privately."

JJ was surprised to hear Petty's name, but didn't let down his guard.

"What's going on?" the ambassador asked.

"SOP, Mr. Ambassador, something's not right here so we're going to check this guy out," Jackson responded.

As Wilson passed Michelle, he put his left hand on her shoulder. "Everything's okay, Sis. We just need to figure out who the hell he is. Sit tight and we'll be right back."

With his hands up, the stranger walked around the table and out the door.

JJ's gaze never left the man as he backed out of the room, the rest of the team following closely behind. Michelle stayed seated. Before today she had never seen her brother or her husband in action. She had only heard stories and imagined what they might look like at work, based on movies and TV shows about Marines, Seals, and Rangers. JJ had only one question, was this actor friend or foe?

Closing the bunker door behind them, the Marine consulate security force remained in place as JJ continued to back down the hallway toward the stairs. "Frisk him," he ordered. White slammed the actor against the wall, arms straight up, legs spread. She pulled his identification from his jacket pocket and tossed it to JJ. Wilson's rifle sight never left the actor's head.

"Army Captain Kyle Morrison," JJ read aloud.

White completed her pat down and turned the actor around to face them. "He's clean. Giblin, State Department my ass!"

The four were silent for a moment and then Morrison told his story. He knew Captain Scott and General Brooks back at the Pentagon. He was an Army Ranger and, after being severely injured during an operation in Iraq, he was transferred to Brooks' staff. The General liked being surrounded by heroes and knew having "Mo" there with him would be a good thing—like Jackson, Morrison was a strategic genius and that made him invaluable to the Army. While at the Pentagon he got to meet and interact with the Generals, Admirals, and support staffs of the Joint Chiefs and developed a strong bond with Colonel Petty. Both were from Brooklyn, and New Yorkers tend to stick together.

"So why the hell are you here, following my wife?" JJ asked.

Morrison smiled. "Petty made me a part of BOTM a long time ago. He assigned me to BOTM security—to keep an eye on everyone, to make sure nobody got himself, herself, or the program in trouble. I watched from a distance."

"Okay, *Morrison*," White said, "why the hell were you partying with Scott at the bar the night we were celebrating Moretti's birthday? And why did you say you were with State on the jet?"

"Any chance you can lower your weapons?" Morrison asked.

Nobody moved.

"Okay, you guys never got along with Scott and neither did I. Hell, I don't even think his mother liked him."

Wilson chuckled. "Yeah, he was a real asshole."

Morrison went on to explain that he and Scott had bumped heads at the Pentagon. Brooks had ordered them to go have some drinks and get to know each other better. "Petty had told me where you guys were headed, and the General told me to go out and try to make peace, so I figured I could kill two birds with one stone."

JJ studied Morrison's face as he spoke. Training had taught him how to read a liar's facial expressions, eye movements, breathing, and body language. His instincts told him this guy was telling the truth. Slowly, he lowered his rifle and asked again, "So why were you following us on the jet? The mission was over. We were on R&R."

Morrison seemed happy to answer. "I was at Colonel Petty's side the entire time you were missing. I asked him if I could come along covertly to make sure you got to Michelle and also to make sure you were all okay. You'd been away for such a long time—just throwing you on a jet and back into modern society, and particularly into the mess that is the Middle East, might put you at some risk either to yourselves or to the program."

Wilson and White lowered their weapons further and further with each sentence. "He approved my shadowing you. When the shit hit the fan upstairs, I thought it best to maintain my cover and keep an eye on Mrs. Jackson. Having an Army Ranger in plain clothes in the bunker couldn't hurt, right?"

"Just goes to show we can count on the Army when we

need to," JJ said with a smile. "Brooks and Scott were the only two bad Army apples I've ever encountered."

White laughed. "JJ, if you want to start swapping spit with Mo here, go for it, but Michelle's going to get jealous. We need to find out what's going on up above and what the hell's going on back home."

Everyone took a breath and relaxed for a few minutes. They shook hands with Morrison, thanked him for what he had done, and agreed it is time to get an update and develop a plan. "As far as anyone else is concerned I'm still with State, at least for now," Morrison said. "We have no idea how far this latest attack might spread or who's behind it."

The team led him back into the bunker.

"Everything's AOK folks," Wilson announced, nodding first to his sister and then to the Ambassador.

Morrison took a seat and focused on the monitors. Wilson sat down beside Michelle and gave her a big smile. Morrison seemed to be okay, but JJ could see that Tommy intended to add himself to the security inside the bunker, just in case.

JJ headed back up the stairs, with White following him. He wanted to get Petty on a secure phone ASAP to confirm Morrison's story. If he checked out, they'd embrace their newfound friend. If not, Wilson would see to it that he never left Jerusalem alive.

Four hours later, reinforcements arrived and the security detail was fully enhanced. After placing calls to Petty at the White House and to the Pentagon, they finally received a call back from one of his aides. The message was blunt: Yes, Mo was legit. And no, intel was not yet being released on the President.

The team picked up their belongings at the hotel and stopped by Michelle's apartment to grab whatever they could. There is a C-17 coming in from Qatar to pick up personnel heading for Andrews, and the Tel Aviv departure time was two hours out. The same security crew that had greeted them at the airport escorted them back to Ben Gurion for the long flight home.

The huge Air Force transport wasn't anything like the personal jet they'd come over on, but it was headed to the States and comfort was their last concern. Captain Morrison sat all the way in the back with White and talked about all the things that had happened in the world since T1 was stranded.

JJ turned to look at her. "I can't believe you are the one saying, forget Greece."

She laughed. "It's not going anywhere, boss. Somebody tried to kill the President and that's all I'm thinking about right now."

Wilson was looking forward to spending some alone time with White and seeing where their budding relationship might take them. But this was big, and they all wanted in on it.

On arrival at Andrews they quickly cleaned up and changed clothes before boarding a military vehicle that would take them to see The President. Security at the base was tighter than they had ever seen.

It had been a few years since they were there and, as they neared the exit gate, JJ pointed out their old apartment in the distance. "A lot of good times in that place," Wilson said with a smile. He then asked Michelle about Anne. He and the rest of what was left of T1 had debated her possible role the night they went missing. Michelle said she hadn't seen her in years. Not since she'd moved back to Montana. The last she'd heard, Anne had met someone and moved to Orlando.

Michelle held JJ's hand tighter. Her memories of Andrews were sprinkled with laughter and good friends, but mostly she remembered how very sick she had been and how much time she'd spent alone, waiting for her men to return.

As the driver prepared to leave the base, he suggested to his guests that they sit back and relax. It would be two hours before they arrived at their destination. Petty had ordered the Marines to the Presidential Retreat at Camp David in Maryland. Morrison was headed to the Pentagon.

Turning to look back at the gate one last time, Michelle thought about the night she had almost died there. "I'm so lucky Anne was there with me. She called 911 and got me to the hospital. If it hadn't been for her I might not be here today."

JJ wrapped his arm around Michelle and looked over his shoulder at Wilson and White. Someday they'd continue that conversation but for now they were together and back home again.

20

"MR. PRESIDENT, I am so happy to see you standing," JJ greeted President Stewart at Camp David. "You scared the hell out of us."

The President gave JJ and Michelle each a hug. With their assistance, he sat down in his leather recliner, wincing from the pain. He asked everyone to sit and relax. A steward brought coffee, water, and a selection of nuts and chocolates, which they are happy to devour. The two hours on the road had felt long without any stops. They all expressed concern over Stewart's health and recovery.

"What's this I hear, Mr. President, about not wearing your seat belt in the limo?" Michelle asked with a frown.

Stewart took a slow sip of his coffee and rubbed the side of his head. "Never thought I'd need to wear one while riding around DC at ten miles an hour. But when that explosion flipped the car, I was tossed around like a towel in a dryer. I hit my head so hard it took me a day to see straight. Hell, while we were tumbling around I broke three ribs and even stuck the pen I was writing with into my Chief of Staff's leg. I'm going to hear about that for at least a year."

Some laughed and others shook their heads. "I'm still dealing with a pretty good headache and bouts of blurred vision, but I'm told that's to be expected." Stewart laughed but then his tone turned serious. "Now, about the bastards that did this. Those sons of bitches must have planned this for months. The blast tore up the damn intersection. The count so far is twelve dead and forty-seven injured. When analyzing the fragments of the landmine they recovered, the FBI found traces of the same material used at Oklahoma City. The same damn stuff delivered the force needed to flip the Beast." The President sighed but then insisted they talk of other things, like the team's reunion with Michelle in Jerusalem and the personal plans they had been making before the attack occurred.

"Well, I had expected to see you three Marines back in the Oval Office in a few months. I'm happy to see you here now, but I wish it were under better circumstances. The world has always had good guys and bad guys. It is the growing threat that made me seek this office, where I thought I would have the best chance of taking the fight to them—to be aggressively and relentlessly proactive rather than reactive."

JJ listened to his every word, knowing the others in the room were thinking as he was—that this man was both impressive and inspiring. This was the brave, confident leader the nation had needed and voted for. And now that he had survived an attack on his life, that same confidence, passion and determination would pursue justice.

"They might have punched our country in the face with this latest escapade, but I can assure you, just as Truman responded with the biggest hammer American scientists had ever designed, this President is going to use every asset available to step on these bastards and leave nothing but a stain in the dirt."

The team nodded, but Michelle shook her head slowly. She knew that her men would be back in this fight. She wanted them home in Montana, out of harm's way, but this was their job, so she waited for the shoe to fall.

"Now Michelle, I see that look on your face, but I want you to know I'm not planning on asking any of these Marines to sling a rifle over their shoulder and go stomping around looking for bad guys. My intention, my hope, is that you will all stay the night here and enjoy this place. In the morning, I'd like to speak with JJ and exchange some ideas. After that, unless we catch Wilson here stealing a bottle of scotch from the bar, you're all free to go wherever you wish, and Uncle Sam will get you there without delay."

The joke cut the building tension. Wilson smiled, looking at the President as if he had just read his mind.

Early the next morning, after the President's daily physical and his national security briefing, he asked JJ to sit with him and spend some time catching up over coffee.

"Son, I know you pretty well and I also know that your father was very proud of you before he died. If he were here today he'd be beaming." Stewart paused and let that sink in. "I also know you are probably totally conflicted inside. Unless you've changed after spending such a long time away, you want two things. You want to go home with your wife and enjoy some peace and quiet." JJ started to speak, but Stewart waved him off. "The other thing you want to do is kill the bastards who attacked me and continue to attack our way of life."

JJ nodded. Every day since the motorcade attack he had been torn. He felt much like the football player who played his last game and was focusing on the next chapter of his life, only to hear the team needed him to suit up. A big part of him wanted back in the game, back in the action, but how could he after being separated from his wife for such a long time? Especially after all that had happened to both of them?

He was concerned about the President's security; videos of the assault on the motorcade played over and over in his head, and it was clear to him that a lot of planning went into it. Could someone on the inside, someone from Stewart's own security detail have been involved? Could Brooks somehow have had anything to do with it? Did he need to suggest that the President surround himself with a corps of hand-picked Marine Raiders?

JJ had already led an extremely fulfilling and successful life. He rose to the top in the Marines, shot Hitler, saw Gladiators fight in the Coliseum, talked to George Washington before beating a hasty retreat, and did so much more. He had found a wonderful woman he was lucky enough to call his wife. He kept reliving that night in the Garden. He still can't believe he asked the Man for a miracle and got one. That, in of itself, was enough adventure for a lifetime. When he and his team sat in the Israeli desert all those nights thinking of what they had done in their lives, what they had seen and accomplished, they would always be caught between laughter and tears. Their experiences had run the extreme from high to low. The loss of their friends and fellow Marines would remain with them forever. They were all still young, but what could they do with their lives that would make the future something to look forward to, instead of living in the shadow of their proud past?

The words "vengeance is mine" replayed in his memory. He knew that America was in harm's way. Innocent men, women, and children were at risk. How could he sit back with his wife while others fought and died?

"One big problem, JJ," Stewart cautioned. "The bastards that tried to blow me up weren't from overseas or of foreign descent." JJ looked at the President with surprise.

"Yep, they were white. Two men and one woman. Caught them on video footage, planting explosives but it wasn't reviewed soon enough to grab them."

JJ shook his head. In past battles, the enemies wore different uniforms. The Asian features of the Japanese during World War II made it easy to identify the enemy. Going after domestic white terrorists, killers who didn't look like they were from the Middle East, was going to make this harder. In this instance, profiling would be useless.

"So, were these assholes brainwashed traitors or three pieces of shit who didn't like your politics?"

The two talked for another thirty minutes before an aide tried to interrupt. Stewart waved him off and went on to tell JJ what he had in mind for him. JJ had chosen five warriors and led them into areas of conflict using the BOTM technology. Now, his mission would be to hand pick one person from each of a list of agencies: the CIA, NSA, FBI, Secret Service, the Army, Marines, Navy, Air Force, Homeland Security, and State. "I want you to be the commander of this newly formed, top-secret security force.

The President assumed that Tommy Wilson would want in too. That would make them a band of twelve with one objective. The entire United States government and twelve pulses would be at their disposal. All roadblocks would be removed. This group would be active players in counter-terrorism field operations and have carte blanche, an all-access pass to their agencies' assets. Anyone who got in the way would be reported to the President. Assets, money, authority, and BOTM's time-travel technology would be at his disposal.

Stewart said, "I'm certain you know the difference between right and wrong, JJ. And you won't let yourself or anyone in your charge take advantage of your newfound power and capabilities. Unlike the two who were sent to the top-secret lock up at Guantanamo Bay. You and your team will have only one goal in mind, only one agenda. Eliminating any and all threats."

JJ drew a deep breath. "This is quite a responsibility, sir."

"It is. But we've never seen such a massive threat to our freedom and safety. Generally speaking, dogs are born, but some contract rabies and have to be put down. Nowadays, deadly animals are born and bred every day, here and in all parts of the world. From the first day these bastards were able to understand anything, they were taught to hate and destroy our way of life. Now they are the biggest threat to our people and the lives we wish to lead. This time, again with the help of an American scientist, we've got another hammer to help drive these animals into the ground once and for all."

JJ looked at the President, acknowledging the challenge. "If I accept the assignment, I'd prefer to use the BOTM space at Andrews. The White House is a target, and the team would be able to operate more discreetly from the base. Also, the position must give me access to all intelligence sources and to the offices at the White House and at the agencies you just mentioned. While that is going on we can use BOTM to gather intelligence and some leverage on all branches of the government and the media."

The President nodded in agreement and encouraged him to continue.

"We need to know who we can trust and as this expands beyond going after terrorists. We need to be able to keep the media off our asses so we can get the job done. The hawks on the intelligence committees will support the effort, as long as nobody goes rogue and starts stomping on things they shouldn't. We need to be able to operate like a combined FBI-CIA-Special Forces. We'd need to be able to operate on any soil. I'm pretty sure Tommy will want in and if he does I'm ahead already. I'm not sure about two teams of six running 24/7. That's a lot of exposure and more missions mean more chances for problems. We will work through that. I noticed that you have never mentioned the Vice President. Do you trust her?"

It was early in the day but Stewart was clearly growing tired. The weight of the office and the trauma from his injuries wore on him. JJ could clearly sense that but needed to continue the discussion so once they agreed on the mission and the tactics he would not have to bother the President much after that.

Stewart smiled. "First off, the Vice President should be fine and we will bring her in on this once you've had the chance to BOTM her if I can use that phrase without getting into trouble. She's smart and a hundred percent behind the platform I ran on. Back to the legal issues, some will say what we are going to do violates our Constitution, but we live in a much different world than when those men wrote it two hundred forty years ago. To get things done in this new world you may have to bend a few rules. If you need to disrupt the damn Facebook or CNN then you'll have the ability to do that. Steer the blame toward the North Koreans, if you must. You'll do it through BOTM sabotage so it will be discreet and untraceable. The end will be justified by the means. Someday when we have more time I will tell you how I've already used the technology to advance the good. It's time we set *some* of the restrictions aside and give our fighting men and women the chance to annihilate the threat under any means possible. To follow trails wherever they may lead. Forget about waterboarding. If a terrorist has intel, we need to save lives then stick a hot piece of rebar up his ass. He'll talk. It's kill or be killed time, JJ, and you will be operating directly under my orders as your Commander in Chief. You will be protected under emergency orders and given full immunity from prosecution in the United States. However, no matter what, I must trust you and you must trust your people to stay within certain boundaries. No undue harm is to come to anyone. Evil doers need to be dealt with firmly and with finality." He paused to let his words sink in. "After it's all said and done, JJ, I'll be ready to join you in that beach house counting beer bottles. Do you remember saying that to me a very long time ago?" JJ smiled. He did. "You in, *Colonel* Jackson?"

JJ smiled and was just about to respond when the First Lady entered the room.

"Elizabeth!" JJ shouted. He stood and embraced her. He hadn't seen her since she moved to Florida. She left to get away from the uniforms, the salutes, and the never-ending sound of taps at Arlington, everything that reminded her of the son she and the President lost. Michelle came in behind her and, while happy to see them reunite, she seemed concerned. JJ's talk with Stewart had gone on twice as long as promised and she probably knew that wasn't good.

The President's aide returned to remind him of an important call. Stewart acknowledged him and looked to JJ for his reply.

JJ smiled again. He remembered the words that were spoken to him in the Garden about vengeance. When his life was over he might need to justify what he had done and was about to do. God had to deal with Lucifer, and the fight JJ was about to embark on would be a monumental one. He had met Christ once already, and hoped that, if he were lucky enough to meet him once his time on earth came to an end, his actions would be understood, or at least forgiven. He put his arms around Michelle and the look she gave him said that she knew he was getting back into the action.

"You're going to have to get Michelle another puppy, young man," Stewart joked.

"Looks that way, Mr. President. It'll be fun watching the pup grow up with the baby we plan on adopting. I guess that means you and Elizabeth are going to be grandparents!" Michelle wrapped her arms around her husband as the Stewarts shared the intimate moment with them.

After a few minutes of celebration, JJ asked The President if he might have a few words in private. The two left the women by the fireplace and walked to the large bay window that revealed the beautiful woods surrounding the retreat. America's leaders and foreign dignitaries had shared this same view since Franklin Roosevelt hosted England's Winston Churchill in 1943, in the midst of World War II, as they fought to defeat Hitler in Europe and Japan across the Pacific.

"I'll accept the assignment on one condition," JJ said. "Remember that I lost both my parents to cancer, and I would have lost Michelle as well if it hadn't been for Dr. Moretti's technology."

"Of course. I'll be forever—"

The sound of automatic weapons outside the cabin cut off the President's words. Both men tensed and stared out the window. Within seconds a group of Secret Service agents rushed in through the cabin entrances, guns drawn.

"Mr. President," the lead agent shouted, "you and the First Lady need to get down into the bunker."

The Agents rushed the Stewarts down a hallway and into a stairwell. The Jacksons followed close behind.

Michelle called out to JJ, "Where are Tommy and Christie?"

"Their cabin is near where the gunfire started. Our people are trying to secure that area. We don't know whether they are hurt or not."

"Who is doing the shooting?" JJ shouted. "How many of them are there?"

"Unknown!"

JJ's mind shifted into high gear. He knew the protocol. By now a sizable contingent of uniformed military guards and additional Secret Service Agents should have surrounded the Presidential cabin. But he'd seen no sign of reinforcements.

Once down the stairs, the group was ushered through a

vault door and into a room that looked just like the White House Situation Room. A staff of four was already in place, manning the phones, monitoring the closed-circuit security feeds and initiating contact with the Pentagon, the Secretary of Defense, the Vice President, and the Secret Service Command Center.

"They have people down here 24/7?" Jackson asked.

"Only when POTUS is on site, sir," one of the staffers responded.

The lead agent prepared to shut the vault door, but the President held up his hand indicating he needed to wait. He looked at Elizabeth, and then Michelle, and finally to JJ. "I'm getting *very* tired of retreating. This is the second time I've been rushed into a God damned bunker in as many weeks."

"But, sir," the agent began. Stewart silenced him with a look. It was clear that this President was much different from those who had come before him.

Stewart walked over to the tall metal storage cabinet at the far end of the meeting room. He looked to the agent and asked, "Does this thing have anything worthwhile in it?"

The agent looked worried but nodded. "M-16's, MK-18's, and .45 automatics." At a signal from the President, the agent moved to the cabinet and opened it.

"Elizabeth, you still a better shot than me?" Stewart asked. The tension in his wife's face transformed to a look of confidence and anger. She'd had enough of watching people try to hurt her husband.

Michelle walked over, put her hand on the President's elbow and smiled up at him. "You better have something in there for me, too." She looked back at her JJ. "I'm a damn good shot. Probably about as good as that young man."

The agent shifted nervously on his feet. "Mr. President, Colonel Jackson, we have protocols to follow. This is the safest place for the President to be right now. Colonel Jackson, we gave you Marines a very wide berth that morning in the Oval when you took out the trash, but there weren't threats running on the property firing at us."

JJ walked to the cabinet, pulled out an MK-18, handed it to Michelle and took one for himself. The look on the President's face let the agents and everyone in the room know that the protocols were being rewritten, effective immediately.

"The reinforcements haven't shown up. That means protocol is out the window. Long before this man was President of the United States, he was a United States Marine. He always will be. We don't let people jump fences. We don't run from anything or hide in bunkers. We run *toward* the trouble and we're getting ready to do that right now. Got that?"

"Got it, Colonel. I'm in. So—" JJ could see the agent was struggling not to smile "—what are the President and the First Lady going to lock and load with?"

Stewart's confident grin lit the room. "I think we'll start with Semper Fi!"

JJ nodded and slapped the agent on the back. "Oorah!"

21

JJ PEAKED OUT the front window of the great room. Secret Service agents had formed a defensive circle around Aspen, the Presidential cabin. He counted nearly twenty terrorists running from the cover of one tree to another, firing automatic weapons at the agents. More would be attacking from the rear. The amount of firepower directed at the cabin reminded JJ of some of the worst firefights he had fought in Iraq. The emergency alert button had been pushed in the bunker below the building. Air and land reinforcements should arrive at any moment. But meanwhile, time and ammunition were running out.

"Where the hell are the tactical teams?" Agent Hill yelled in his wrist microphone. He and JJ were on opposite sides of the large bay window the President had been standing at just minutes before. From Hill's expression, JJ assumed he'd gotten no answer through his earpiece.

JJ assessed their situation. Luckily the walls of the cabin were reinforced; windows and doors were military grade bulletproof. Even armor-piercing bullets could not penetrate the exterior. But if the terrorists made it past the last tier of security outside they could probably breach the doors with explosives. With no reinforcements in sight, Hill shouted for everyone to return to the stairway so he could secure the bunker entrance. From the extent of the assault, JJ realized they had underestimated the enemy.

"Go, go, go!" Hill yelled at them as they crawled toward the entrance, back down to their last line of defense.

Suddenly two explosions shook the Aspen cabin. Dust and debris filled the air. A lack of sound in their ears, caused by the concussion, made the scene inside the President's living quarters even more surreal.

JJ aimed his weapon toward the front door while Hill gathered himself and took aim at the gaping hole that used to be the rear entrance. A stun grenade suddenly hurtled into their airspace and further dazed everyone in the room. The sound of gunfire erupted outside. As his head cleared JJ determined from the sounds of the weapons that reinforcements had finally landed.

One terrorist and then another ran through the front entrance. JJ fired, hitting the first. Michelle, and Hill took out the other intruder. It was her first time in combat and JJ was relieved to see her perform like a veteran. A rookie mistake could have cost them dearly.

"You go, girl!" he shouted to her. Hill had known what to do but Michelle must have been paying attention all those nights in the apartment. Terrorists have to be headshots.

Within minutes the massive back-up teams were on scene and fully engaged. They outnumbered the remaining terrorists ten to one and were able to eliminate the threats with surgical precision. A third terrorist attempted to breach

Aspen but fell dead into the doorway, shot from outside by a specialist from the Quick Response Team.

Michelle edged closer to JJ, looking alert and ready to do whatever she needed to protect her family and their President.

"Quantico!" was shouted from outside the rear entryway.

"Fuck that!" Hill shouted in return. "Nobody's coming through either doorway until we're sure you're with us!"

A familiar voice shouted, "Clusterfuck!"

Michelle looked at JJ. "I know that voice."

"Wilson!" JJ called out. "You good or does some ass wipe have a gun at your head?"

"Mykonos!!" White shouted.

"They're with me," JJ told Hill as he checked to make sure the bad guys they'd dropped were dead. "We need to get everyone the hell away from here and to a safe haven."

"Right."

While Hill attempted to re-establish coms and assemble a protective detail JJ waved Wilson, White, and the reinforcements inside. But when he turned around he saw that those who had been in the underground bunker had come up into the cabin. And something was very wrong.

There on the floor, leaning against a bullet-strafed wall, was the President of the United States. He held the First Lady, his dear Elizabeth, in his arms, and the expression on his face crushed JJ's heart.

"Medic!" JJ shouted. He looked at Michelle. "Help them," he choked out.

Michelle bent down and gently took Elizabeth from her husband, laying her down on the floor and quickly checking for wounds. The expression on the fallen First Lady's face was peaceful. Her eyes barely closed. While medical teams gave aid to wounded Secret Service agents another was admitted to the cabin to do whatever they could for her.

Hill returned, took in the situation, and offered a hand to help the President to his feet. Stewart waved him off. "No. I want to be here with her for a few minutes more."

"Yes, Mr. President, of course." Hill cleared his throat, shot JJ a worried look, then announced, "We've found our tactical teams. Both teams are KIA; repeat all U.S. tactical are KIA. All guard posts including the main entrance are KIA. It looks like they were gassed."

"Good Lord," Stewart murmured, although it wasn't clear to JJ whether his response was to Hill's news or his beloved wife's passing.

For now, as JJ stood over the medics, watching them go through the motions of trying to resuscitate Elizabeth, HE KNEW that she was dead.

The President's physician was escorted in and attempted to check the President's vital signs, but Stewart pushed him away. "She had the heart of a lion, but a sick one in these last few years. The shock of what happened here was too much for her."

Hill stood by respectfully, but JJ could tell the Secret Service agent was anxious. Hill needed to get the President the hell out of there. Nobody had any idea what else the terrorists might have planned.

JJ looked at Hill. "Can we give the President a few minutes' privacy? Let's clear the room, step outside."

Marines who had been checking the dead intruders quietly pulled the remains from the room.

Outside the cabin, JJ and Michelle reunited with Tommy and Christy. "What the fuck," was the extent of their conversation. The camp looked like a war zone. Rubbing the shock and emotion from his face, JJ muttered, "This is unbelievable."

Hill waited a full five minutes before re-entering Aspen with the doctor and a quickly assembled security team. The First Lady was pronounced dead and carefully placed on a stretcher.

The President covered her with a blanket, pausing for one last look before he let it fall over her face. "Agent Hill," he said, "if there is an evacuation plan that is secure, perhaps now is the time to make our move."

"I agree, sir. Camp David is no longer a retreat let alone a safe haven."

Stewart gave him a stiff nod. "Take me to the White House. I've had enough of this."

JJ had already started to move when a voice called out, "Where do you think you're headed?" He turned to see a medic approaching Wilson. JJ hadn't realized until that moment that his friend had taken a round in his side.

Michelle and White flanked Wilson. The medic insisted he sit down to be checked out.

"What's the verdict?" JJ asked.

The medic looked up at him. "It doesn't appear to be life threatening, Major. But a bleeding hole is always a concern."

"Unless it's in the head of a terrorist," Wilson joked, but then winced. "Really, I'm fine. Just a scratch is all."

But JJ could read pain in his friend's eyes and stiff posture.

"Sir, I wouldn't be doing my job if I didn't insist on this Marine coming with me to Andrews for tests and x-rays."

White stepped forward. "I'll go with him, JJ. Make sure he doesn't give 'em a bad time. Call you soon as I know something."

Within minutes three Marine helicopters had lifted off and headed toward the nation's capital. Aside from transporting the most seriously wounded, they would create a diversion. The President and his protectors would travel by stealth. Meanwhile, the terrorists' bodies strewn across this sudden battlefield needed to be checked for booby traps—explosives, and chemical weapons. This would take time. Medical and support troops attended to the remaining wounded and the dead. Only two terrorists were still alive, and everything would be done to save them. JJ glared at them both, uttering to anyone who could hear him. "I wish Benny was here to deal with that scum. He'd have known how to handle them." The U.S. Intelligence community would do anything and everything to discover what they could about the operation. Who was involved and what else might be planned?

Communication with Secret Service HQ was re-established, and procedures authorized. Hill led JJ, Michelle, the President and a small, heavily armed security force back down into the bunker and then nearly 300 yards through an underground passage. The tunnel opened inside a maintenance shed deep in the woods. Waiting for them was a rolling fortress. Operational specialists and Marines were already on board. The tractor trailer looked like any other on the nation's highways. But, inside, was a bombproof containment center that combined the safety of the Beast, the communications capability of Air Force One, and the ability to operate as a submarine, if necessary. They were headed for a loading dock at Andrews.

There was nothing more to say about what had just happened. After taking a few private minutes to gather his thoughts Stewart got on a teleconference with the Vice President, the Secretaries of Defense, State, and the Treasury. He told them he was headed to a secure location, that the First Lady had died, and that he was not hurt.

"I want you all to remain at your safe havens and wait for a videoconference call from me within ninety minutes."

It had been seventy-five years since the United States was attacked from the air at Pearl Harbor. It had been fifteen years since airplanes were used to attack the homeland. Today would mark the first time a small army of fighters had launched an assault on United States soil.

They had used bullets and poisonous gas to try to take the President. His son and now his wife were gone. His entire focus would be on finding and destroying anything that threatened innocent American citizens. He had Jim Jackson and the assets of the federal government at his disposal to wage an epic war. He also had the BOTM program. In his mind, it was not going to be a fair fight. And he was damn glad of it!

A month after the Camp David assault, the President was doing everything he could to focus on the country and his declaration of war on terrorism. But JJ knew that Stewart desperately needed something that would keep his mind off the loss of his dear Elizabeth and relieve the constant pressure of his office. Unlike presidents before him, he couldn't leave the White House. Security measures had become so stringent that even taking a mind-clearing nighttime walk on the South grounds became an event. Helicopters overhead, at least twenty-four armed Secret Service agents spread across the property, and four Belgian Malinois dogs trained to attack on command erased any chance of finding solace. In a handful of years, Stewart had buried his son at Arlington and survived two assassination attempts, only to return to Arlington again to bury the First Lady.

As to the Jacksons, Michelle had returned to the family ranch in Montana. Her brother Tommy accompanied her and was under strict orders from JJ. "Rest up and help her shut that place down for now. Get back here in a month and your orders will be waiting for you."

Bunker was chasing a squirrel the afternoon Michelle returned home. The dog jumped a four-foot tall fence to get to her. White was also given a thirty-day leave and told to relax and recharge. Her concern and her interest in Tommy was still strong but she wanted to give him time with Michelle to reconnect and to also to rest. She planned on getting into an Oakland Raiders jersey and sleeping for at least two weeks. Sharif had managed to reach them all. He wanted back in the action but wanted, needed, some time. "None of us can forget that we all just came in off a three-year mission overseas and need time to be sure our shit is together."

JJ remained at Andrews, assembling the team the President had directed. He called the President every night around seven o'clock to see if he wanted company. Some

Thank you very much for
purchasing Found In Time.

If you enjoyed it please
let other booklovers
know by taking a moment
to write a review on
Amazon.com or perhaps
sharing on Facebook or
other social media.

If you would like to contact
me or receive information
about my other books please
visit jkkelly.com

Very sincerely,

JKelly

nights Stewart invited him to join him for a late dinner and perhaps a ball game on the TV.

"This old place is big and lonely. I can stay the night and we can stroll the hallways looking for old JFK and anyone else who might be wandering around," JJ would joke.

Some nights the President accepted the offer. Other nights he'd wave JJ off. "Too many God damned reports to read." Or he'd simply say, "I still can't believe she's gone."

Two weeks after the Camp David attack, newly appointed and fully empowered National Security Commander Jim Jackson addressed his first White House security meeting. "In the old days you would see dumb asses climb the White House fences and three guards would chase the guy until a dog brought him down," Jackson said matter of factly. "Effective immediately, anyone jumping that fence or running a gate is to be shot dead on the spot. Head shot whenever possible so we don't set off any explosive vests. People, especially the bad guys, will know we mean business. We don't have time to evaluate the threat so end it! There's a new sheriff in town, a war-hardened Marine, and he's not putting up with the ACLU or anyone else getting in the way." He looked around the room to check the facial expressions of the staff he would lead. "The best of the best, Marine Raiders, will now stand alongside the uniformed guard positions at the White House, and the Army's Rangers will share in protecting the Capital and any other structure considered a target." He had everyone's attention and he could tell they were behind him one-hundred percent.

"The men who attacked Camp David were highly skilled, well-trained fighters. They used stealth and state-of-the-art weaponry. They also exhibited a drive that I haven't seen before. I've seen killers on my tours overseas, but these assholes were like hungry wolves on Red Bull. Super intense. They will be the most dangerous enemies we've ever seen. We'll have to bring to the fight the best of our best, operating at the highest level of efficiency. They may be like hungry animals but we've got Seals, Raiders, Rangers, and some very dedicated people at Langley. We also have technology on our side. As of today, we're declaring Terrorists an officially endangered species and I, we, will eradicate them."

At 19:00 sharp, 7pm in laymen's terms, the President welcomed JJ to the dining room in the private residence of the White House. To his surprise, many familiar faces were already seated at the table. Everyone was dressed casually except for one person.

"Looks like we've got the band back together, Mr. President," JJ said with enthusiasm. "I know Petty, Buchanan, and Morrison but you'll need to introduce me to this young lady and the padre."

Stewart rose from his chair to shake JJ's hand and then walked him around the table. "Commander Jackson, let me introduce you to Air Force Captain Frances Devine. She's Frankie to her friends. Frankie is Elizabeth's niece. She was a star at Colorado Springs and then kicked the crap out of some badasses in Afghanistan before coming home for Arlington."

The two exchanged greetings and then Stewart moved him along to meet the cleric. "This is Father Thomas Jefferson. Don't let the collar fool you, JJ, he's got an incredible sense of humor and his frankness can make a Gunny blush."

Pleasantries exchanged, the group sat quietly in their chairs as the Catholic priest blessed the meal. After two hours of laughter and good food, the assembled knew that the next day would be the first in a thousand. The U.S. Military and the American government would focus on putting an end to any evil the forces could touch.

Taking a moment to look at each of his guests, the President offered a final toast. "My grandfather was from Scotland but I'll borrow this from his Irish neighbors. May those that love us, love us. And those that don't love us, May God turn their hearts. And if he doesn't turn their hearts, May he turn their ankles, so we'll know them by their limping."

After exchanging good-byes, Jackson and the others left the White House dinner party and headed for their cars parked at the EOB.

"Father Thomas Jefferson. Seriously?" JJ said with a laugh as he opened the priests' car door for him.

"Yep, the parents were history professors, so go figure." They shook hands and as the priest rolled down his window and put his car in reverse he said one last thing to JJ. "We have a lot to talk about, young man. I spent time in Jerusalem teaching at the Catholic University. Stew said we might enjoy exchanging stories sometime."

JJ just smiled. "Yep, but it'll need to be in a confessional, Padre."

THE END

Made in the USA
Columbia, SC
30 April 2018